DEADLY
Conscience

Amy Lane Williams

Cover Artwork by Dave Wandell

ISBN: 0615695116
ISBN-13: 9780615695112

LCCN: 2013901830
Amy Williams, Baton Rouge, LA

To my friends and family, thank you for your unwavering love and support. Most especially, I would like to thank my parents for supporting me my entire life. And to Meghan who had such a hand in the design, your talent and enthusiasm are appreciated more than you know. I would like to thank my original editors: my friends. Last but in no way least, Kara. I would not be here if you would not have encouraged me to write this book. Because whether you wanted to read the story or you only wanted me to stop narrating it to you, you opened this world to me. I cannot thank you enough.

Chapter 1

BALANCING A POLITICAL career and a drug distribution empire could be problematic. Especially when Jovan Nasser was throwing one of his infamous campaign parties at the same estate he used for his cocaine warehouse. But this estate was the most magnificent of his properties. Besides, what senator would notice drugs when the guest list was filled with stunning, exotic prostitutes?

Sounds of the revelry stretched across the mansion infecting all those present. Nasser played the perfect host and made a great impression on his honored guests. The elaborate decor and champagne were outshined only by the beautiful, powerful people holding their crystal glasses.

He greeted each of his guests with a beautiful model on his arm. His dark hair and eyes, not to mention his extreme wealth, made him attractive to all women. His favorites were the beautiful ones hoping that he could somehow advance their careers, just like Brandi, his date for the evening. The pair made their way over to the once honest Senator Jenson. Amid the jumble of small talk, Nasser's assistant Robbie approached them.

"Excuse me, sir, but there is an important phone call for you from Austria." Robbie's use of the code word "Austria" let Nasser know the matter was important.

"You will have to excuse me for just a moment. Business never waits." With that, Nasser left his date and followed Robbie out of the party.

"What is so important that it requires me to leave my guests?" Nasser inquired calmly.

"Patrick found out that Lance stole some merchandise. He has Lance in the garage."

"This couldn't have been handled without me?"

Nervous, Robbie paused to regain composure before responding. "Since he's your cousin, we thought you might want to handle this personally."

They entered the garage, where they found Lance. Nasser's second-in-command, Patrick, and three of his men were waiting with him. Lance was annoyingly calm in a situation where he should have been terrified. Nasser walked up to the men, and Patrick handed him a gun. Nasser pressed the gun to Lance's forehead, forcing him on his knees.

"What were you thinking, stealing from me? I looked past it the first time you betrayed me, and how do you thank me? By stealing my drugs!"

Lance began to sweat and shake, as all men did when Nasser unleashed his temper.

"I'm sorry, Jovan. I wa-wasn't thinking. We're family. I would never hurt you. Please forgive me. Please."

Nasser lowered his gun and patted his cousin on the shoulder. "It's OK. Of course I forgive you, you're family." As he said that, he pulled Lance to his feet and embraced him. "Let's just make sure this doesn't happen again. OK?"

"Thank you, Jovan. It won't happen again," Lance told him.

Nasser handed the gun back to Patrick and looked in his eyes. "Patrick, make sure this doesn't happen again." Patrick gave Nasser a smile and a quick nod.

Nasser walked away from the garage to the sounds of his cousin pleading which were abruptly cut off by the sound of gunfire. Lance would never cause problems for Nasser, or anyone for that matter, again.

Returning to the party, Nasser found Brandi sitting alone at the bar, finishing off a glass of champagne. She was a beautiful woman with long blond hair and dark blue eyes, which gazed at him from under an expanse of thick lashes. She was not as tall as the other models he dated, but her perfect body made up for the lack of height. Unlike most models, she had a full chest and a luscious backside.

Nasser approached his stunning date and ordered them both another drink. The rest of the night was filled with shameless flirtation, which turned to drunk flirting as the hours passed. Near two in the morning, most of the guests were gone or had passed out wherever they fell. The good Senator Jenson left the party with one of the many prostitutes Nasser had hired for the evening. Nasser liked to ensure that all of his guests were completely satisfied. It made them easier to bribe later. If one of the guests suddenly had an attack of conscience, a few pictures of them with a hooker would ensure their aid in his endeavors.

Nasser and Brandi retired to his room for something other than sleep. After they entered, Nasser closed the door behind them. He grabbed Brandi's arm and spun her around into a kissing embrace. As he held her, she moved her hands up his arms to his shoulders, twining delicate fingers into his thick hair.

"You're so tense," she told him. "Turn around."

As he turned, Brandi slid the jacket from his shoulders. She leaned against his back and began massaging his shoulders. He felt her move forward and kiss his neck. Blond hair fell across Nasser's chest as her hands kneaded the muscles in his neck.

Nasser reached behind him to slide his hands up her thighs. He began pushing her dress up toward her waist. Brandi's hands abandoned their massaging and wrapped around his shoulders. Pressing herself firmly against his back, she ran one hand through his hair while the other embraced his neck. He felt her soft lips press against his ear and heard her whisper one word: "Good-bye".

Chapter 2

I LOOKED DOWN AT Nasser's lifeless form and let out a sigh of relief. *Thank God I used enough force to break his neck.* The first time I ever snapped someone's neck had gone horribly wrong. I had done everything right. I had sneaked up behind my target and grabbed his head in a firm grip, but I did not twist with enough force to break his neck for an instant kill. I had to slit his throat to finish the job. Blood poured out of the body and covered the entire scene. It was an incredible mess. This time, like every time since, had gone beautifully.

I stepped over Nasser's body and walked around the bedroom, my heels clicking softly against the hardwood floor. Nasser's room was an elaborate example of how he perceived himself. He had a bed big enough for five people to sleep comfortably, which I'm sure had happened on occasion. The bed was dressed in royal blue fabrics, so plush and exotic they probably cost more than all the furniture in my condo.

On the nightstand next to the bed were only pictures of him at different locations. I walked to the closet and opened the French style doors. Inside were some very expensive suits from some of the most sought-after designers. *These suits would put the red carpet to shame. Tank would love one of these. It's not like Nasser will be needing any.* No, I couldn't fit one in my purse. *Shame.* I closed the doors and walked to the other side of the room, where a giant armoire stood. I wasn't looking for anything in particular; I just needed to pass time. I didn't want to arouse suspicion by leaving too quickly.

I tried to open the doors but found them locked. Locks had never been a problem for me. I reached inside my purse and pulled out my lock pick kit. I found the appropriate tools and went to work, and in a matter of seconds, I had the doors open. Inside the armoire were documents, along with thousands of dollars in cash.

In the back of the armoire was Nasser's gun collection. *I can't believe he has this.* I picked up the third one from the left. *M203 Grenade Launcher! The gun from Scarface!* I badly wanted to pick it up and yell "Say hello to my little friend" while waving the gun at no one in particular. *I've always wanted one of these. Oh well. Sometimes I wish I was a thief. It's about time I leave anyway.* I put the gun back and walked toward the door.

I walked out of Nasser's room and quietly closed the door behind me, then turned and began tiptoeing toward the exit.

"Hey, you there," someone behind me said.

I nearly jumped out of my skin. I stopped in my tracks and turned toward the voice. It came from a guard stationed near Nasser's room. He was a mountain of a man who wore a nice pair of black pants and a blue button-up shirt. He had a dress jacket on, which made him look very professional. He was a fairly average-looking man with dark hair and eyes.

"Shhh-," I told him, giving him a judgmental look. "You will wake Jovan. He just fell asleep."

"What are you doing?" he asked me, in a much lower voice.

I noticed the gun strapped to his chest beneath his jacket. *This could get messy.* "Oh, I'm so embarrassed," I told him, as I moved closer to him and gave him my most innocent smile. "I never do this kind of thing. You must think I'm a slut."

Hopefully my flirting can get me out of this. It had many times before (it had also gotten me into quite a few unpleasant situations). If that didn't work, I would be close enough to get his gun.

He smiled at me and replied, "No ma'am, I don't think that at all." *Yes, chalk one up for flirting!*

"Call me Brandi," I said, as I laid a hand on his arm. "I have an early photo shoot, so I have to leave. Would you mind giving Jovan a message for me?"

When he smiled back at me, I reached in my purse and pulled out a piece of paper and a pen. I smiled at the guard and made a circle motion with my index finger, so he would turn around. The guard did as I indicated and turned his back to me. I place the piece of paper on his back and wrote:

> *I had fun last night.*
> *Give me a call. 555-6948*
> *Luv Brandi*

I handed the paper to the guard. He folded the paper and placed it in his pocket.

"Thanks," I said, giving his arm a not too subtle rub before I turned and began to walk toward the doors.

"Brandi. Wait." *Oh, crap. I was hoping to get out of here without trouble.*

"Yes?" I replied, as I was beginning to asses my defensive attack. I reached in my purse and let my hand rest against the small 22mm. I carried in case of emergency. It was not my favorite gun but my 45mm would not fit in my purse.

The guard approached me. "I will have someone bring your car around."

"That would be great. It's a red Mercedes convertible." The guard got on the radio and told someone to bring my car to the door.

I left the guard for the second time, but this time no one stopped me. I got in my car and drove off. As soon as I was safely off the estate, I pulled my blond wig off and put it in my purse. I combed my fingers through my long brown hair and continued driving down the road.

I pulled down the visor of my car and opened the vanity mirror. Reaching in my purse, I retrieved my contact case. I steered with my knee as I filled the case with solution, spilling a little as I made a right turn. When my knee slipped, I quickly grabbed the wheel and continued the turn. Using my mirror, I removed my colored contacts and placed them in the case. I glanced back at the mirror and saw my eyes had turned from blue to my natural green. I placed my contacts back in my purse and pulled out my cell phone. I flipped open the phone and dialed 1-800-555-9022, extension 24.

"Computer tech support," a woman answered disinterestedly.

"Blake Morgan," I told her my name. "ID number 483860."

"I'll connect you to your controller," the operator replied. After a minute on hold, a man picked up the phone.

"Tech support," he said. Controllers always answered the phone with that greeting, in case a civilian dials their extension by accident.

"Hey, Tank," I replied.

"Blake, how is the assignment going?" he asked, in a deep voice.

"Done. I just left the estate," I told him.

"Good girl. Your money will be wired to your account on confirmation of kill. How did you do it?"

"I was Brandi," I answered.

"Enough said. I'm scheduling your flight out now." The sound of Tank's typing on his computer came through the receiver.

"That's a good idea. They will start looking for me tomorrow morning."

"Tommy was asking about you," he told me.

"Yeah, he called me and left a bunch of messages on my voicemail," I said, after letting out a long sigh.

"Do you want me to handle him?" Tank asked.

"No, that won't be necessary. I will talk to him when I get back."

"OK," Tank said. "I scheduled you on the red-eye to Houston under the name Heather Wilson. Then you have a flight from Houston to Chicago under the name Sarah Mooney. And don't forget to ditch the car."

"When have I ever forgotten to do that?" I asked him.

"Good point. I'm also scheduling you an appointment with Dr. Harris on Tuesday for one o'clock. And please don't fight me on this one. You know it's policy to see a therapist once every few months."

Two years back, an employee went crazy after a mission. He had stormed the office and took out six assassins before he was finally brought down. Ever since that incident, management required all assassins to talk to a therapist a few times a year to make sure such incidents did not reoccur.

"Very well. I guess an hour with Dr. Harris won't kill me," I reluctantly agreed.

"Good. Then I will see you on Tuesday," he said.

"See ya, Tank."

As soon as I hung up with Tank I called the cab company and requested a cab to pick me up at the nearby mall. I pulled into the parking lot and cleaned the car of all prints.

I grew bored as I waited for the cab, so I pulled out my cell phone and texted my best friend.

Want to grab dinner later? I'm on my way home.

I had to wait a few minutes for the reply.

Can't. Tabitha wants to check out the new restaurant next to my house. Want to join?

I laughed out loud, as Mark had most likely intended. He and I had dated for a few months when I was recruited by Tank. We both decided we did better as friends and had been very close ever since. However, his girlfriend, Tabitha, thought that I was harboring strong feelings for him, therefore hated our relationship. She was delusional.

Yeah, that sound fun. No wait. I was thinking of a lobotomy. I'll pass.

LOL. He texted back

Just as we finished our written communication, my cab pulled up. I got in and left for the airport.

Chapter 3

I STARED AT THE ceiling of Dr. Harris's office. Although she told me that I did not have to lie on the couch, I felt the need to anyway, probably from all the times I'd seen this in movies. Dr. Harris had short dark hair that looked lighter due to the gray streaks running through it. She looked too young to be graying but some people's hair ages faster than their bodies.

She had a normal office, equipped with a large oak desk facing two cream-colored suede chairs and one large, dark brown leather couch. She took one of the chairs facing me. "Let's see, Ms. Morgan, last session we were beginning to talk about your childhood. Why don't you begin with your parents?" said Dr. Harris.

I took a deep breath and began. "My parents were killed in a car wreck when I was five years old. I don't remember too much about them, other than quick flashbacks. I can remember helping my mom in the kitchen and sitting in my dad's lap as we watched *Cheers* after dinner. My mother was an only child whose parents died before I was born, and my dad's only living relative was my Uncle James, who was sent to prison for murder before my first birthday. When they died, I went into the system and was placed in an orphanage in Lansing, Michigan. It was called a group home, but that is just another name for an orphanage." I looked at Dr. Harris while she was taking notes. When she didn't say anything, I continued.

"The first few weeks I tried to keep to myself. I ate alone, played alone, and slept with a stuffed giraffe I've had since I was born. One day, while sitting under a tree, watching all the other kids play, a boy named Henry and his friends walked up and started picking on me. When I tried to run, they pushed me down and took my giraffe.

"Then these other kids came over. A girl named Courtney with her four friends walked up to Henry, and Courtney snatched my giraffe back from him. Henry just stood there. He looked really scared of her. I didn't realize it until later, but Courtney ruled over the orphanage. Though she was small, no child dared test her wrath. She told them to leave, and they did, without saying a word. After that she gave me back my stuffed animal. She introduced herself, along with her four friends. They were the twins Jake and Janey, a girl named Brooke, and Finn. His real name was Bradley Monroe, but everyone called him Finn, because he was obsessed with the book *Huckleberry Finn*. Courtney and her gang took me in and taught me the ropes of the home."

The doctor noticed my air quotes around the word "home" and asked, "How did you feel about the group home?" *How do you think I felt about it?*

"I hated it until Court and the guys became my friends. They showed me which lunch lady I could suck up to get extra dessert, they kept kids from messing with me, and they showed me how to defend myself from those who did try to pick on me. Only a few ever did, though after I got a hit in, the rest of the guys would join in to make sure that kid and anyone watching would not start anything with us again."

Dr. Harris interrupted me to ask, "So these friends became your family?" Although it was more of a statement than a question, I answered anyway.

"Yeah, I guess they did."

She followed by asking, "So what happened? Did any of them or you get adopted?"

"No," I answered. "We didn't want to get separated, and we were a lot older than the babies that everyone seemed to want, so we made sure we didn't get placed in foster care." Before she could ask how we avoided foster care, I answered for her. "Court would break into the office at the orphanage and alter our records to state that we were too unruly to be placed in foster care. Of course, we had to act that way to keep up appearances. Even most of the adults were afraid of us by the time I was thirteen."

"What kind of things did you do to appear unruly?" Dr. Harris asked.

"Well, we would hurt any kids stupid enough to give Court a reason, and if we didn't have anyone to fight, we would fight each other. Court called it 'staying prepared.' She would pair us off and we would fight. Nothing too violent, it was more like sparring."

Dr. Harris interrupted me to ask, "So Courtney was the boss?"

"Yeah, pretty much," I responded. "She thought of everything to keep us together, and she basically ran the house. But one day when I was fifteen, the house mother, Ms. Roberts, called me into her office and told me that my uncle was released from prison because the police found DNA evidence that proved he was innocent. She said he was coming to take me to live with him. Even Court couldn't figure a way out of that one."

Dr. Harris then asked, "You didn't want to leave the orphanage to live with your uncle? Why not?"

"Like you said, Court, Finn, Brooke, and the twins became my family. I didn't know my uncle. I had never met him."

As Dr. Harris jotted down information in her notebook, she asked me, "Uncle James, was it? How did your Uncle James treat you? Did you like living with him?" *I really hate when people ask me numerous questions at once.* I never know which one to address first. I guess that quirk comes from years of prying information out of unwilling people. Asking one question at a time gives the best results.

"He was OK. He was a quiet man and kept to himself, mostly. I had to move to Chicago and go to a public school here. I would wake up, fix myself breakfast, go to school, come home, fix dinner for both of us, and go to bed. We would go days without talking to one another. Then one day at school, a boy made a crude comment to me, and I responded by breaking his nose. I got suspended for fighting, but my uncle was proud of me. He was surprised I knew how to fight and decided I should learn more.

"He sent me to a martial arts school, where I began my training in martial arts. Being a fast learner, I impressed my sensei, so he moved me up in my classes. Uncle James had me attending class every day after school and working longer on the weekends.

"One day, Uncle James decided to take me with him on a job. Up to this point, I didn't know what he did for a living but I had an idea that it wasn't legal. On the way, he told me that he was a freelance enforcer. That's just a fancy name for a hired gun. He was supposed to meet this guy for a pick up.

What we were picking up, I never found out. We waited until dark and drove to an empty lot outside of town. Uncle James pulled up to a black van and parked. We got out of our car, and my uncle approached the driver, who was leaning against his door. I noticed four other men walking around the van to position themselves behind us. After Uncle James and the driver exchanged a few words I couldn't hear, Uncle James punched the driver, knocking him to the ground, and began kicking him sharply in the ribs. When the other four men moved toward Uncle James, I was able to trip one on his way to my uncle and knock him out before the others noticed. I quickly grabbed another by the arm and spun him around. Using his own momentum, I threw him into the side of the van. The blow to his head knocked him out instantly. My uncle pulled out a revolver and shot the other two. I stood there in shock, staring at the rapidly pooling blood flowing from the two dead men, while my uncle grabbed a nondescript cardboard box from the back of the van. He told me to get in the car, and we left."

When I looked over at Dr. Harris, she had stopped writing and was staring at me. For a second, she forgot that she was working and listened to me like it was story time. She sat straighter in her chair when she realized I was a patient and not Mother Goose. Clearing her throat, she paused to regain her professionalism before asking, "How did you feel when your uncle killed those two men?"

"At first I thought I was going to be sick, but as soon as I got in the car, I realized I was OK. These men obviously intended to hurt us, so I didn't feel that bad. My uncle was so impressed by the way I handled the situation that he took me on more jobs. That's how I ended up here. I met Tank on one of Uncle James's assignments. I was nineteen when I accepted a job offer from Tank."

When I finished talking, I sat up because I was tired of lying down. Dr. Harris was busy writing in her notebook when the one-hour alarm went off on her desk clock. She stood up and said, "Well, that looks like all we have time for today. We can pick up here next time." I thanked the doctor for her time and exited her office.

Chapter 4

I LEFT DR. HARRIS'S office and headed down the hall. Her office was located on the second floor of our building. Our agency disguises itself as Chicago Security, a security system installation company. Assassins are very good at breaking into buildings, so logically assassins would know the best way to secure a building.

I took the elevator to the fourth floor and walked down the hall until I stopped at room 428. Behind the door was a giant room filled with twenty adjoining desks paired up in two long lines. This room had an office in the back where Tank resided. From his office, Tank kept a close watch over all the assassins for whom he was responsible.

I walked through the room and sat at my desk, which was located near the back. A blond man sat at the desk adjoining mine.

"Hey, Tommy," I said, as I sat in my chair. Tommy kept his head lowered.

"I called you," he told me, in a low voice.

"I know, I had four voice messages."

"Why didn't you answer?" he asked. I looked down at my desk and took a deep breath for the conversation I knew was coming.

"How many times are we gonna have the same argument? We are not dating anymore. You can't call me whenever you want-and especially not while I'm on a job," I said, trying to keep my voice down so the conversation would not include the sixteen other people in the room.

"I was worried and just wanted to make sure you were OK," he told me.

"I know, but calling me like that only jeopardizes my cover and puts me at a greater risk," I said. *I really don't want to be mean, but he does not understand this. I hate wearing the pants in a relationship.* "We broke up. We are not getting back together. You have to accept that," I told him, a little more forcefully.

He looked up at me with clear blue eyes and said, "I know, but it's hard. I still really care about you."

I looked back at him and softened my voice. "I know you do. And I still care about you, but it won't work. We tried, but every time I had a job, you would worry about me. I would do the same thing when you were gone. And if we are thinking about each other, then we are not thinking about our jobs. People in our profession can't afford to let their guard down. That's how they get hurt." We both sat in silence until someone walked up to us.

"Hey, guys," said the man standing by our desks. Peter was a skinny man, with dark hair and a forgettable face. He had a bad temper, which made him a bit of a wild card at work, but he was loyal to those he respected. When we didn't respond to his greeting, he asked, "Am I interrupting something?"

A couple seconds of silence passed before I answered, "No Peter, you're not. What's up?"

His eyes shifted curiously back and forth between Tommy and me before he responded. "Oh, not much. Just finished a job. It was a simple breaking in and making it appear like a burglary. How was yours?"

"It went well," I told him. Before I could finish explaining my job to Peter, a tall, mean-looking man walked up to us.

"So, the Pack Rat is back from his assignment. What did you steal from your mark this time, Pack Rat?" said the grumpy man standing in front of me. He called Peter that because he took an item from each of his victims and had developed quite a collection over the years. I stood up and stepped between the man and Peter.

"David, why do you always have to mess with Peter?" I asked him. David was tall, with light brown hair, a square jaw, and a bad attitude.

"I wasn't talking to you, Morgan. Keep your nose out of other people's business," he said. I knew it wasn't a good idea to anger a professional killer but sometimes I couldn't help myself.

"I know you're aggravated because you haven't had a date in a while. And when you did pay someone to go out with you, you had a technical malfunction. But if you don't walk away now, I will make sure you don't have anything left to malfunction, if you know what I mean," I told him. He made an aggressive step toward me but stopped to stare at Tommy, who was now standing behind me.

"Oh, so I guess you're gonna try and threaten me now too?" David asked Tommy.

"No" Tommy replied, with a smile. "I was just getting a better view for when Blake knocks you out with a single hit, like she did last time." That seemed to do the trick.

David's face turned red as he shouted, "She didn't knock me out! I tripped over the mat when she came at me."

"Is there a problem?" Tank's door opened, and a large bald man stuck his head out. His scalp was covered in intricate Celtic tattoos-in fact, there wasn't much of Tank that wasn't covered in ink. David glared at me before turning away and leaving the office.

"Blake, a word please?" Tank said.

I walked into his office and took a seat in one of the two chairs facing his desk. Tank's office was a very typical office. The walls were lined with filing cabinets, and in the center of the office was a desk with two chairs facing it. The only decoration was a picture of a bird, flying over a beach setting. I think he stole it from a tacky hotel room. "What was all that yelling about out there?" he asked, as he sat down at his desk.

"It was nothing, just David being a jerk again, so I stepped in before Peter pulled the Glock from his desk and killed him," I said.

Tanks smiled and shook his head. There was a rumor going around the office that I was psychic. The truth is, I have a photographic memory, and I pay close attention to things in my peripheral vision. I had seen the gun in his desk drawer a few weeks earlier and assumed it was still there. It always startled people when I predicted things or recalled facts I should have known nothing about. I didn't mind, it added a little mystery. It was always good for people to be slightly intimidated by me. I was five foot six and weighed one hundred and fifteen pounds, a small girl working alongside large, testosterone-filled male assassins. There were not that many women in my company, so I had to show the boys that I was not afraid of them; otherwise, they would walk all over me.

"Well, I got conformation of kill on Jovan Nasser. Your fifty grand will be wired in small amounts to your bank account," Tank said.

I know it may not seem like fifty thousand dollars is enough money to kill someone. Our payment fluctuated depending on the target, and Nasser was about middle of the line. Freelance kill-for-hires tend to make a lot more money. The difference is, one kill-for-hire may have five or six jobs a year at most, whereas working for a corporation like I did meant I had more like twenty jobs a year. In the end, it worked out in my favor.

"Also," Tank said, "my connection in the LAPD said they found an interesting note at the crime scene. The murderer left a phone number."

I couldn't help but smile as he continued, "Do you know whose phone number was on the note? Betty White's." Unable to restrain myself, I let out a giggle. "How did you get Betty White's private phone number?" he asked.

Before I could answer, he added, "You know what, I don't want to know." He allowed himself a tiny grin and then asked, "How are things going with Tommy?"

I sighed and slouched in my chair. "Well, they're not great. He doesn't seem to understand we broke up, and I don't want to be mean to him but..." I let my sentence trail off.

"Do you want me to talk to him?" Tank asked.

"No thanks, I will handle it. And you don't have to say 'I told you so,'" I replied.

"I wasn't going to," he said, with a grin. He wanted to say it.

"I now know not to date people I work with," I told him.

"Good. Also, I have to ask you for a favor," Tank said.

"Sure, what can I do for you?" I asked.

"Well, I have a new girl joining our group and I am assigning her first job tomorrow. Would you mind going with her to make sure things go well?" he asked me.

"Sure," I answered. "It will be no problem."

"I know you just got back from a job, but I don't have many veterans here that I trust to train a new girl," he said.

"Really, Tank, it's not a big deal," I assured him.

"Thanks, Blake, I owe you one."

Chapter 5

TANK WALKED A tall girl with long auburn hair to my desk. She looked like she could be a runway model. Her graceful walk along with her perfect face easily drew the eyes from everyone in the room as she approached my desk. She was a person who would be hard to forget, which was not always a good thing in our line of work.

"Nicole, this is Blake Morgan. Blake, meet Nicole Watson," Tank said, as I shook hands with the new girl.

"Nice to meet you," she replied politely.

"Blake is one of my best assassins," Tank told her. "Listen to anything she says."

He turned to me. "She has already been to Human Resources so she has all of her IDs and credit cards. Just show her how we do things." With that, Tank walked back to his office.

"So, did Tank show you around the building?" I asked Nicole.

"No, not really. We just went down to Human Resources," she answered.

"Well, each group has a different office, and this is our group's office," I explained. "You can pick any of the available desks to claim, but for today you can just pull a chair up to mine. I can show you the rest of the building later."

As she went to find a chair at a nearby abandoned desk, I saw Peter staring open mouthed at her. I crumpled a piece of paper and threw it at him. When he looked at me, I mouthed the words "Stop it" to him. He rolled his eyes at me and got back to his paperwork.

Nicole returned to my desk and sat in her borrowed chair. "Do you mind if I see the kill order?" I asked her.

"Not at all," she said, as she handed me the file. I opened the folder and saw the target. His name was Ethan Lambert. He had dark hair and a strong face. He was fairly attractive. He lived in Denver and ran a paper corporation. *Seems like a good beginner's job.*

"OK, first thing we need to do is get plane tickets to Denver. It's not very important to be too cautious on the way to the mission, but you have to be extremely careful on the way home. When we leave Denver, we will have to schedule separate flights, and we must make at least one stop before arriving in Chicago. It's important to use different names and airlines. For example, you can fly to New York and then book a separate airline under a different name to fly you here. That makes you harder to track. But we will worry about that later," I said, as I ordered our tickets to Denver to leave at the beginning of the next week. "All right," I said, "we are all set to leave on Monday."

I glanced at my clock on the computer and saw that it was ten o'clock in the morning. "Oh, crap! I forgot I am helping out with Bando lessons today. I can't show you around the building-but don't worry, Peter would love to show you around. Wouldn't you, Peter?" I asked. Bando is a form of martial arts that focuses on footwork and technique. The fighting style is modeled after different animals' mode of attack. It was one of the fighting styles I had studied, and I had promised my sensei I would help him with a few classes.

Peter shot out of his seat with a huge grin on his face. "I will meet you here Monday morning at nine o'clock a.m. to leave for the airport," I called back to Nicole, as I ran out of the office.

We landed in Denver and headed for our hotel room. The flight had been enjoyable; I had always liked flying, and Nicole turned out to be pleasant company. She was beginning to come out of her shell, and by the time our flight landed, she was cracking jokes. I was glad I ended up getting along with her. There were so few women in our company, and most I didn't like. We picked up dinner on the way to the hotel and ate as we discussed the job we were there to complete.

"You are going to make all the decisions," I told her, "I'm just here to make sure things go well. Have you ever done this before?"

"Yes, but not professionally," she said. I assumed that meant that she had killed before but did not get paid for it. Most assassins started out that way. I was a rare exception. My first kill was my first assignment.

"OK, well, the first thing you need to do is surveillance. It's not fun, but it's important," I replied. "We need to figure out Lambert's routine. Then you can decide how to execute the kill order."

The next morning we got in our rental car and drove to Lambert's house. We parked on his street, a few houses down from his, and Nicole grabbed the binoculars. I stretched out to rest because, like I told Nicole, this was her job, not mine. I slept in the car for close to five hours, until Nicole nudged me to wake up.

I leaned up and saw a man in a suit, who could only be Lambert, being followed by four large men. I guessed these men were his bodyguards, due to their attire. They were wearing all-black suits, which made them look like they came straight out of a bad film. The five men got into two black SUVs and pulled out of the driveway. Nicole and I followed behind them, making sure we stayed a couple cars behind so they would not realize they were being followed.

They led us to a warehouse, where all five got out of the vehicle and went quickly inside. They were inside for the remainder of the day and well into the night. After they left the warehouse, we followed them to a club called the Gray Area.

Lambert and his muscle went into the club and did not return for a few hours. When they left the bar, we followed them back to Lambert's house. After that, we went back to the hotel so Nicole could get some rest, because the next day, we were going to do the same thing.

The next day Lambert followed the same schedule, but this time, we followed him into the club. The club was called Gray Area, but the inside was decorated too dark to fit the description of "shades of gray." The decorations were a cross between a new age club and a dungeon. Neon lights were placed around the club, intermingled with chains that looked like props from a bad Dracula film.

We walked in and sat at the bar where the bartender was advertising shots dedicated to the seven deadly sins. Lambert and his guys went to a private area reserved for them.

The private area contained a table and a couple of couches. A sheer curtain surrounded the space to give it the illusion of privacy while still allowing the occupants see the rest of the club. There Lambert sat, drank, and watched the hard rock band that was playing there that night. We took our queue from Lambert and left the club around one o'clock in the morning and headed back to our hotel.

The next morning we went out for surveillance again and found Lambert repeating the same schedule. It became obvious that this was what he did every day. While we were in the car in front of Gray Area, I asked Nicole, "So how do you want to do the hit?"

She leaned back in her seat and stretched her long legs. "Well, we can't get into the house or the warehouse. Security is way too tight there, so that leaves the club. I was thinking I could pose as a waitress and simply poison his drink," she said.

"That's not a bad idea, but there are a lot of people in a club. What about something quieter, like a sniper shot?" I asked.

"I'm really good with a knife and close combat but not a rifle, so that rules out sniper," Nicole replied. That surprised me. I did not think she was the type to get too close to the mark. Close combat, especially with knives, has a tendency to get messy. Most women prefer something cleaner.

"Well, OK then, we can go with your idea," I told her. When I said that, Nicole opened her door. "Where are you going?" I asked, surprised.

"To get a job as a waitress," she said, with a confident smile.

The next morning, we drove down the streets of a suburban neighborhood. I looked out the window and saw a few children running through the front yards of their cookie-cutter homes.

"Are you sure this is the right neighborhood?" Nicole asked, as she turned down a street called Mountain Peek.

"Yeah, I think so," I answered. A pair of housewives jogged past us as we pulled up to a brick house. I checked the address I had written down earlier. "Yep, this is the address Tank gave me."

We exited our car and walked along the stepping stones through the established flower bed to the front door. I rang the doorbell and noticed out the corner of my eye that Nicole was growing anxious.

"Calm down," I said. "Things are fine."

A lady opened the door, and a child darted past us. "Danny, don't play in the street, and be back for lunch!" She was of normal height and had short blond hair. She had a tan, indicating that she spent time in the sun to perfect her look, and wore a plain black apron that had flour rubbed on it. "Can I help you?" she asked us.

"Yes," I said. "Tank sent us."

"Of course, come in." She stepped aside, allowing us to enter her home. I walked in and noticed nothing out of the ordinary. The front door opened into the living room, which was connected to the kitchen.

"Right this way...and you will have to excuse my appearance, I was baking a cake for my son's birthday tomorrow," she said. "We have to hurry; my husband is outside, and he doesn't know anything about my side job." She led us through the kitchen and into the laundry room.

"You have a lovely home," I said. I did not know what to say but felt the need to be polite.

"Thank you. I just redid the kitchen with granite countertops. I hate remodeling; it is such a nightmare." She obviously did not feel awkward with having strange assassins walking through her home. She walked past the washer and dryer and opened the door to a laundry closet. The closet appeared large enough to hold only detergent and a few boxes.

The woman removed a key from behind a large bottle of Tide and opened a small lock connected to a hidden door.

"I have to hide the key somewhere my husband will never look," she said, with humor in her voice. She opened the secret door in the wall, which was so small that only one person could squeeze through at a time.

She led the way through the door, and I followed, with Nicole close behind me. Once we made it through the door, we were in a small room, lit by a single light bulb. Along the walls were guns of all shapes and sizes. There were also knives and choke cables. *I need a room like this.*

"So what type of equipment do you need?" she asked. Nicole and I exchanged a quick look before I walked around the small room to examine the variety of weapons she had.

"I won't have a place to hide a gun," Nicole told her, "so I will need a thin knife I can tape to the bottom of a serving tray."

The woman walked past me and picked up a thin dagger and handed it to Nicole. Nicole tested the weight and balance of it. After flipping it in the air and catching it with ease, she decided it would do the job.

"How about you?" she asked me.

I picked up a 9mm and tested the feel of it. "This will work; also, I will take that forty-five and ammo," I told her, pointing to the Taurus on the opposite wall.

"Good choice. Is there anything else I can do for you?"

"Actually, yes there is," I said, "We need some poison. Do you have anything?"

She walked to the side with the choke cables and lifted a small vial off the shelf.

"This should do the trick. A few drops in any liquid and the consumer will be dead in about thirty minutes," she said, as she handed the vial to Nicole.

"What is it?" Nicole asked, looking at the clear liquid.

"I don't really know. I get it from a source at the market. He says it's some kind of dehydrogenating alpha-keto something. It's a type of arsenic, really. It's something like two hundred times more potent than normal arsenic. It will work."

After we gathered our things, she led us out of the room; then she locked the door and hid the key. As we were walking back to the front door I turned to mention payment, but she beat me to it.

"Tank already contacted me and told me to give you anything you need, and he will handle the cost." She smiled at me, as she opened the front door. "Good luck with everything," she said. I thanked her, and we left with our goodies.

Chapter 6

WE ARRIVED AT Gray Area at seven forty-five in the evening. Nicole's shift started at eight o'clock. This was her third shift, so management did not keep a close watch on her like they had the previous couple of nights. Her first two shifts, she averaged close to two hundred dollars each. Not bad for a six-hour day.

Nicole was wearing the required uniform: black shorts that were hardly bigger than my swim suit and a white button-up shirt left unbuttoned and tied across her chest. All in all, she was dressed to draw male attention (although her natural looks did that on their own). Her clothes were too tight to hold an ink pen, much less anything else, so she taped the dagger to the bottom of her serving tray like planned.

I wore my typical bar clothes. I had on low-cut jeans and a skimpy black halter top with a low v-neckline. I was not there to impress but wanted to blend in with the crowd. I carried a purse, where I kept the 9mm and the 45mm safely within reach.

I found a seat at a round table near Lambert's reserved area, so I could be close enough to keep an eye on the operation. Nicole went to work flirting with the customers, and I could tell she had been employed by a bar in the past by the way she handled the male clientele. She would frequently approach my table and "see if I needed a drink." I ordered my favorite drink, Belvedere and 7, to keep up appearances. Around ten o'clock, a man, or should I say *boy*, approached my table.

"Hi there, I noticed..."

"No," I interrupted him.

He had a confused look on his face but kept talking. "I wanted to buy..."

"No, walk away." I interrupted him again. Over the years, I have found the only certain way to get men to leave you alone was to be the quintessential bitch. He still didn't quite understand what I was saying, so I continued. "Look, I'm sure you find yourself very interesting and think I am stupid enough to fall for your 'charms,' but I am not interested in anything you have to offer me. Walk away now," I told him.

He stared at me for a second, obviously never having been handled that abruptly. Finally he turned and sulked back to his friends, but not before calling me a vulgar name. I just smiled to myself and sipped my drink.

Finally around ten-thirty as scheduled, Lambert and his cronies walked into the bar.

He left a guard near the door and walked with his other three guards to his reserved area. He went through the curtains with two guards and left the other at the curtain entrance. He sat down and signaled to Nicole that he needed a drink. She walked over to him, and they exchanged a few words before she went back to the bar to fetch his drink. She placed the drink order, along with a Belvedere and 7. She delivered mine first.

"Here we go," she told me.

"Don't worry, I got your back," I assured her and handed her a ten-dollar bill wrapped around the arsenic vial. She swiftly overturned the vial, pouring the contents into Lambert's mixed drink.

She was walking back to the curtained area with the altered beverage for delivery, when I saw the guard at the door. He started to move quickly toward the curtains while talking into his wrist. He must have had a small two-way radio at his wrist. He was telling the other guards something urgent. *Oh crap, he saw her.*

The guard at the curtains grabbed Nicole by the wrist, knocking over the serving tray along with the arsenic laced drink. He swung her around so her back was against him and held her in a firm grip. *Shit!*

I jumped up and grabbed the first gun I could out of my purse, it was the 9mm. Nicole stared at me straight in the eyes. She looked calm. She tilted her head to her right. I aimed, exhaled, and fired my weapon. My bullet flew straight and hit the guard in the chest, just to the left of Nicole's head. I saw blood splatter on the left side of her face as the guard went down, pulling her with him.

The gun-fire caused the packed bar to erupt in panic. People were fleeing for their lives and knocking others over, trying to get to the door-which worked out well for us, because they were delaying the door guard from reaching us quickly.

One of Lambert's guards near him pulled his gun and pointed it at me, but before I could react, Nicole pulled her knife off the tray and threw it. The knife landed in the side of the guard's neck. *She wasn't lying about being good with a knife.*

She stood up, and I threw her the 9mm I was holding. She caught it and sent a few rounds into the chest of the guard still standing in front of Lambert. I pulled the 45mm out of my purse to prepare for the door guard, but a concerned bouncer decided to step in.

He grabbed my arm holding the .45 and twisted it behind my back. He knocked the gun out of my hand and held me tightly against his chest. He was stronger than me, but I knew how to handle him; after all, that is why I took all of those martial arts lessons. Quickly, with as much force as I could, I managed to elbow him in the face with my free arm. When he backed off, I turned to Nicole and saw her shoot a few rounds, which landed in Lambert's back as he was running for the back exit.

I turned my attention back to the bouncer, kicked him in the stomach, and finished with a right elbow to his face. I grabbed my purse and searched for the .45 but was unable to find it. I decided to leave it when I noticed the door guard was making his way out of the crowd toward Nicole. Completely oblivious to the approaching guard, Nicole was checking to make sure Lambert was dead. I yelled out to her but she could not hear me over the screams of the crowd. The guard lifted his gun toward Nicole. She could not hear my warning, so I made a split-second decision. I ran to Nicole and dove for her at the same moment the guard shot his weapon. I slammed into Nicole, and we both fell to the floor. I looked up and saw Nicole take down the guard with her 9mm.

I felt a stinging sensation shoot through my body, and my right arm felt like it was on fire. I looked down and saw blood pouring from my shoulder. *SHIT!*

Nicole pulled me to my feet. "Blake, you've been shot!"

I looked at her and gave her the stupid look her statement deserved. "No shit! I hadn't noticed!"

I glanced around and saw the bar was beginning to clear out. I spotted my .45 underneath my former stool. As quickly as I could, I maneuvered over and picked it up.

"Come on, we have to get out of here before the cops show up," I told her, and we left through the back exit that Lambert had been unsuccessful in reaching.

I climbed in the passenger seat of our rented Nissan Altima, and Nicole sped out of the parking lot. "We need to get you to a hospital," she told me.

"No, we can't," I replied. "Hospitals mean questions. Hand me your phone."

She grabbed her phone out of the console and handed it to me. I removed my left hand from the bullet wound in my right shoulder and took her phone. I dialed the office and our extension. When the operator picked up, I yelled my ID number at her, and she connected me to my controller.

"Hello, Tech..." he said

"Tank, I've been fucking shot," I yelled at him, trying to sound calm. Obviously it didn't work.

"What! What happened?"

"I was shot in the shoulder, but otherwise I'm fine," I said, in an aggressive, sarcastic voice.

"Where are you?" he asked.

"Leaving the scene. Target's been taken care of," I told him.

"I don't care about that, Blake. Give the phone to Nicole," he told me, so I gave her the blood covered smart phone.

"Hey," she said. I couldn't hear what he was saying because he wasn't yelling. That made me more nervous. Tank is unusually calm in serious situations.

"She is bleeding pretty bad," I heard Nicole tell Tank. "OK, yeah, I know where that is. We'll be there," and with that, she hung up the phone.

"What did he say?" I asked Nicole, as I let my head rest against my seat.

"He said to go to a drug store and get something to stop the bleeding. Then we need to get our stuff out of the hotel. He is sending a private plane to pick us up in about two hours. Can you make it that long?"

"Yeah, no problem," I answered, trying to sound optimistic. I wanted to keep Nicole calm, because it looked like she was about to crack.

Nicole used some napkins we had in the car from our fast food to clean some of my and the guard's blood off of her face before going into the store for bandages. She still looked a little rough but at least she wasn't bloody anymore.

My shoulder felt like it was on fire, and a thousand tiny swords were stabbing into it over and over again. I turned on the radio and tried to take my mind off of the fact that a large amount of my blood was flowing out of my shoulder-but surprise, surprise, the music didn't help.

Nicole got back in the car and ripped the rest of my halter top off my shoulder to expose the full wound. She pressed the bandages against it, and I held back a scream when she applied pressure. I held the bandages in place as she drove to our hotel. Again I waited in the car while Nicole gathered our bags and made sure we didn't leave anything too incriminating. While she was in our room, I had to change bandages twice. I wasn't certain that the bullet had exited my back, but I pressed my back against the seat, hoping the cushion would stop any bleeding in case it had. *SHIT! Bad idea!* I quickly released pressure between the seat and my shoulder. Nicole jumped back in the car and looked at me with concern.

"What?" I asked her, with my eyes still closed.

"Nothing," she said. "You just look a little pale."

I smiled. "Yeah, getting shot will do that to you."

Nicole drove just slow enough to keep from getting a speeding ticket. She pulled in the park Tank told her to go to. She parked the car and turned to face me.

"How are you doing?" she asked.

"Great," I answered "I think I will go bowling when we get home."

That made her laugh a little, but that ended when I cringed from the pain laughter caused. I changed my bandages for the sixth time.

"I'm so sorry," she told me, on the verge of tears. "I should have seen him coming."

I opened my eyes and looked at her. "Don't worry about it. It wasn't your fault, besides it's not the first time I've been injured on a job and it probably won't be the last."

We waited for another twenty minutes before we saw the plane approaching in the distance. Nicole got out of the car and ran to my side. I opened the door before she reached me.

The small plane landed about a hundred yards from us, and Tank and a tall, handsome assassin ran out of the plane. Mark had dark hair that was short but thick, which women often found themselves wanting to run their hands through. He was muscular, not in the body-building sort of way, but more like a swimmer. His eyes were so blue they almost looked black, like a sapphire. His smile caused girls to go weak in the knees. He knew how handsome he was, and reminded me of it often.

The sight of Mark made me feel a little better-but, at the same time, nervous. Tank would only bring him if he was worried my injury was very serious.

They ran up to me, and Tank pulled me carefully out of the car. Once I was standing, I was very aware of how weak I was. I could hardly stand on my own, and I was blinking away the dark spots that precede fainting. I knew it wouldn't be long before the pain caused me to black out completely, but I would fight it as long as I could.

Tank and Nicole carried me to the plane because they knew I would have a hard time making it on my own. Nicole gave Mark the keys to the car, and he pulled the car away from the plane. As we were walking up the stairs to get on the aircraft, I heard sirens in the distance.

"The cops must have seen us land, we have to hurry," Tank told Nicole.

When we got into the plane Tank set me down on the couch. Our company doctor was there and still in his pajamas. *Tank must have woken him up for this.* He cut my shirt off and removed the bloody bandages.

"She looks like she lost a lot of blood," he told Tank, as he turned to retrieve something out of his bag. At that time I heard Mark running up the stairs. He sat across from me as the doctor began to administer an IV. Tank told the pilot to get going and the plane began to pull away.

"Did you take care of the car?" Tank asked Mark.

"Yeah, I set a timer on the bomb. It will go off in fifteen minutes," Mark answered. "How is she doing, Doc?"

I answered before the doctor had a chance. "I'm fine Mark."

"Blake, sweetie, I was not asking you," he said, in his playful tone that sounded like he was talking to a puppy. I knew he was just trying to keep me calm, but I hated when he talked to me like I was an infant. I would normally have made a smart-ass comment to him, but I didn't have the energy.

"What happened?" Mark asked.

"My back was turned, and Blake jumped in front of a bullet intended for me," Nicole explained.

"Who the hell are you?" Mark asked aggressively. I hadn't realized that Mark had not met Nicole yet.

"Stop it," I told Mark, with as much strength as I could muster, but it came out only a little louder than a whisper. "It wasn't her fault."

Mark moved to the couch by my side and took my hand. "I'm sorry, Blake, I didn't mean to upset you," he said.

"We will discuss what happened later; right now you need to rest," Tank told me.

I leaned my head back and closed my eyes. I guess the medicine in the IV was kicking in, because the pain lessened as I sat with my eyes shut. I listened to Tank and the doctor talk as he worked on my bandages, and slowly the sound of their voices faded away.

Chapter 7

I WAS HALF ASLEEP when I tried to roll over onto my side. I let out a moan when the pain in my right shoulder reminded me not to move. "That's not how I remember your moans sounding."

I smiled at the sound of his voice. "Mark, you really shouldn't say things like that. If your girlfriend heard you, she would literally kill you."

I opened my eyes and saw Mark sitting in the chair next to my bed. I instantly realized that I was in the hospital wing of our building. All hospital rooms look the same-but Tank would not take me to a real hospital; they ask too many questions, especially about a gunshot wound.

"How are you feeling?" Mark asked.

"Surprisingly, not that bad," I told him. "It just hurts to move my arm."

"I'm shocked you can feel anything, with the amount of drugs they pumped in you." I looked down to see my shoulder, but I was dressed in one of those tacky hospital gowns that opens at the back. "I brought you an ICEE, but you were still asleep, so I drank it." I gave him a threatening look. "Well, I didn't want it to melt," he said, with a grin.

ICEEs have always been my comfort food. One of the few memories I had of my mother was buying me an ICEE after a bad visit to a doctor.

"Hey, I was wondering if you would put in a good word for me with Nicole?" Mark asked. A sly grin slowly made its way on his face.

I gave him a confused look. "What about Tabitha, your girlfriend?" I asked, as I raised my eyebrows.

"I'm just keeping my options open, and she's hot," he joked.

"You're a pig." I rested my head on my pillow and closed my eyes.

"Yes, but I'm a good-looking pig," he said, with a smirk. I could only laugh at his conceded self-image.

"How is she?" I heard. I opened my eyes and saw Tank standing in the doorway.

"You know it will take more than that to hurt our Blake," Mark told him, as he winked at me.

"Mark, do you mind if I talk to Blake in private?" Tank politely asked my friend. "Sure, I better get going anyway; Tabitha will kill me if I'm late for our lunch date." Mark kissed me on my forehead after promising to visit me later and left Tank and me alone.

Tank closed the door and stood at the foot of my bed. "Really, how do you feel?"

"I'm fine," I told him. I was beginning to get annoyed with people asking me if I was all right.

"Good. In that case, Blake Annabel Morgan, what the hell happened?" I was a little shocked by Tank's outburst but I kept my face from showing it. "You were supposed to make sure nothing bad happened, and you end up getting shot!" After I did not respond he asked "Well, are you going to say anything?"

"I'm just waiting for you to calm down. Did you just three-name me?"

"Sorry," he said, as he walked over to my side and sat down in Mark's abandoned chair. "What happened?" he asked again, trying to remain calm.

"Well, I'm sure you already have the story from Nicole, but if you must hear it again...Things were going well until a citizen decided to step in." He gave me a confused look, and I realized that Nicole did not see what happened. I told him everything that had happened from the moment we entered the bar to the second I spotted the plane coming to my rescue.

When I finished, Tank took a moment to digest the information. "OK, I'm sorry I yelled at you, but you scared the crap out of me. Anyway, the doctor said that you need a few months to recover from the gunshot wound and the surgery, then rehab for the arm. So it looks like desk work for a while."

"Months? How many? No, I can't be cooped up in the office for that long. I'll go crazy."

"I don't know how many months; that's up to your arm. And you will stay in the office until your arm heals. I won't let you damage it any more than it already is," he firmly stated, as I gave him an argumentative glare. "Now, get some sleep. The doctor says you need rest."

Tank left my room, and I turned on the television because I was too stubborn to sleep when he told me to. I watched the DVD of the first season of *I Love Lucy* that Mark had left for me. *I Love Lucy* was one of my favorite shows, and I made Mark watch them all the time when we were a couple. After a few episodes, I decided I had protested long enough and drifted off to sleep.

Chapter 8

I LET THE WATER cover every inch of me that I didn't need in order to breathe. My Jacuzzi tub was large enough that I could relax and be completely submerged by hot water. It had been over two months since my doctor cleared me for activity. Ever since then, I had been spending every waking moment either at work, physical therapy, or my dojo. My arm was growing stronger every day, and my sensei told me I was showing rapid improvement. Sensei Hayato had given me some type of bath salts to use, which he said were supposed to heal and rejuvenate; so I had been using them every night and every morning. I wasn't sure if it was really making a difference but it gave off a pleasant lavender scent, so I continued to use it.

I raised my head out of the tub and noticed that my finger tips had aged nearly sixty years. That, combined with the sun brightly shinning outside, told me that it was time to get out of the Jacuzzi. I drained the water and hopped out of the tub, then jumped in the shower. I always took a shower after a bath. I felt dirty after a bath; the idea of sitting in the water used to clean the dirt from my body didn't seem sanitary. That, plus the bath salts left my hair greasy, so a shower was a quick fix.

Afterward, I did my hair and dressed in a pair of jeans and a white button-up shirt. I had bought a new Llama .45 pistol the day before and was anxious to try it out at the gun range in out building, so I put it in my briefcase with my workout clothes, got in my Range Rover, and drove to work.

I parked in my normal parking spot and walked down the sidewalk to my building. I greeted the guards as I walked past the security desk. "Good morning, Walter. Good morning, Lance."

"Good morning, Ms. Morgan," Lance replied, as I moved to the side door.

Our lobby was an empty room, with a door off to the left and a pair of double doors located in the back used for the hospital wing. On the side of the left door is a hand print reader. I placed my right palm on the screen, and it scanned my hand. Once I was identified, the door opened. I walked through the door and to the elevator.

I realized that in my excitement about my new gun, I had forgotten to grab my coffee on my way out of the house. I cannot function without my morning cup of coffee, so I decided to head straight for our lunch room to grab a cup. I exited the elevator and walked down the hall. At the end of the hall was a room with a stove, microwave, refrigerator, and the most important appliance of all...the coffee maker.

I retrieved my coffee mug from the cupboard and filled it with coffee but left enough room for cream and sugar. After adding the final ingredients, I headed back to my office.

"Good morning, Peter," I said, as he stepped out from around the corner.

"What the hell? I can never sneak up on you. How do you always now I'm there?" he asked, as he turned around to walk beside me. I just smiled at him. We walked through the door of room 428 and to our desks.

"I was getting ready to head down to the mats," he said. Not only did our building have a shooting range beneath it, it also had a weight room and a gym equipped with mats, so we could spar. "David and the new kid in Jones's group are going to fight. We are all going to watch."

Jones was in charge of close to a dozen assassins including Mark. Jones and Tank had never gotten along, and a sort of rivalry had formed between the two groups.

"Well, that sounds more interesting than the paper work I had planned-I think I'll join you," I replied, and we both walked out of the room together. "Has David aggravated you anymore with that whole 'Pack Rat' thing?" I asked.

"No, but I like the name. I think I'm going to keep it," he answered. I gave him a funny look, so he explained. "I mean, I kind of am a pack rat, so the name fits. I do store a lot of souvenirs," he said.

"Well, all right; if you like it, that's fine with me," I replied.

We walked into the gym and found a large group of people circled around the mats. *Apparently the fight already started.* We moved through the crowd until we were positioned near the action. David was dodging a punch by a twenty-something-year-old named Ryan. I looked across the mat and saw Mark smiling at me. His current girlfriend Tabitha saw him smile and gave me the meanest look she possessed.

I returned the smile and turned my attention back to the fight, where Ryan received a blow to the stomach. When he got off the ground, David gave him a right hook that sent him back to the floor.

David turned toward our group and began to jump up and down in celebration, while our team cheered him on. While David's back was turned, Ryan got up and hit him from behind, sending David into the crowd. Our group began to boo and yell obscenities at Ryan, calling him a coward for hitting David while his back was turned. They began to push toward the mats. I could see a riot was about to break out. *Crap!* I had to do something, or there would be a bunch of killers fighting.

I walked onto the mat, trying to think of some way to keep the mob from tearing each other apart. Before I could make a move, Mark walked up and got in Ryan's face. "What the hell are you doing?" he yelled. "You do not hit an opponent while his back is turned. That's poor form. Do you understand me?" Mark was the senior assassin in Jones's group, so he had authority. David started to cheer Mark on, but I cut him off.

"Shut up," I told him, hoping my reputation and seniority had some sway in my group. "You never turn your back to an opponent. You know better than that. You deserved to be hit. Now leave, all of you." When neither David nor Ryan said anything, the crowd began to disperse. David lingered a moment to stare me down, but when I didn't flinch, he turned and sulked away.

I turned toward Mark. "Thanks for that," I said.

"No problem; I didn't want a fight to break out, either," he replied. Tabitha quickly walked up to stand close to Mark.

"Why, aren't you the little hero," she sneered.

Don't anger a killer. Don't anger a killer...oh what the hell? "No, Mark is the real hero. If he hadn't come up to help me, I don't know what would've happened. Of course, all white knights are heroic," I replied, trying to channel

Scarlet O'Hara (without the accent) as I walked up to rub his arm. Tabitha gave me a death stare and clung tighter to Mark.

From behind us, a few girls called out to Tabitha, "Hey, let's go. If we want to grab brunch before the mall, we need to leave." Tabitha did not move an inch; she was in a staring match that I refused to lose.

"Go," Mark told her. "You've been excited about this all week. Besides, I have an appointment with Dr. Harris in fifteen minutes." She stared at me for another few seconds, then turned toward Mark.

"OK, honey. I will call you later," she said, before she reached up and gave Mark a passionate kiss intended to aggravate me. It made me laugh silently and proved how easy it was to get under her skin. She gave me a smile designed to anger me then left to join her friends.

"Why do you have to do that?" Mark asked, as we walked toward the elevators. "You know how sensitive she is about our friendship."

"I don't know. It's just too much fun, and too easy to piss her off," I said.

"Yeah, well now I'm going to have to have a thirty-minute conversation about how we are just friends, again," he replied.

"I'm sorry," I told him, still grinning.

"No you're not, but thanks," he said, as we boarded the elevator.

"You're right, I'm not," I said, as I leaned against the wall of the elevator.

"So, I saw Tommy yesterday," he said, with a side smirk.

"Yeah, he's been moping around the office. I didn't want to hurt his feelings, but the boy does not understand the concept of a breakup. After my accident, it got worse, and I know I just scared him...but come on," I said, with exasperation in my voice.

"You scared all of us. Tank was a nervous wreck. Just give Tommy some time. He's just taking the breakup hard. He will get over it. I did," he said.

"You were different," I told him. "We both decided to break up."

"That didn't make it too much easier," he said "I mean you're pretty, smart, and funny; and although you have a mean sense of humor, you're really a nice person. There were times when I thought we had made a mistake."

I froze. I didn't know what to do or how to respond. I had no clue he thought that. "I didn't know you felt that way," I told him, standing straighter from shock.

"Yeah, well, it doesn't matter. We were right. You're probably my closest friend. And if we had kept dating, we probably would have killed each other," he said, as the door to the second floor opened. He kissed my cheek and stepped off the elevator. "I'll talk to you later," he said.

I replied, "Good luck with the shrink and the girlfriend."

He gave me a smile and yelled "Thanks," as the elevator doors closed.

I got off the elevator on the fourth floor, still a little shocked by Mark's comment to me. I walked to my desk and began my paper work. *I hate paperwork. Just a few more hours; then I can go to physical therapy.*

Tank opened the door to his office and saw me sitting at my desk. "Blake, can you come in here please?" he asked me.

I walked into his office and sat down in front of his desk. Tank closed the door and sat in his chair.

"I heard there was an incident in the gym," he said.

It always amazed me, how fast he heard things. He must have been able to read my surprised expression. "I figured it out when David came in from his fight, complaining about you. So what happened?"

"Oh, nothing. Things were beginning to get out of hand, so Mark and I stopped it," I answered.

"Good; the last thing we need is a war with Jones's group. How's the shoulder? I talked to your therapist, and he said your arm is excellent and that you can return to missions soon," Tank said.

"That's awesome! I am so sick of paperwork. I think if I have to sit at that computer for another week, I will go 'Office Space' on a fax machine." The part of that movie where the main characters beat up a fax machine was my favorite. I began to shift excitedly in my seat. I felt like a kid finding out he was going to a fair.

"Well, I do have a job that I was saving for you, but if you don't want it..." he said, teasing me.

"What's the job?"

"A woman. Most of my guys have problems with killing women; and those who don't, like David, I don't trust with this job," he said, as he handed me the file.

I opened the folder and saw an address in New Orleans, and under name, it said "The Mother." I looked up from the file. "That's it? That's all the information we have?"

"Pretty much. Anyone who tries to retrieve intel or even a picture of her ends up dead. She is very dangerous. Are you sure you're up for it?" he asked.

For some reason, I was kind of nervous about this job, but I had to get out of the office, so I decided to take it.

"You can take someone with you if you want," Tank told me.

"No thanks. I only worry about the other person, and someone will end up getting hurt. I work better alone," I told him.

"OK, but at the first sign of trouble I want you out of there. Do you understand me?"

"Yes, Dad," I joked.

"I'm serious."

"I know you are. I promise."

I left Tank's office and picked up my brief-case. *It's time for some target practice.*

Chapter 9

AFTER FIRING TWO hundred rounds with my new 45mm, I felt so much better. It's amazing how shooting a powerful weapon helps someone to relax. I went back to my office to work on some plans for my assignment. I walked through the door and saw Tommy at his desk. I sat at my desk (which was joined to his) and, remembering what Mark had told me in the elevator, decided to be nice.

"Hey, Tommy, how are you?" He kept his head down and stared at his paperwork. "Fine," was all I got out of him. *OK, I tried.* I turned to my computer to begin a search on "The Mother."

"You know what?" Tommy suddenly said, as he looked up at me. "I am fine. You, however, are not." I gave him a looked that showed how shocked I was by his outburst. "Yeah, that's what I said. You are all screwed up. And the funny thing is, you have no idea. Let me ask you a question. How long is your longest relationship?" Before I could get a word out he answered it for me. "Wait, let me guess. Hmm about three months. Am I close?" *Damn, he was.*

"Yeah, so what?" I asked him.

"So that's my point. You are so damaged that you can't trust anybody. You think that if you allow yourself to get close to someone, you will end up hurt. And I get it. Really, I do, it makes sense. Your parents were ripped from you at an early age, and then you were torn apart from your orphan family by the only living relative you have. And then he dies. It makes sense-but if you don't let people in, you will be miserable the rest of your life. I mean, you don't even have any friends. The closest people to that are an ex-boyfriend and your boss. Don't you see how messed up that is? So to answer your question, I'm great, because I won't die alone. You, I'm not so sure about," he finished, as he got up from his chair and walked out the door.

I was so shocked that I could hardly move. I sat there staring at his empty chair. *What the hell just happened?* After a period of time (how long, I'm not sure) I turned back to my computer.

I don't have issues. Yeah, so I haven't had a long-term relationship, but that doesn't mean anything. Does it? My mind started working in overdrive, trying to sort out my life. Everything he said was true. My best friends were Tank and Mark. I had not had a lasting relationship. *Maybe I do keep people at a distance. Holy crap, could he be right?* I started to have trouble catching my breath. *Oh great, now on top of psychological problems, I'm having an anxiety attack. Perfect.* I put my head on my desk and took in a few deep breaths.

After a few seconds, my breathing returned to normal. *OK, I need to just relax and not think about Tommy or what he said.* I typed in "The Mother" in Google and checked out the results. I got passed the first result about a film and drifted into a daze, thinking again about my relationship phobia. *He was right, shit, he was right. It makes sense.*

I saw a hand wave in front of my face. "Hello, Blake?" I looked up to see Nicole leaning across my desk. "You OK?" She asked, as she got off my desk and sat in Tommy's empty chair.

"Yeah," I lied, as I rubbed my eyes back into focus.

"What are you working on?" She asked.

"Just my new assignment," I told her. She kicked her heels up on the desk.

"Hey, what are you doing tonight? There is a movie out I want to go see. You want to come?" I turned to look back at my computer screen.

"No, I can't. I have some things to do before I leave for my job," I said.

"Oh, OK, that's fine. Maybe next time," she said, a little hurt. As she stood to walk away I heard Tommy's voice saying "You don't even have any friends".

"You know what, I would love to go to a movie tonight," I said suddenly. *I refuse to let Tommy be right.* "I can just push that other stuff till later," I told her.

"Great! The new Johnny Depp movie is showing, and everyone is talking about how good it is," she said, sounding as excited as a child who was going to a circus for the first time.

"I'll pick you up after Bando class," I told her, and I went back to work.

"Everyone was right, that movie was awesome!" Nicole exclaimed, as I dropped her off at her apartment.

"Yeah, it was pretty good. Well, thanks for inviting me. It was just what I needed," I told her.

"Anytime. And good luck on the job." She smiled and closed the door. I drove back to my condo and began packing for my assignment in New Orleans. I had always heard the weather in Louisiana was hot, so I went to pack a bunch of tank tops, and then decided against it. Instead, I grabbed a handful of designer t-shirts that would cover my scar from the gunshot wound. I packed the usual: jeans, some dressier clothes, and a couple of dresses. You never know what you will need on a job. I added a few new songs to my iPod for the plane ride before getting into bed. As I tried to sleep, I kept thinking about what Tommy had told me earlier. I knew I would not be able to sleep, so I sat up and grabbed my cell phone. I dialed Mark's phone number.

"Hello," he said. He sounded like I woke him up. I looked at my alarm clock. It read twelve-oh-eight in the morning.

"Do you think I have relationship problems?"

"Blake, what are you talking about?" he asked, like I was being ridiculous.

"I'm serious. Tommy said I have relationship problems, because my parents died and I was pulled away from Court and the gang, and then Uncle James died. I mean, I haven't had a long-term relationship, and I don't really have friends..." I was rambling.

"Whoa, hold on, slow down a second. Tommy said what?"

"Weren't you listening? I'm screwed up!"

"No, you're not. You just have had a rough life."

"Gee, thanks."

"You know what I mean. Besides, Tommy is just mad you broke up with him. You shouldn't take anything he says seriously."

"So you don't think I'm damaged?"

"Yeah, I do. But not like that," he joked

"Ha, ha, very funny," I replied.

"So are you OK?" he asked.

"Yeah, I guess so. But I still think he may have a point."

"I don't. You just haven't met the right person. It's hard finding someone who could replace me."

"Yeah, I don't think I will be able to find someone with a bigger ego," I retorted. He laughed for a second. "Well, I guess I better try to get some sleep," I said. "I have a flight to catch in the morning. Thanks for letting me vent."

"Anytime."

Chapter 10

I ARRIVED IN NEW Orleans a little after five o'clock pm. on a Sunday. I got in my rented Acura and headed for my hotel. I checked into the W Hotel under the alias Jessica Morales. I ignored the soft sofas and beautiful art that lined the walls of the four-star hotel. Since becoming an assassin, my job sent me to hotels all over the country. It took a lot to impress me. One thing I did notice was the bar. I normally didn't drink during an assignment, but I decided to take the day off and begin work in the morning, so I sat down in front of the cute twenty-something-year-old bartender.

"What can I get you?" he asked, as he leaned forward on the bar.

"I would love a Belvedere and 7," I told him, with a little too much desperation in my voice.

He smiled and turned to fetch the vodka from the top shelf. "Been a bad day?" He handed me my drink in exchange for cash.

"More like a bad yesterday," I replied.

"Anything I can help with?" he asked, with a serious amount of flirtation in his voice. OK, he was cute, a little too young for me, but with the stress I was having with recently figuring out I was emotionally damaged, I could use some company. Before I began to return his flirtation, my common sense broke in and I decided that a one-night fling would not be a good idea.

I answered his question with a sigh. "Oh, well, I just recently figured out that I have some serious relationship issues- which was brought to my attention by my ex-boyfriend, by the way-stemming from my parents' death and quickly followed by the abandonment of everything I knew and loved. Then, once I found a stable loving family, I was wrenched from them and forced into a world devoted to pain and agony. Every relationship I've had since then has ended in a flash of a heartbeat, and all I want to do is scream, run for the hills, and knock out every happy couple I see on the way. But, I refuse to let my emotions make my decisions for...me so instead, here I am, drowning my sorrows in a glass of vodka. Anything you can do for that?"

Once I finished my rambling, the bartender looked at me, and I saw terror flash in his eyes. "Yeah, I didn't think so," I told him. He gave me a nervous smile and walked off to busy himself with washing glasses instead of looking at me. You mention something about a relationship, and guys flee.

I decided that I didn't want to sit there anymore, so I quickly finished my drink and got up from the bar. "Thanks for your help," I said, and walked to the elevators, towing my bags behind me. I used my access card to enter my room.

I walked into my room and dropped my bags at the foot of one of my two queen-sized beds and threw myself on top of it. Sometimes I can be a little dramatic, but I'm OK with it. After a moment on an incredibly soft bed, I decided to walk around and explore the city. I grabbed my purse and headed out of the hotel. On my way out, I passed the bar and saw the bartender trying to avoid making eye contact with me.

I left the hotel and decided to head north. I found myself walking through the French Quarter. It was incredible. Jazz music could be heard from bars, and occasionally I would find people playing jazz on the street. One entire block was devoted to artists portraying their work and psychics offering to tell my fortune for a small fee. After five minutes of walking down the street, I was engulfed in the essence of the town and falling in love with the city.

I found myself standing in front of a cute little café. I walked in, searching for a cup of coffee. As I sat down at a table to await the waitress, I realized I hadn't had dinner yet. A waitress with long brown hair, pulled up into a tight pony-tail, walked up to my table. "Hi, how are you today?"

Deciding that my ramble of my recent issues would not be needed here, I replied with a normal answer. "Fine; can I have a cup of coffee and," I glanced at the menu, "beignets?"

The waitress let out a little laugh. "You're not from here, are you, sweetie?"

I gave her a confused look and answered. "No, I'm not. I'm from Seattle," I lied. "How did you know?"

"They are pronounced *ben-yaes*." I smiled my thanks to her. "I'll be right back with your order."

I leaned back in my chair and looked out at the city. Two women were perched on stools outside the café. One played a steady rhythm on her guitar, while the other used her violin for the vocals. It took only a second for me to recognize Annie Lenox's "Waiting in Vain."

I saw many couples walking down the street hand in hand. Not all of them were lovers. I noticed a woman walking with a shopping bag in one hand and her daughter's hand in the other. I couldn't help but smile at the picture. The daughter was a mini-clone of her mother. They both had long blond hair; they wore similar outfits; and the little girl even held her own mini shopping bag. I never wanted children. I guess I always thought I would be a horrible mother. It makes sense, I'm a trained killer. How compassionate could I be? But as I watched the mother and daughter walk down the street, I felt something begin to stir in my chest.

The waitress interrupted my maternal debate and delivered my coffee and beignets. Beignets are fried bread with powdered sugar on top of them. I took a bite of my first beignet, and if I hadn't been sitting down, I'm sure the taste would have knocked me to the ground. They were amazing. I was instantly addicted to them. I devoured the order I had and quickly placed another order. The waitress laughed at my enthusiasm about the delicious treat and brought my second helping. As soon as I finished, I debated over another order of beignets but decided to pass. I paid my bill and returned to my city exploration.

I walked down the famous Bourbon Street and was stunned by the amount of people there. It was eight-thirty, and there were people everywhere. I knew this was a major party city, but this seemed excessive. I walked into a karaoke bar but turned back to the door when I realized I didn't feel like fighting the crowd at the bar.

"Is it always this busy?" I asked the security guard sitting at the door.

"No, it's just because of Mardi Gras," he answered, without turning to look at me. I had heard about Mardi Gras and had always wanted to experience it.

"Oh, was Mardi Gras today?" I asked, slightly disappointed that I had missed it. He turned his head and stared at me with a confused look. "No. It's next Tuesday. If it was today, you wouldn't be able to walk through here. People get a little nuts anticipating it." I looked around the street, and as crowded as it was, it was nowhere near being packed. "Where are you from?" he asked me.

"Seattle," I lied. I had never felt like I stood out so bad in my life. Part of my job was to blend in, but here it was as if I had a neon sign over my head that flashed "Out-of-Towner."

"Yeah, the town gets pretty busy before Mardi Gras, with everyone coming in for it." He turned his attention to a guy trying to start a fight, so I left.

I walked down the street to sounds of people yelling for beads that were being thrown from balconies. *This is crazy.* I knew the concepts of Mardi Gras but never understood why people would go crazy for a string of plastic beads.

I turned off of Bourbon Street, trying to circle back to my hotel, and a few blocks later I realized I was lost. The crowd dwindled, and soon I found myself alone walking down a dark street. *How can this street be so deserted when, only a block away, the street is crowded with a bunch of drunken maniacs?* I made another turn and felt an uneasiness forming in my stomach. My pace quickened, and I knew that this was somewhere a girl shouldn't travel alone. I was stopped in my tracks when I heard a couple of guys call out to me.

"Well, well. What do we have here?" one asked the other. "It looks like an out-of-towner may have gotten lost. How horrible." This only proved my neon light above my head theory. They laughed as they approached me. "My, you are a pretty little thing, aren't you?"

The uneasy feeling was replaced by anticipation when one guy pulled out a switch blade. I loved knives. Most girls are afraid of them. I guess it's because, one, it is more painful to die from a knife wound than a gun (although, after my recent accident, I was not so sure that was accurate) and two, if you survive a knife attack, there is a great chance of scars. I know all girls are not vain, and I considered myself among those who were not, but I was embarrassed by the scar left from my bullet wound.

I liked knives, because I felt they were a fairer way to fight than guns. I smiled at them. "Could you tell me how to get back to the French Quarter?"

The guy holding the knife laughed at me. "Oh honey, you're not going to the French Quarter. You are gonna stay here and entertain us."

I looked at him and smiled. "I don't think so."

"Get her," the knife-wielding guy yelled, and the other ran straight at me.

I stood my ground, and when he lunged at me, I side-stepped his grasp but kept my foot placed in front of him. Using his momentum, I easily tripped him and sent him flying to the ground. I turned my attention to the knife-wielder and his advance.

He swung his knife at my face, which I kept out of his reach. When he brought the knife back up, I grabbed his arm with one hand. With the other, I grabbed his weapon hand and pressed my thumb down on a pressure point located on the back of his hand. He screamed and released the weapon. I punched him with my left hand, sending him away from me, and turned just in time to duck a punch from the other would-be rapist.

I came around and grabbed the wrist that he jabbed at me firmly with my left hand. With my right hand, I hit the outside of his elbow with as much force as I could. I heard the distinct sound of joints breaking and he fell to the ground, screaming.

I turned back to the other attacker just in time to see him pull a gun that was tucked in his belt. He was still within arm's reach, so I grabbed the hand holding the gun and sent my other elbow into the side of his head as hard as I could. My elbow connected right above the ear and he fell back from me as I managed to pry the gun from his hand. I kicked him in the knee cap, and he fell face-first to the ground. I sat on top of his back and pushed the barrel of the gun to the back of his head. "Again...How do I get back to the French Quarter?"

Chapter 11

I FOLLOWED THE DIRECTIONS the hoodlum gave me back to my hotel. *What an idiot. He pulled a knife while he had a gun the whole time. That is just stupid.* I walked past a trash can and stopped to throw the pistol in it before continuing on my way. Once I got back to my room, I pulled out the bath salts my sensei gave me and took a long bath. I felt exhausted after the bath and went straight to sleep. I would need the rest. Tomorrow I would start reconnaissance on the Mother. *I hate stakeouts.*

I woke up from a wonderful night' sleep (the beds at the W are amazing) and took a shower. I pulled on a pair of jeans and a t-shirt. I pulled my hair into a ponytail and put on my Chicago Cubs baseball cap. The Cubs were my favorite major league baseball team. I remembered my father watching the Cubs when I was young. I would curl up in his lap and watch the great Ryne Sandberg. I had such a crush on him. My mom liked Mark Grace, but he couldn't lay a finger on my Ryne.

I left the hotel, got into my rented Acura, and drove to the address listed in the kill order. I drove past the Mother's address. It was a large Victorian house completely surrounded by an iron fence, and at the entrance stood a security gate house. It was a guard house with one or two guards to monitor who entered the premises. The house was in the middle of a suburban-looking neighborhood. It did not blend in with its surroundings. I parked down the street in front of the neighbor's house to begin my stakeout. I stretched across the backseat of the car with my binoculars and watched the house for hours. For close to six hours, I watched the house steadily, and absolutely nothing happened.

The only time anyone entered or left the premises was early that morning, when a delivery truck stopped at the house. It was a white van with the words "Crescent City Produce" written on the side. I opened my laptop and typed "Crescent City Produce" in the search bar. I wrote the address down and made a mental note to stop by later. I watched people walk around the yard inside the premises. The men and women were all dressed similarly, wearing khaki cargo pants and tight black shirts. After six hours of nothing, I decided to grab something to eat and make a bathroom stop.

I returned to my post after picking up a fried shrimp po' boy. A po' boy is similar to a hoagie with fried shrimp on it. I was a little skeptical but decided to give it a try. I settled in my back-seat with my sandwich and a Coke, took my first bite of the New Orleans po' boy, and was amazed. *This is delicious!* I scarfed down the rest of my sandwich. After another four hours of nothing happening, I left the house belonging to my target and headed back to the hotel.

I decided to stop at Crescent City Produce before going back to the hotel. It was ten o'clock at night so the produce stand was closed and boarded up for the night. I pulled my car around and parked behind the building. I got out of my Acura, grabbed my pick set, and headed for the side door where I bent down to examine the lock. It was a simple lock, so I searched through my tools and withdrew the appropriate pick. In a few seconds I had the door unlocked. I slowly opened the door looking for a security system. When I found no security wiring, I entered the building and realized why they did not have a security system. A huge German shepherd was standing in the doorway, staring intently at me. *Crap!*

I quickly jumped on top of a nearby counter as the dog lunged at me. The beast was unable to reach me on the counter, so I took a second to catch the breath the dog had scared out of me. On and off assignments, I dealt with various types of security systems. The one type of security system I had never cared for was the use of a guard dog. I never felt it was an adequate way of keeping unwanted visitors away, but as I sat on the countertop, I finally understood how effective it can be.

I crawled off the back of the counter, making sure the angry guard dog could not walk around to attack me again. I turned to find an office and entered the room quickly. It was a small room with a few chairs, a desk, and a filing cabinet. The desk held a computer and a disorganized pile of papers. I was only fair at computer hacking, so I headed for the filing cabinet. I thumbed through the files, not knowing exactly what I was looking for. Then I found it.

I pulled out a file named "Deliveries." I opened the file and found a single outstanding order. The order was for a delivery of produce to the address matching my target's. It was a large order, big enough to feed a lot of people. The order consisted of all types of produce. The file also revealed that the order would be delivered every Monday and Thursday. *One order is more vegetables than I eat in a year. OK, maybe not a year, but at least a few months.* I scanned down the page and found the section titled "Payment." I scanned for a name but did not find one. Service was paid for in cash.

I read the file again to make sure I hadn't missed anything and placed it back where I found it. I peeked out the door to make sure the guard dog had not made his way around the counter. After concluding it was safe to leave the office, I stepped out the door and jumped back onto the counter, which was the only place I knew the dog could not reach.

I looked down and saw the dog sitting between myself and the exit. I moved toward the door, and the dog's ears perked up. I stopped where I was and decided I would not be able to leave the way I had arrived. I looked around the produce area for another exit. It was a large, rectangle-shaped room that had two rows of fruits and vegetables running through it. The two rows created three aisles for patrons to walk through. The outside of the room was completely boarded up. There was no exit except for the door I had arrived through.

I quickly weighed my options. I could jump for the door, but the dog was in the way, so I knew my chances of actually making it through the door were slim. I couldn't shoot the dog. My silencer was still in my car, so the gunfire would draw unwanted attention. My other option was to run around the aisles, making the dog chase me. The dog would be behind me, and hopefully I could get back to the door before it took a bite out of my neck. I was fast. I was not conceited, I just knew I was fast. I had to be fast, for the career I had chosen. Was I fast enough to out run a German shepherd? Absolutely not. However, I might be able to stay in front of it for the few seconds I needed to get to the exit.

I slowly moved to the other side of the counter to get far away from the dog. Wrapping my fingers around the edge of the countertop, I slid the end of one foot to the same edge to give myself a strong push off. I looked back at the dog and saw it stand up. I took a deep breath and pushed off.

I ran down the first aisle as fast as I could. As I ran, I glanced behind me and saw the dog was close on my heels. I reached to my right and pulled a crate of Satsumas off the first row to land behind me. I was hoping the crate would slow the dog down, but it dodged the tangerine-like fruit easily. I turned the first corner, skipping the second aisle, and went straight to the last aisle. I needed to get out fast, or I would be puppy chow. As I turned the last corner, I pulled a barrel of potatoes down behind me. The dog jumped over the barrel and landed on my ankle causing me to stumble. I tried to regain my footing but was unable to do so. I braced myself for the fall.

I hit the ground with a jolt that shot up my arms and rolled over on my back to fight off the attack. As I rolled, the large dog wrapped his teeth around my calf. I bit my cheek in anticipation of the bite and to keep from yelling.

But the dog did not bite down. He let go of my leg and jumped up and down. I sat up on my hands and looked at the dog in confusion. He jumped at me and nipped at my hand. *Is he playing?* I stood up and the dog laid his chin on the ground and wagged his butt in the air. *Holy crap! He's playing!*

I leaned over and cautiously extended my hand to the dog. He nipped at my hand again. He was not a mean guard dog. He just looked scary enough to get the job done. I looked around the room and noticed the mess I had made in our race. Not wanting the dog to get in trouble for messing up the place, I began picking up the spilled produce. The dog stayed by my side throughout the cleaning.

When I was done, I walked to the exit. I sat on my heels and stroked the dog's head. "I think I will call you Satsuma," I told him. As the dog no longer filled me with terror, I noticed how cute he actually was. He was golden, with black fur covering his back and his nose. After a few seconds of petting his dark nose, I left the produce stand and heard the dog whining as I locked the door behind me.

I drove back to my hotel and let the valet park my car. Once back in my room, I headed straight for my bathroom, drew my bath water, and dropped in some of my special bath salts. After my bath I fell down in my extremely comfortable bed and turned on my TV. I scanned through the channels until I found something that caught my eye. *The Goonies* was one of my favorite movies when I was younger, so I could not pass up watching it, no matter how tired I was. I fell asleep sometime before the movie finished.

I decided to sleep in the next morning. I drove out to my stakeout spot a little after ten o'clock. The stakeout was very similar to the day before. No one left the confines of the fence, and the only ones who entered or left the house were the people dressed in the khaki cargo pants and the black shirts. The day was incredibly boring.

The only interesting thing that happened that day was at two o'clock in the afternoon, when a group of the soldier lookalikes decided to play a game of football. I watched from my car as the guys split into two teams, the shirts verses the skins.

These guys were fit. That is to say, some of these guys were fit. Some were incredibly muscular. I could see every line and indentation of their muscles from my car. I watched as the game continued. About half-way through the game, one team kicked the ball over the fence. The ball landed about twenty-five yards in front of my car. One of the players left the field and the gate to retrieve the ball. Even though he was a ways from me, I could see how attractive he was. He was built like a professional surfer, with perfect blond hair that was a little long on top. He ran across the street to where the ball had landed, but a neighborhood boy had beaten him to it. The hot player called out to the boy and held his hands up for the pass. The boy threw the ball with all his might, and it barely reached his receiver. The player cheered the boy on as if he just threw a winning touchdown pass. I couldn't help but smile at how happy the little boy was. The player turned and ran back to his game. After the game, nothing of interest happened. I staked-out the house until one in the morning, when I retired back to my room for a bath and sleep.

The next day I called Tank to check in and to find a weapon supplier. Tank was protective, especially with me. He thought of me as a daughter, which I didn't mind. After I had convinced Tank that I was OK, he gave me the address of a nearby supplier he was in contact with.

I drove to the address of a guy named Garrett. I pulled to the curb in front of a house that looked like it had been divided in two; it had two front doors, and the porch had two different sets of patio furniture on it. I learned that this was common in New Orleans. A long time ago, the house had been built as a double shotgun house, which is two shotgun houses built side by side, with a connecting wall. A family that owned a double shotgun house would normally rent one side out for extra money.

I walked up the driveway and knocked on the door on the right side of the house. The man who answered was not what I expected. He was not very tall, skinny, and had curly red hair. If I saw him on the street, I would have guessed he had never touched a gun in his life. *Where does Tank find these people?*

"You must be Tank's friend. I'm Garrett," he said, stepping aside so I could enter.

I walked into the house and looked around his living area. He had a massive computer set up instead of a television set. He had a couch on one wall, facing the computer. Nothing else occupied his living room.

"Nice to meet you," I said, with a smile, unable to tear my eyes away from the cluster of freckles on his nose. I never gave my name to suppliers, as a precaution. His cheeks turned pink when I smiled at him, and he quickly looked away.

"Right this way," he said, as he started walking down the hall.

I followed him to a room in the back. He stepped inside the room and turned the lights on. I walked in and noticed he had a fairly decent collection of weaponry. He had more guns than the woman in Denver had, but I liked her secret room better.

I walked around the room and carefully examined his collection. I decided on my favorite caliber and picked up the 45mm in the center of the room. Once I decided on my weapon, I turned to Garrett and noticed that he would not make eye contact with me. He was extremely introverted. I wanted to ask how he got involved with professional killers, given his incredible shyness, but I thought that was too personal a question. Instead, I asked for a few cases of bullets and headed for the door.

"This is a nice set up you have here," I told him, as I examined his computer center. He blushed again at my compliment.

"Thanks," he told his feet. I thanked him and left his house.

I drove back to the Mother's house and parked outside. I stayed there for five hours, watching the same things I had watched the previous two days. As I left, I decided that I would learn nothing through future stakeouts. I would have to break in and search the house if I wanted information. Although it was incredibly dangerous, I was excited to be doing something other than a stakeout. I drove back to my hotel, where I took an extra long bath and went to bed early. I would need the strength because tomorrow I would break into the Mother's house.

Chapter 12

I WOKE UP THE next day and got dressed in jeans and a dark shirt. I pulled my hair into a ponytail and grabbed my 45 pistol before leaving the room to drive to Crescent City Produce. I tucked my gun underneath my shirt at my lower back and exited my car. Walking through the produce stand, I took note of everyone who worked there. The employees consisted of kids who were not old enough to drink but were probably out of high school. I noticed the delivery van in the back and slowly made my way over to it. I stopped by the counter when I saw an apron hanging on a hook. The apron was green, with Crescent City Produce written in white across the front above large pockets. I glanced around and noticed no one was looking, so I quickly grabbed the apron before making my way to the van.

I was halfway to the van when I heard a dog barking. I turned to see the German shepherd jumping on the fence door of his small prison. No one else heard the bark, or at least no one cared. "Satsuma, sit," I told the dog. I smiled to myself as he slowly sat down. "Good boy."

I walked to the van and noticed the back was fully loaded. I looked around for suspicious eyes of workers. No one was looking, so I opened the back door and climbed inside the van. I quietly shut the door and found a good hiding place behind a crate of bananas and covered myself with the apron.

I could not tell how long I was waiting, because I had forgotten my wrist watch in Chicago, but I guessed it was around twenty minutes. I heard the driver's side door open and someone climb in the front seat of the van. I stayed as still and silent as I possibly could as we drove to make the delivery.

After a few minutes, we slowed to a stop, and I heard the window roll down. "Name," someone outside the van said. I guessed it was the guard at the gate.

"Jared Stephens, from Crescent City Produce," the driver said.

There was a ruffle of papers, followed by the guard's response. "Go straight through the gate and around back to the kitchen entrance."

"Thanks," Jared said, as he drove through the gate. He parked the van and exited the driver's seat. He walked around to the back and opened the door. I stayed as still as I could and hoped he wouldn't see me hidden behind the many crates. He picked up the first crate and turned to bring it inside the kitchen.

Once he left the van, I quickly jumped out and brought my stolen apron along with me. I put the apron on and poked my head inside the kitchen. I saw Jared walking out of a walk-in pantry, heading my way. I moved from the door and pressed my back against the wall. Jared walked out the kitchen and passed by me without noticing me. Once he passed me, I walked calmly into the kitchen.

It was an industrial-sized kitchen, like one might see in a large restaurant. The counters were completely stainless steel, and there were stainless steel pots hanging from the ceiling. There were about ten kitchen workers, busying themselves with their daily chores.

I walked through the room and into the hall without anyone stopping me. I moved down the hall and passed a room with the door open. I stopped and looked in the room to find the security office. One wall was full of TV screens, showing images from security cameras that were placed all around the house. I scanned the TV screens and saw everything, including Jared and the delivery van. There were two guards monitoring the screens, but they were not paying close attention. I quickly continued down the hall before a guard could see me lingering at the door. The hall ended abruptly, forcing me to turn left or right. I chose left. I had just begun walking when I heard a door open and close down the hall behind me.

"Excuse me, are you lost?" I froze as soon as I heard a man's voice. I knew that voice.

I turned toward the voice but kept my head down and was glad my long bangs were covering most of my face.

"You're not supposed to be here. Deliveries are to stay in the kitchen," he said to me. I could hardly breathe.

"I'm sorry," I told him, trying to disguise my voice. "I was looking for the bathroom," I lied.

"Oh, well, if you go back the way you came, there is a door on your right. It's labeled 'Restrooms,'" he explained, as he took a step toward me.

I took a deep breath as my heart began to beat faster. Before he could reach me, I heard someone walking up to him. "Excuse me, sir, the squad completed their exercises like you asked. Would you like me to take them through the next drills?"

"No," the familiar voice said to him. "I'll be there in a minute."

I used the distraction as my chance to escape. I turned down the first hall and walked as quickly as I could but stopped once I turned the corner. *That couldn't have been him.* I turned and peeked around the corner to where he was standing, to see if I was losing my mind.

He was still talking to the army-looking guy, who was now blocking my view of him. The army guy turned and walked away, and I was able to get a good look at him.

He was tall, maybe a little over six feet, and had long, thick dark hair that fell in front of his eyes and just below his ears. A strong chin held perfect lips just below a nose that showed no sign of ever being broken, although if he was who I was thinking he was, I knew it had been broken before. He had strong cheekbones under the most unique eyes I had ever known. They were bright blue with a hint of green in them. They always reminded me of the ocean surrounding an exotic island, the kind of water that was so clear you could see the ocean floor. To say this man was handsome would be a lie. He was gorgeous. My heart fell to my stomach. *Finn.*

I watched him walk back into the room he had just left before I turned to leave. I couldn't catch my breath. *What is he doing here? I haven't seen him in ten years and this is where I find him?*

The trip back to the van was a blur, but somehow I made it there. Jared had one crate left. After he pulled it from the back I sneaked through the kitchen and into the back of the van. I lay down and pulled a tarp over me to hide, taking deep breaths to prevent the panic attack I felt quickly approaching. Jared soon entered the van and drove back to the produce stand. It was the longest ride of my life.

I waited a few minutes after he parked before peeking out the window to see if it was safe to exit. I saw someone close by, so I waited. Once the coast was clear, I left the van and all but ran to my car. I don't remember the drive back to the hotel. It was as if my mind was in a haze. I threw myself on the bed as soon as I was in my room and covered my face with the pillow. *What was Finn doing there? Could he be working with the Mother? He looks so good.*

Chapter 13

As I soaked in the bathtub, I decided that I could have been mistaken. I had been thinking about Finn and the rest of my orphanage family so much lately that I could have imagined him. I decided to find out if that was really him. I got out of the tub, dried off, and got dressed. I got my car from the valet and headed to Garrett's house. After I knocked on the door, he answered.

"Oh, hey! I didn't expect you back. You need something else?" He stepped away from the door so I could enter.

"Actually, yeah. I need surveillance equipment. Do you have anything I could use?"

"I have some things. What kind of surveillance do you need?"

"I need to see what is going on inside a building. How can I do that?" He looked at me for a long time before answering.

"Does this building already have cameras or not?"

"Yes. This building is full of cameras," I answered.

"Can you get in?"

"Yeah, no problem," I sounded a lot more confident than I was about being able to get back inside the house. After I answered, he walked to his wall of computer gadgets and pulled out a small black clamp with a tiny antenna and a pair of wire cutters.

"Ok, here is what you have to do. Once you're inside, find a camera you would like to use. Take these wire cutters and strip the wire of the rubber coating, but do not cut any wires. Clamp this transmitter around the wires. The transmitter will send the video to my laptop. I assume you need that too?" I nodded.

"Anything the camera sees, I will be able to see?" I asked. He nodded. "Will the security guards still be able to see what the camera records also?"

"Yep, it will have no effect on their screens."

"What about sound?" I asked. He walked back to his computer and pulled out a tiny round disc about the size of a penny.

"This is a bug. Stick it underneath a desk or a chair, and it will pick up any sound nearby. I have the sound equipment for it too," he told me, as he handed me the bug.

"This is perfect," I said, as I took it from him.

"You want me to bill Tank?" he asked.

"Yes, please," I said. I began taking equipment to my car.

"Hold on, I'll help you with the gear," he said. He took the laptop from his desk and helped me load my car with my new supplies.

Crescent City Produce wasn't scheduled to make a delivery until Monday, so I would have to think of another way into the house. I drove to the nearest clothing store I could find and searched the store until I found a plain black shirt. The cargo pants took a little longer to find. After a couple of hours and a few stores, I found clothing close enough to match the army-looking girls at the house. I had the supplies I needed. Now all I needed was a way through the gate.

The next day I drove out to the house and parked down the street. I searched the yard full of army clones and made sure my wardrobe matched the others. I stayed in my car until I figured out how to get through the gates. I looked around the neighborhood until I found what I was looking for.

There was a house with a front yard full of children's toys. I tucked in my gun at the small of my back under my shirt, in case things went wrong, and got out of my car. I walked across the street and quickly picked up the football that was lying in the grass. I walked to the gate and held up the ball for the guards to see. I held my breath as the guard's eyes shifted from me to the ball.

"Those guys are so careless. If it goes over the fence again, they are gonna have to get it themselves," I told the guard.

He looked away from me and let me through. I let out a deep breath and walked to the back of the building. I decided to go in the only way I knew so I headed for the kitchen entrance. I tossed the ball on the ground before I walked inside, where I got a few strange looks from the kitchen staff. It was obvious that the army guys normally did not travel through the kitchen. I ignored the looks and confidently walked through the hall.

I only had one transmitter, and I knew where I wanted to put it. I got to the end of the hall and turned right instead of left. I stopped in front of the door that Finn, or his lookalike, had used. I noticed the PRIVATE sign on the door. It was obvious that most people were not allowed in this room, so I pushed my ear up against the door. I strained to hear any voices inside the room but was unable to do so.

I slowly turned the door knob and entered the room. I was relieved to see the room was unoccupied. I scanned the room and noticed a couch, a few chairs, and a desk surrounding a coffee table. There was another door on the other side of the room.

I walked to the coffee table and stuck the bug underneath the surface. I looked around the edge of the ceiling, searching for a camera. I found it in the top left corner of the room. I knew any watching guard could have spotted me on the camera while I surveyed the room, but I hoped they would assume I had a legitimate reason for being there. I pulled up a chair and stood on top of it to get close enough to install the transmitter. As soon as I climbed on the chair, I pulled my face out of the camera's scope. I reached in one of the pockets of my cargo pants and pulled out the wire cutters. Being careful not to cut the wire, like Garrett told me, I slowly stripped the rubber cover of the cable, leaving the camera wires. Once the rubber was removed, the internal wiring was exposed. I reached in another pocket and retrieved the transmitter. I securely clamped it on the exposed wires and made sure the transmitter was hidden behind the camera. I climbed down from my chair and picked it up to place it back where I found it. As I was putting the chair back in place, I heard the door open behind me.

"What are you doing in here?" It was the same familiar voice but this time it sounded more aggressive. There was nothing I could do. Nowhere I could run. I slowly turned around and lifted my face to him.

"You know this room is off lim-" his words were cut off as his eyes settled on my face. "Blake?"

His eyebrows pulled down in confusion. His hair was slightly in his face, but I could clearly see his mesmerizing eyes. *He is so cute.*

"Hi, Finn," I said, as my heart threatened to beat out of my chest.

"Blake," he said my name as if it was an answer to a question. A huge grin spread across his face, reaching his eyes. It was the same little-boy grin that I had known and loved so long ago. He closed the distance between us and scooped me into an embrace. It was a sincere hug that involved his whole body. It was the kind of hug that, combined with his smile, made my knees wobbly.

"Blake, I can't believe it's you. What are you doing here?" he asked, in an excited voice as he let go of me.

I had an answer prepared. It was something about security technician, but as I stared at his happy face, I couldn't remember my lie. I just stood there unable to keep my face from betraying me. When I did not answer, his smile faded.

"And why do you have a gun at your back?" he asked. *How did he know I had a gun?* I was unable to say anything. I just stared at the hurt look on his face. I was going to have a panic attack if I did not get out of there fast.

"I can't," was all I said before I ran out of the room.

This time I did not walk out. I ran down the hall toward the door. I could not look back, but I did not hear anyone following me. He did not follow me. He let me run out of there without trying to stop me.

I ran through the kitchen and out the door. I continued running through the gate. When the guard yelled after me, I yelled back, "I just need some fresh air." It was not a lie. I was hyperventilating.

I jumped in my car and gripped the steering wheel as hard as I could. *It was Finn. Holy crap it was Finn.* I took deep breaths, trying to calm myself before driving. I looked in my rearview mirror and did not see anyone coming after me, so I took a few more seconds to regain composure. I pulled my car around the corner and then stopped. I looked at the laptop in the passenger's seat and decided I had to know what was going on. I wasn't entirely sure I wanted to know what was going on, but I needed to know.

I leaned in the back seat and flipped the switch on the sound system Garrett had given me for the bug. I did not hear anything. I opened the laptop and clicked on the camera icon. The room appeared on my screen and I held my breath. Finn was leaning on the desk with his head down. I had not noticed what he was wearing while I was near him. I could not take my eyes off of him.

Now I saw that he wore a fitted red t-shirt. Not one that looked like it was painted on, but it was tight enough to show the muscles in his chest and arms. He was muscular. Not like those guys that think it's attractive to be so muscular that they have no neck, but you could tell he was in shape. He had the body of a swimmer or a soccer player. He had on cargo pants, identical to the others' khaki cargo pants, only his were black. After a second, I heard him sigh and walk out the room through the door that I had not used.

I closed my eyes and tried to stay calm. I was about to close the laptop when I heard a door open. I looked at the screen and saw a girl with short black hair enter the room, pulling a man in behind her. She held him close to her as he wrapped his arms around her waist. I heard her giggle as she pushed him against the wall. I only saw the back of the woman but I could see the face of the man. It was the extremely attractive football player.

She pulled his head to hers and began kissing him. His hands slid down to grab her bottom, and suddenly I felt dirty for watching. I closed the laptop, but I could still hear what was happening.

"We could get in trouble for this," said the man. I was leaning in the back to turn off the sound when I heard her reply and her voice.

"Oh, I don't care. They know me well enough to know that I wouldn't follow stupid rules." *You have got to be kidding me. Brooke?*

I opened the laptop and saw the couple kissing. I looked closer at the girl. She was about the same height as I was but had short, sassy black hair. They stopped kissing and she led him to the couch. When she turned and faced the camera I saw her dark brown eyes and the sly grin that never left her face. *Brooke. Why not?* I'm even sarcastic in my head.

She was naturally tan. We always assumed she had Native American blood somewhere in her line, but because she never knew her parents, we were not sure. I let out a sigh as I saw the second person from my past. Brooke pushed him on the couch and lowered herself on top of him. They continued kissing for a few seconds until the other door opened. A girl with long curly light brown hair walked through the door. *You are freakin' kidding me!* She stopped and stared at Brooke and her man.

"Hey Brooke. You really shouldn't do that where anyone could see you," Janey said, and her voice was as familiar as the others.

"Where would the fun in that be?" Brooke asked, as she let the man off the couch.

He looked embarrassed at being caught with Brooke. Brooke didn't seem to care at all. She had always enjoyed breaking the rules. Janey laughed at Brooke and walked to the desk.

"Run along now," Brooke told the man, as she swatted his bottom. He quickly left the two girls alone, clearly anxious to be out of that awkward situation.

"What are you working on?" Brooke asked Janey, as she fell on the couch.

"Finalizing the guard rotation for next week," Janey replied, without lifting her head from her paper work.

"You really should get your mind off of work and get some use out of all these hot guys we have around here," Brooke said.

"I don't think so."

"Oh, come on. We have all shapes, sizes, and colors. You could have your pick-well, except for my man, of course," Brooke joked.

"Nah, I'll leave the man-handling to you," Janey said, as she looked at her watch. "It's two o'clock. Aren't you supposed to be in the gym?"

"Oh, shit!" Brooke yelled, as she jumped off the couch. "I totally forgot all about that."

"Hold on. I'll go with you. I have got to get Finn to look at this rotation," Janey said, as they both got up and left the room.

I quickly closed the laptop and leaned back to shut off the sound. I'd had enough ghosts from my past for the day and did not want to see who else would appear. I put my car in drive and headed back for my bath. I desperately needed some relaxation.

Chapter 14

I LEANED MY HEAD back as the hot water settled over my skin. *This can't be real. It's got to be some kind of a bad dream.* Finn, Brooke, and Janey were at the house. I could only assume Jake and Courtney were there too. That group was too strong to break up. *Are they working for the Mother? Courtney doesn't take orders well, even worse than Brooke does. At least Brooke will pretend to accept the rules and later see which ones she can break; Courtney would absolutely refuse to abide.*

I began to get a sinking feeling in my gut. No, I refused to think Courtney was who I thought she might be. I cleared my mind from that thought and my mind drifted to Finn. I closed my eyes and saw his smile. It lit up his entire face. It was the same smile he'd had when he was younger. It looked even better on him now, which I would not have thought possible.

Finn and I had connected from the first day we met. He was the only one of us who knew his parents, besides me. His mom was a high school teacher and his dad was the principal at the same school. When Finn was five, a few students brought guns to school and went on a rampage killing students. They killed twenty-six people, including Finn's parents, before turning the guns on themselves. He was the only one who understood the grief I felt at my parents' death. We were inseparable for the duration of our childhood. He was the first guy I ever cared for and the first I ever kissed.

When I saw him again, all the old feelings came back to me in a flash. I realized I had been fretting over Finn and the others too long. My bath water had turned cold, so I got out of the tub and dressed.

I sat down on the bed and tried to sort out my thoughts. My head began to throb, so I pulled some ibuprofen out of my purse and grabbed a bottle of water. I took the pills and threw myself back on the bed. While consumed in thoughts of my orphanage family, I heard the faint sound of a cell phone ringing. I looked at the caller ID and saw Tank's name. *Great, this is all I need right now.* I thought about ignoring his call, but that would make him worry, so I answered.

"Hello," I said, trying not to sound as upset as I was.

"What's wrong?" Obviously my voice failed me.

"Nothing, just a long day. Intel is not going so great," I said. "Plus I have a headache."

"Are you sure that's it? How's your arm?" I had completely forgotten all about my shoulder during the last few days.

"It's fine. I haven't even noticed it lately."

"I've been worried about you," he told me.

"I'm fine," I lied, as I pushed my fingers to my temple.

"I know this is a hard assignment, so I decided to help you," he announced. My forehead wrinkled in confusion.

"What? What does that mean?" I asked, completely exhausted from the stress of the day.

"I have been doing my own intel on your mark. My source told me that she has a group of five people who stay by her at all times," he said, proud of himself for his new information.

Five. That means Finn, Brooke, Jake, Janey, and Courtney. Those are the five. Courtney is not the Mother. I closed my eyes and let out a sigh. I felt like a small weight was lifted off of the larger one on my brain.

"Yeah, it looks like you're going to have to go through those five to get to the Mother," he told me. "In fact, the bosses have added them to your kill order."

"What?" I felt my breathing begin to quicken.

"Yeah, they feel that those five are as important as the Mother. But don't worry. I have talked to them and they have decided to pay you sixty-five thousand a piece and seventy-five for the Mother. That's four hundred thousand dollars total for the job." I closed my eyes and tried to stay calm.

"And I've found out something about the five," he said, as I held my breath. "Well it is actually only two of the five. Two have criminal records so I was able to pull their files. The first is named Bradley Monroe." *Finn*. "He was arrested for assault seven years ago. Served a little time but not much. The other's name is Lee Chauvin. He was arrested for theft but didn't serve any time just got probation."

"Thanks," I said, trying to sound appreciative but unable to do so. Tank took a pause before continuing our conversation.

"Look, Blake, this is a dangerous job. All the people who went after this woman died. And now you have five new targets. I think I'm going to send you some help."

"What? No. I don't want any help. I can handle this. Other people will just get in the way," I pleaded with him.

"All right," he sighed. "I won't send anyone, but you have to check in with me every night. Is that clear?" he asked.

"Yeah, no problem."

"OK, well, please be careful, and take care of yourself, Blake."

"I will, Bye, Tank"

"Bye."

I hung up the phone and dropped it on the bed beside me. I threw one arm over my eyes and replayed the phone conversation in my head. So now I have to kill my family. And who the heck is Lee? If he is one of the five, that means... *Shit, Courtney is the Mother.*

I felt tears forming behind my eyes. I took a deep breath and remembered what Courtney told me when I was five years old. I was upset over my parents' death, and Courtney had told me how to handle it. I could still hear her voice in my head. "Can you do anything about their death? No. So take that sadness and push it to the corner of your mind. Lock it away. Tears can't solve problems." Courtney had never been a child. She was born an adult.

We knew about Finn's parents, and we knew the twins were left on the steps of a hospital, and Brooke was left at a church; but Courtney's past had always been a mystery. She never talked about how she ended up in the orphanage-but I heard some of our caretakers talking about her one day. I was sneaking off to meet Finn at our favorite tree when I passed the office. Like any good future assassin, I eavesdropped.

One of the ladies was complaining about Courtney. The other spoke up in her defense, saying that Courtney had a rough life. She then explained how Courtney's mom was a severe alcoholic and how her dad was physically abusive. One day her father went too far and killed her mother in front of Courtney. Her father received life in prison, and Courtney received the orphanage.

I ran from the office to meet Finn but I never told him or the others what I heard that night. I could not imagine what Courtney went through, and if she did not want to talk about it, then I would respect that. I guess she had personal experience with locking her emotions away. Her voice played in my head again, and I gained control of my tears. They would not fall; I would not allow it.

Courtney's words may have sounded harsh, but they got me through tough moments. I don't know if I could have become an assassin without her advice. *And that is what I am. I am a trained killer. I will lock away the feelings I have about these people and do the job I was hired to do.* As depressing as my decision was, I made it, and I planned to stick to it. I felt a wash of relief at knowing what I was going to do.

I turned on the television to keep from changing my mind. I was searching for mind numbing sitcoms. I found an episode of *Friends* and stopped channel surfing. I loved *Friends* and it would do the job of distracting me. Ross was playing the bagpipes when I heard a knock at my door.

I stared at the door for a second before standing. I was not expecting anyone, so my visitor alarmed me. I walked along the wall and slowly stepped in front of my door so I could look through the peep-hole. Finn was standing in the hall with his head tilted down. He had his hands in the pockets of his jeans. *What was he doing here? How did he find me?*

I felt those pesky butterflies fluttering in my stomach as I opened the door. I waited in silence for him to say something, anything.

"Hi, Blake," he said, as he continued to stare at his feet. I couldn't figure out what to say. My brain would not work.

"You changed clothes," I said, looking for some type of response. *You changed clothes? I'm an idiot!* I wanted to kick myself. He was wearing jeans, a long-sleeve white shirt, and a brown leather jacket.

"Yeah," he said, without looking at me. We stood there for a few seconds in silence, but it felt like an hour. *I wish I had taken the time to fix my hair.* He finally looked up at me.

"Would you take a ride with me?" I couldn't answer. I just stared into his blue-green eyes. "You can bring your gun if you want," he added, as he went back to staring at his shoes. I hated to see him like that.

"OK," I replied, and turned and walked to the counter. My gun was sitting next to my purse. I could feel his eyes on my back as I debated on whether or not he was serious about me bringing my gun. I knew he was. I picked up my purse and left my gun on the counter.

I left my room and closed the door behind me. He gave me a small smile that did not attempt to reach his eyes and turned to walk down the hall. I walked beside him in silence, rode the elevator in silence, and walked through the lobby in silence. In my peripheral vision, I noticed the desk clerk was staring at us but I ignored him and continued to follow Finn.

He held the door for me and I walked out of the hotel. I stopped outside the hotel, but Finn didn't. He walked past me and headed straight for a black Tahoe parked on the curb. I followed him to the SUV, and he opened the passenger side door for me. I climbed in, and he shut the door before walking around to the driver's side. He climbed in and started the engine. I waited patiently until I could no longer stand the silence.

"How did you know where I was staying?" I asked.

He gave me a sly smile and reached in his pocket. He pulled out a small metal object. He flashed it at me and I saw it had N.O.P.D. engraved on it with some other designs. "You're a cop?" I asked. I couldn't keep my eyes from widening in shock. *That's all I need.*

"No," he laughed, "but your desk clerk thinks I am. People are a lot more eager to answer your questions if you have a badge." We drove in silence for a few blocks.

"Where are we going?" I asked, as I began to pick at the strap of my purse to keep my hands busy.

"Nowhere, really. I just like to drive. It helps clear my head," he replied, as he turned down a side street. "So," he locked his eyes on me. "How have you been?"

That was not the question I was expecting. "Good," I replied. "I've been good," I said again, not being able to pull my eyes off of his handsome face.

At my response, he turned his attention back to the road. When he turned his head, I noticed the tiny scar above his right eye and I couldn't help but smile. He had received the scar when he was thirteen. He chased me up a tree at the orphanage. I was always a much better and faster climber than he was. When he tried to keep up with me, he slipped and fell. I had to tell him the scar made him look rugged to soothe his thirteen-year-old pride.

"I'm glad," he replied, giving me a sincere smile that faded too quickly. "Are you going to tell me what you were doing at my house?" he asked. That was the question I was expecting.

"No," I answered. I couldn't tell him the truth; that I, as a hired assassin, was there to kill him along with everyone he loved. But I had never been able to lie to him. He had always been able to tell when I lied, and even though I had significantly improved my lying abilities, I was not in the mood to test him. So I answered him the only way I was able to.

He combed his fingers through his long dark hair and set his hand back on the wheel. *If I kill the others, can I let him live? He is way too cute to kill.*

"OK, why can't you tell me?" he asked.

"I'm sorry Finn, I just can't," I told him. A moment of silence followed my answer.

"Is our family in danger?" he asked calmly, without looking at me. *He said "our family." He still considers me family.* That thought caused a huge smile to spread across my face. He saw my smile and looked at me in confusion.

"What?" he asked.

"You called me family," I told him, with the smile still across my face.

"Of course you are. Just because we haven't seen you in a while doesn't mean you are no longer a part of our family," he said, with a small smile. I stared at him and knew he was telling the truth about how he felt.

"No," I said. He looked at me and wrinkled his forehead. "The answer to your question is no. Our family is not in danger of me."

The moment I said it, I knew it was true. I couldn't hurt these people. They saved me from losing myself in the orphanage. They were there for me when I had no one. I would not hurt them-or allow anyone else to, for that matter. I would have to find some way to deal with my assignment. It felt as if a weight was lifted off of my conscience. My answer seemed to make Finn feel a little more at ease. His grip loosened on the wheel and he leaned back in his seat.

"So are you gonna come back to the house? The others would freak out if they knew you were here," he told me. Then he noticed my concerned face. "They would freak in a good way," he quickly added.

"You haven't told them I'm here?" I was surprised. I figured he would have told the others by now.

"No. I didn't know if you would want me to. Besides, I didn't know what you were doing here. I still don't know what you are doing here," he said, as he pulled up to the curb in front of my hotel.

"I can't tell you. I wish I could, but I have to work some things out first," I told him. More specifically, I had to work out how I was *not* going to kill them.

"OK," he said. "I can deal with that." He got out of his car and walked around the SUV and opened my door.

"What are you doing?" I asked him, when he opened my door.

"I'm walking you to your door," he said matter-of-factly.

"Oh, yeah, I forgot. You're big on the whole manners thing," I told him, as I rolled my eyes.

Finn's father had grown up on old southern manners. He treated his wife as if she was a queen, and Finn never forgot that. Even when we were young, he was always opening doors and pulling out chairs. I guess it was the only way Finn was able to stay connected to his father.

"You always did give me such a hard time," he said, reaching out his hand to help me. I took his hand and stepped out of the car. His hand was warm against mine.

"Old habits, you know." I smiled at him.

He walked me to my room, and I opened the door. I turned back to him to say good-bye, and he pulled me into a hug. As I stood there in his embrace, I could not keep myself from inhaling his scent. He wasn't wearing cologne, and that was probably a good thing. One; he smelled amazing without it; and two, I'm a sucker for good cologne. If he had some on, I would have had to insist that he follow me into my room. OK, I may not be that bad, but I love cologne. He released me, and I said good-bye before awkwardly stumbling back into my room.

Chapter 15

I CLOSED THE DOOR behind me and walked to my bed before throwing myself on top of it. I closed my eyes and replayed the ride with Finn in my head. I couldn't help but grin when Finn's smile crossed my mind. My happiness was abruptly ended when I remembered that I was supposed to kill him. I felt the surge of panic rise through my stomach. *No, I can't allow anyone to hurt them.* I had to figure out what I was going to do about this situation.

I pulled open the drawer of the nightstand and retrieved the complimentary notepad and pen. I sat back on my bed and pulled my knees up to my chest. Leaning my back against the headboard I set my notepad on my knees and stared at it. *OK, what are my options?* I liked to make list when trying to solve a difficult problem. It helped to see it written out. I set my pen on the paper and wrote:

1. Complete the job I was hired to do.

I stared at my handwriting and felt the swell of panic forming as I thought about killing my family. No. I would not be able to complete option one. I quickly scratched a line through it. I thought a second and wrote:

2. Tell Tank.

I sat back and thought about this option. What would happen if I told Tank that I could not complete the job because the marks are my family from the orphanage? I knew exactly what would happen. Tank would make me leave New Orleans. He would take the job from me, because he would not force me to do something that would hurt me. He thought of me as a daughter and would want to protect me from that kind of pain.　　However, Tank would do his job. Tank would not assign one of his assassins to the job, because I would know who it was and hold a grudge against whoever killed my family. Instead, he would hand the job, along with all the information on my family over to another controller. That controller would give the job to someone else, and my family would be in danger again. No matter how much Tank cared for me, he cared for his job more.

The only way I would be able to keep my family safe in this option would be to kill the next assassin assigned to the job. I could move to New Orleans and protect them. I had been working with this company for a long time and would know most of our assassins by sight. If they chose to send someone I did not know, I still know what kind of signs to look for. I could easily kill the first person they sent. But my company always got their mark.

They would send more people, probably some I would know and care about. If we survived that, they would send more, and eventually I would have to face the might of the entire company-and I was not naive enough to think we would survive that. I was not Angelina Jolie, and I did not have Brad Pitt helping me, like in the movie *Mr. and Mrs. Smith*. There was no way my family or I would survive that type of assault. I thought about all of this and decided that option two was no good. I scratched out number two.

3. Run.

We could run. I could come clean about why I was in New Orleans. I could explain everything to Court and the gang, and we could run. I had a lot of money acquired over the many years of contract killing, not to mention the millions my uncle left me. That could help us. But my company had an unlimited amount of money, supplies, and people. They would search for us.

We could move to a different country. Somewhere that would take my company a long time to find. If we kept moving, never staying in one place long, they may not be able to find us. But would my family run? I had never known Courtney to run from anything.

I left the third idea unscratched and continued to think of more options. I stared at my notepad for hours but could not think of a number four. Running was our only option. Options one and two ended in theirs or our deaths. Option three was our only chance to stay alive. At the very least, we would live longer if we ran. I would have to make Courtney run. I would have to explain it to her in a way that she would understand how important it was to run. I let out a sigh at finally having some idea how to handle this situation. I would have to withdraw my money. I would need a lot of cash, because my company could trace all of my accounts. It would take some time. I would have to delay Tank while I got my affairs in order.

I thought about Tank and grew very sad. I would never see him again, or Mark, or my sensei and the other friends I had made. I would never return to Chicago to say farewell. I buried my face in my pillow and fought back the tears that were forming behind my eyes. I don't know when it happened, but I fell asleep with my face in the pillow.

I woke up the next morning with a crick in my neck from the awkward position I slept in. I saw the notepad next to me but did not feel like looking at it anymore. I decided to go for a run to clear my head. Maybe after my jog, I would be able to think of another way to handle things, so we didn't have to run away.

I dressed in my workout clothes and headed for the lobby. I tried not to think about anything as I ran. I turned my iPod louder to drown out my own thoughts. I ran a few blocks before deciding that I wanted a cup of coffee. I turned around and started back for the hotel. Once I was back in my room, I started the coffee pot and sat down on my bed. The run made me feel a little better, so I decided to give our options another glance.

It didn't do any good. I couldn't see any other options that I couldn't see the night before. I put my face in my hands and fell back against my pillow. I had only been lying there a minute when my hotel phone rang. I was immediately confused. Tank was the only one who called me on a mission and he never used the hotel phone. I leaned over and answered it.

"Hello?"

"Hey Blake, it's Finn."

"Oh. Finn. Hey," I said. Finn completely caught me off guard. I was not expecting the call would be from him.

"Did I catch you at a bad time?"

"No, I just got back from jogging."

"Oh, OK. Good. Well, its Sunday, my day off, and I didn't want to stay home. I was wondering if you wanted to go do something."

"Like what?"

"Umm, I don't know. Anything."

"Yeah, ok. I could use a break from work. That would definitely help my sanity," I said.

"I doubt anything could help that."

"Ha, ha." I laughed sarcastically.

"How soon can you be ready?"

"How about an hour. Is that good?"

"Yeah, that's perfect. Well, I will see you in an hour."

"K, bye."

"Bye."

I hung up the phone and ran to the shower. While I was in the shower, I thought about telling Finn everything and felt my butterflies flutter nervously around in my stomach. I decided to wait. I wanted to figure out how much money I could get and where we should go first. I wanted to get as much information as I could before dropping this bombshell on them.

I jumped out of the shower and began getting ready. I didn't know what Finn had in mind for the day, so I pulled on a pair of jeans and a green shirt. Green made my eyes a little brighter. I straightened my hair and began applying makeup. I normally didn't wear a lot of makeup, so I just applied eye shadow, mascara, and lip gloss.

I was putting the finishing touches on my lips when there was a knock at the door. I gave myself one last look in the mirror before running to open it.

I opened it to find Finn standing in front of me. He was wearing jeans as well and had a yellow shirt on underneath his brown leather jacket. His brown hair fell a little in front of his eyes and he had my favorite smile on his face. His boyish grin brightened his gorgeous eyes.

"You ready?" he asked, as I smiled at him.

"Yeah, let me just grab my jacket and my purse," I said, as I spun around and grabbed my brown jacket that was lying on my spare bed next to my purse. I picked them both up and left the room.

As I left the room, I noticed there was an intoxicating scent in the air. I walked to Finn's side and realized he was wearing amazing cologne. I thought I would melt right there, but somehow I managed to walk beside him without attacking.

We walked through the lobby, and I noticed a few people watching us. It was not as many as the night before but word had spread through the employees of the cop and the lone guest. Finn walked me to his Tahoe and opened the door for me. I got in without complaint and buckled my seat belt. Finn did the same before turning to me.

"So, what do you want to do today?"

"I have no idea. I'm not from here. What is there to do?" I asked.

"Well, I don't know. We could walk around the French Quarter."

"I've already seen that," I said a little smugly.

"Oh, excuse me," he replied, with a smile. "How about the Aquarium?"

My eyes lit up. "I would love to go to the aquarium. I have never been to one before."

"Really? Well then, the Aquarium it is." He pulled the car away from the curb and turned toward the Aquarium of Americas. I was so excited. I loved the ocean and all ocean life-except for jellyfish. I hated jellyfish. Finn parked the Tahoe, and we made our way to the entrance. I could not keep the excitement from my face. Finn noticed it and laughed at me. "You look like a little girl," he said.

"I can't help it. I'm excited!"

Finn beat me to the ticket box office and bought two tickets. I glared at him when he handed me mine.

"What? I'll let you buy the tickets next time we come here," he said, with a smirk.

"Right, because we come here all the time," I replied sarcastically. Finn just smiled at me and held the door open. "Well, thank you for the ticket," I said, as we entered the Aquarium.

"You're welcome."

We walked around the Aquarium, observing the different life forms in the tanks. I quickly scooted past the tank of jellyfish and stopped at the shark tank. I was mesmerized by the vicious creatures. I felt connected to them. They were the killers of the sea, and I was a killer on land. They killed for food and enjoyment. I killed for money.

I watched a large shark swim around the tank. The other sharks would not swim near him, and I wondered if he was the most deadly of the group. He turned and began swimming in my direction. I looked into his jet-black eyes and wondered if he could see into mine. I wondered if he recognized me as a killer. I thought about how we were both born to be killers. I genuinely felt I was born to kill. I was very good at it and picked it up quickly. I watched the underwater assassin with intensity and was engrossed with my own thoughts when I felt someone suddenly grab my sides. "Hey!" Finn yelled.

I jumped and screamed out loud. I turned to find Finn laughing hysterically. He was successful in scaring me half to death. "Holy crap! You scared the bejeezus out of me!"

He was still laughing when I walked up and slapped him in the chest. I looked around and saw a bunch of people smiling at me. Apparently they were watching as Finn snuck up behind me and witnessed my reaction. I felt my face flush and knew it would be turning red soon, so I walked away from the shark tank. I heard Finn running behind me trying to catch up with my pace.

He didn't say anything as he began walking next to me. I was embarrassed and wouldn't look at him, but I could see him in the corner of my eye. He was smiling and squeezing his lips together, trying to contain his laughter.

"I can imagine how funny I looked," I finally said, deciding the incident was amusing. That did it, and he cracked. He was laughing again.

"You jumped so high. It's a good thing the tanks are enclosed, or you would have fallen in," he said, laughing. I joined in his laughter when I imagined what I looked like. "I'm sorry, I shouldn't have scared you like that, but I couldn't help myself."

"Don't worry about it," I told him.

Finn took a deep breath to regain control and asked, "So, are you hungry?" I looked around, not knowing where we would eat. "There is a food court here," he answered, knowing what I was thinking.

"Yeah, I could eat," I said, and he guided me towards the food court. We got a couple of burgers, fries, and cokes, which he paid for, and found a table.

"So, why are you about to go crazy from work?" Finn asked, after his first bite of his burger.

"Nope. We are not going to talk about work," I said.

"OK, fine, so what do you want to talk about?"

"I don't know. How long have you been in New Orleans?"

"About six years or so. So where are you living?"

"Chicago. My uncle moved us there after he took custody of me," I said between bites.

"So I imagine you have season tickets to the Cubs."

"Nah," I said, taking a sip of Coke to wash down the burger.

"What? You were crazy about the Cubs. You would be depressed all day after they lost a game."

"Yeah. I still love the Cubs, don't get me wrong, but I travel a lot for work, so I never know if I would be home to use the tickets. I have gone to Wrigley Field and have seen a lot of games, though."

"Well, you know what they say. All work and no play makes-"

"Blake a rich girl," I finished the saying.

"That's not how I remember the phrase," Finn said, with a smirk on his face.

"Yeah, well, I like my version better," I replied, imitating his smirk.

"OK," he said, as he ate some fries. I looked at him and noticed his scar again. I smiled again at the sight of it, but this time he noticed.

"What?" he asked.

"Nothing. I just noticed your scar."

"Oh," he said, as his hand moved to his head and touched his scar. "The scar I got when you pushed me out of that tree."

"I did not push you. You fell out of the tree."

"I did not," he said, with certainty. "We were racing to the top of the tree, and I was about to beat you, so you pushed me."

"No, sir. You followed me up the tree and tried to kiss me. Then you fell," I said, with a small grin. I knew I was right. Finn smiled and quickly looked down at his a French fries.

"Yeah, well, I still got my kiss," he said, in a low voice. I was not sure if he was talking to me or himself.

"I kissed your forehead to calm you down. You were such a mess," I said, still smiling. I knew how to get under his skin and enjoyed doing it.

"I was gushing blood from my forehead! Of course I was a mess. I actually thought I handled the situation well," he said, a little defensively. I kept smiling at him. He looked at me and smiled, realizing what I was doing. "Why do you like to push my buttons?"

"It's fun," I said, as I finished off my Coke. Finn leaned back in his chair and glared at me, but he was smiling, so I knew he wasn't mad. I just beat him in the argument and he knew it. "So, where to next?"

"Penguins."

We got up from the table, and after disposing of our trash, made our way to the penguin exhibit.

"The penguins are my favorite," Finn said, as we walked through the aquarium.

"Why? They are nothing but defective birds." When he gave me a confused look, I elaborated. "They are birds who cannot fly and like to swim. That's not right." He laughed at me but didn't argue.

We entered the exhibit and found a couple of families watching the penguins in an imitation of their natural habitat. There were penguins swimming and penguins wobbling side to side on the icy shore. One penguin would jump off the ice, swim back to the shore, and jump off again. He repeated the same motions over and over again.

"See, I told you, penguins aren't right. I think that one has mental issues," I told Finn, as I pointed out the penguin that was engulfed in his ridiculous routine. Finn laughed with me at the goofy creature.

There was a small boy around the age of four in front of me. He placed a hand on the glass separating us from the arctic birds. One penguin swam to the glass and placed his beak against it where the boy's hand rested. The boy laughed and moved his hand surprised to see the penguin following it closely. The boy began to run back and forth across the length of the exhibit, keeping his hand on the glass. The penguin followed his fingers as he ran. I couldn't help smiling at the boy's excitement.

From behind my back, Finn leaned in a whispered in my ear. "I told you the penguins were great." I could feel his breath on my neck, and heat rose through my body.

I turned to him and smiled. "You were right. They're funny," I said. We turned our attention back to the penguins for a few more minutes before we left the exhibit.

"So, that's pretty much everything in the Aquarium," Finn said, as we made our way toward the exit.

"That was awesome. What's next?" I asked. Finn thought about my question for a second before answering.

"Want to get a drink somewhere?"

I lifted my wrist to look at my watch and realized I left it in Chicago. I hated not having a watch. I seldom forgot to pack one. On the rare occasion that I did, I went out and bought one for the time being, but I had been slightly out of it since I arrived in New Orleans. "What time is it?" I asked.

Finn looked at his watch and answered, "It's three thirty-five."

I gave him a shocked look. "Wow, isn't that a little early to start drinking?"

He smiled at me as he answered, "Not in New Orleans. Drinking is an art here that knows no time limitations."

I laughed at his answer but nodded. "OK, let's go."

We got in his SUV and he drove to my hotel. "I thought we were going to get a drink?" I lifted my eyebrows in confusion.

"We are," he said. "We are just going to park here and walk. The bar I want to take you to isn't far."

We parked on the street next to the W Hotel and started our short walk to the bar. After a couple of blocks we turned onto Bourbon Street. I didn't have the heart to tell him that I had already seen Bourbon Street, so I kept my mouth shut.

He led me past bar after bar without paying attention to any of them. I noticed that there were customers in almost every bar we passed. That many people drinking during the day seemed strange to me, but I didn't say anything to Finn about it; after all, we were going to be some of those people. We walked by all of the bars I had walked passed a few days back and didn't stop in any of them. Finally he led me off the street toward a small dark bar.

We stepped inside the bar and sat at a table against the wall. The bar was dark, with very little lighting around the room. It was the middle of the day, so a lot of light was not needed, but there were a few candles on tables, and the actual bar was lit. Other than that, the sun was the only lighting the customers received. There was a giant fire-place in the middle of the room and a large piano around the back of the bar. There were weird metal tools hanging on the walls that looked like they were hundreds of years old.

"What do you want to drink?" Finn asked, as he stood up from the table.

"I don't know. It's a little early for hard alcohol. What are you going to get?" I asked him.

"Probably a beer," he replied.

"OK, that's fine. I will take that too." I didn't normally drink beer; I didn't care for the taste, but it was too early for vodka, especially if we were going to be there a while. Beer was safer. The last thing I needed was to get drunk and start blabbing about my job.

"What kind?" *Like I know.*

"You pick," I told him. He turned and made his way to the bar. He quickly returned with our drinks.

"It's raspberry flavored," he said, as he handed me the beer. I tasted the unfamiliar drink and liked it.

"It's good," I told him. He grinned at having made a good choice for me. "So, tell me about everybody else. What have they been up to?" I asked Finn. He took a long sip of his beer which was not raspberry flavored before answering me.

"Umm well, Court's been dating this guy, Lee, for the past couple years." *So the mystery target is dating Courtney.*

"Really? Is he a nice guy?"

"Yeah, he's all right. Kind of quiet, but he seems to really care about her, so we're OK with him. Jake dates occasionally, Janey doesn't date at all, and Brooke dates everyone." He laughed as he said the last part and took a sip of his beer.

I remembered the video I had seen the day before of Brooke and the cute army dude. "That seems about right."

"Yeah, Brooke has this two-week rule."

"Two week rule?" I asked.

"She gives a guy two weeks to 'woo' her," he said, applying air quotes to the word *woo*. "If he can't, he's gone."

I smiled, remembering my eccentric somewhat-sister. Before I could ask about his dating situation, he asked a question.

"What did you do after high school? Did you do the whole college thing?"

I knew he was trying to change the subject off of relationships and decided not to push that issue. "Yeah, I went to Northwestern University. My uncle and my boss insisted that I get a degree, so I picked sociology." I had fought that issue with Tank and my uncle the best I could. Why did I need a degree to kill people? That didn't make any sense, but they would not budge on the issue, so I went to college. "How about you?"

"I went to Michigan for engineering but didn't finish. Something came up," he said. He seemed a little hesitant about the last part.

"Do you think you will go back to school?"

"I don't know. Maybe."

"What about the others?"

"Janey went to nursing school. She is a registered nurse now."

"Good for her," I said enthusiastically.

"Yeah. Court decided that school was bogus. She said school only teaches how to think, and she already knew how to do that. So instead she said she would learn from real life. She took different jobs that she could learn things from. She worked for a lawyer for about a year. Once she learned all she could about law and the justice system, she quit and started working at a doctor's office. She has had so many different jobs, I can't even recall half of them; and once she gets everything she can out of it, she quits. It seems to work for her. She is one of the smartest people I know, if not the smartest."

"She always was smart," I said, smiling. Only Courtney would be able to get away with something like that. Finn finished off his beer and excused himself from the table to find a restroom. I took the opportunity and went to the bar to order another round for us. I knew he would not let me buy a round of drinks, so I had to be sneaky about it if I wanted to pay. I had the beer waiting for him when he returned to the table. He sat down and picked up his beer. When he realized it was full and icy cold, he narrowed his eyes at me. I grinned mischievously back.

"Thank you," he said, not wanting to argue with me.

"You're welcome." I took a sip of my beer and looked around the bar. "This is a cool place."

"It's my favorite bar in New Orleans," he said, happy that I liked his choice. "It was opened in the seventeen hundreds by a pirate. He built it as a blacksmith shop, but it was really a cover for his illegal pirate activities." He pointed to the big fireplace in the center of the room. "That is the original fireplace the blacksmith used."

"That's awesome," I said. I had always been fascinated with history.

As I looked around the room, the weird tools on the walls suddenly made sense. They were blacksmith tools. I doubted that they were the original tools used in the 1700s, but they gave the bar an authentic feel. I was admiring the artifacts on the walls when a large group of people walked inside. One woman was directing them to the bar. She had long, blond hair and was very attractive. She also wore a name tag on her shirt but was too far away for me to be able to read her name.

Finn noticed I was looking at the group. "A tour group," he said, in answer to the question that was forming in my head. I looked back at him.

"What kind of tour group would come here? Some kind of historical tour?"

"Yeah, kind of. I would guess it is a haunted tour." I raised my eyebrows at him in a questioning fashion. "They take people to all of the sites that are supposed to be haunted around New Orleans," he told me.

"This place is supposed to be haunted?" I asked, surprised. I was a trained killer; I had entered many situations that would terrify the normal person without as much as a thought crossing my mind. But things like ghosts and demons scared the crap out of me.

"Yeah, but I doubt it is. It's just really old, so they put it on the haunted tour. At least it's not the vampire tour."

"What? Vampires?" I unsuccessfully tried to keep my voice from rising.

"New Orleans is famous for vampires. *Interview with a Vampire* was based here," he said, laughing at my scared expression.

"There are actually tours that bring people to vampires? That's stupid."

"Relax, they are not real vampires. It's just cults who think they are vampires." He was not making this any better.

"There are people who think they are vampires? You've *got* to be kidding me," I said.

"Not kidding; these people really do think they are vampires. They even drink blood. They think it prolongs their life and gives them extra strength or something like that. There are a couple of places, famous vampire hangouts, where people were found murdered and drained of their blood."

"Holy crap, that's insane," I said, wide-eyed. Finn laughed at me. I took a deep breath and a gulp of beer to settle my nerves. "This city is crazy," I said.

"Wait till you hear about voodoo," Finn said, laughing.

"I don't want to hear about it," I said, raising my hands to stop him from explaining.

"Yes, ma'am," he said, as he drank his beer.

We sat there in silence for a minute. *How mentally disturbed do people have to be to think they're vampires?* A visual image of someone sucking the blood out of a person's neck appeared in my mind. I shuddered at the thought.

"Thanks, I'm officially creeped out," I told Finn. He only smiled at me.

"So I take it you don't like scary movies."

"Not that kind of scary. If it's a murderer or slasher movie, than I'm OK, but I can't handle anything demonic," I explained.

"I see," was his response. I picked up my beer to find that our conversation was so captivating (in a scary kind of way) that I didn't notice I was almost done with my beer.

"My turn," Finn said, as he stood up from the table. He walked to the bar for another round. I watched him as he leaned on the bar. He ran his hands through his hair and I couldn't keep from noticing how attractive he was. I was not the only one who noticed his looks. The tour guide was also at the bar.

I watched her as her eyes took in Finn's body and then his face. She stepped closer and said something to him. I wished I was close enough to hear what she said. I didn't have to be close enough to know she was hitting on him. A sudden flash of anger came over me. Finn immediately straightened his back but kept his eyes on the bar. He looked incredibly uncomfortable. He was confident in everything he did but at the same time he was ridiculously shy when it came to women. He was completely unaware of how gorgeous he was, which only made him cuter.

As soon as the bartender returned with our drinks, Finn turned from the woman and walked back to me. The blond's eyes followed Finn to our table and landed on me. I raised my eyebrows and gave her a small grin. She immediately tore her eyes away from mine.

Finn sat down and gave me my beer. I was glad that he didn't notice the death stare I had given the tour guide who was now gathering up her group to leave the bar. From that point on, Finn and I made small talk. We laughed and talked about the different hobbies we liked. We reminisced on old times and drank more beer. After a couple of hours Finn glanced at his watch. "Wow, it's nine-thirty. Do you want to get something to eat?"

"We've really been here that long? Now that you mention it, I am kind of hungry." We left the bar, and Finn led me to a small store that had a deli.

"Have you had a muffuletta?"

"A what?" I asked.

"It's a sandwich. They're amazing."

We walked into the small store, and Finn walked straight to the back. The small deli had a couple of tables set up in the corner. Finn ordered two muffulettas and turned to me. "Would you like a Coke or something?"

"Sure," I answered.

Finn walked to an old metal drink well, slid open the metal door and reached inside. He pulled out two glass Cokes. They were the kind you only see in old movies and on commercials. He paid for our food and drinks at the counter and we sat at a table and waited for our sandwiches. I took a sip of the Coke and couldn't keep myself from sighing at how refreshing it tasted.

"Good, huh? Glass Cokes are the best," Finn said, as he took a sip of his. Our sandwiches were soon delivered, and I took my first bite of a muffuletta. It would not be my last. A muffuletta is ham, salami, and provolone cheese on round Italian-style bread. It also had this amazing chopped olive mix in it. I devoured it.

"This is amazing!" I told Finn.

"The food is the number one reason I love New Orleans," Finn said, before diving back into his sandwich.

After we finished eating, Finn walked me back to my hotel. "Thanks for today. I *really* needed a break from work." I emphasized the word as we walked through the lobby.

"What's wrong? Maybe I can help?" I considered telling him what I was doing there. I had a great day with him and I thought he might understand. I looked in his eyes and decided I couldn't risk telling him. I liked spending time with him and didn't want to chance him hating me.

"I told you I can't tell you about my job," I told him.

"Well, can you tell me what's wrong without telling me what your job is?"

I thought about that. Maybe I could somehow tell him. I thought carefully about how I could state my problem. "The reason I came to New Orleans is no longer the reason I'm in New Orleans."

"That doesn't make much sense," he told me.

"I know, but that's all I can say. The problem is, my boss is not going to be happy with my reason."

"Is your boss the owner of the company?"

I looked at him confused. "No."

"Then go over his head. Talk to the owner. Maybe he will side with you. Then there is nothing your boss can do about it," he said.

"Holy crap, that's it! Finn, you're a genius," I said, as we stopped in front of my room. "Thank you so much for today. I had a blast," I said, as I leaned up and kissed his cheek.

"You're welcome," he said, as he turned slightly red in the cheeks. "I'll talk to you later."

"OK, bye." I turned and walked into my room excited about having another option to solve my problem.

Chapter 16

I PRACTICALLY RAN THROUGH the room, throwing my purse and jacket on the spare bed before pulling open the drawer of the nightstand. I retrieved my notepad and pen and sat down on my bed. I leaned against the headboard and read what I had already written.

> *1. Complete the job I was hired to do.*
> *2. Tell Tank.*
> *3. Run.*

I wrote down my next option.

> *4. Go straight to the source.*

I can't believe I didn't think of this. I would just go straight to the person who wanted Courtney and the others dead. I could reason with him and convince him to leave Courtney alone. *How will I convince him?* I didn't even know why he wanted her dead in the first place. *OK, I will find out who wants her dead and find out why. I will figure out a way to change his mind. I need to know where Tank gets his orders. I will start with that.*

I leaned back and considered my new option. This was the only way I could prevent the deaths of the people I loved and also stay in the country. If I would be able to pull this off, I would not even have to tell Finn that I was an assassin. Life would go on like normal and I could go back to Chicago. That thought hit me like a train. Did I want to go back to Chicago? Now that I found my lost family, I didn't know if I could leave them. *OK, one thing at a time, make sure they stay alive.*

I picked up my phone and called Tank. The sources of our assignments are supposed to remain secret, but Tank had been like family to me. I wasn't sure if he would break the rules for me, but I had to try. Anyway it was time for me to check in with him. I dialed Tank's cell number

"Hello," Tank said, in a harsh and disgruntled voice. I looked at my clock on the nightstand and saw that it was one o'clock in the morning. I hadn't realized it was so late.

"Hey, Tank, sorry to call so late. Do you want me to call back tomorrow?"

"No, Blake, it's fine. Is everything all right?"

"Yeah, just made it back to the room and was checking in with you."

"Ok, good. How is everything going?"

"Good. Oh, hey," I said, trying to sound nonchalant "I was wondering something. Where do we get the kill orders from?"

"What?"

"Well, I know we get them from you, but where do you get them?" I crossed my fingers and waited. There was a long period of awkward silence, which Tank finally broke.

"Blake, you know I'm not at liberty to divulge that information. Why do you want to know?"

"No reason," I blurted out too quickly. I regained my control before speaking again. "I have just been working with the company for so long, and I was just curious, I guess." I should have known he wouldn't tell me. Tank was all business.

"Blake, what's wrong?"

Great now I've tipped off Tank that something is not right. "Nothing is wrong, I'm just curious about the business I have been working with for the last eight years or so."

"You sound stressed out. Let me send someone to help you."

"No!" I yelled. "I'm fine. Really. Please, I can handle this by myself."

After a moment of absolute silence, Tank sighed and then replied. "All right, but you have to check in with me and let me know the second anything goes wrong."

"I've already promised you I would, didn't I?" I said, sounding offended.

"Yeah, you did. OK, be careful."

"I will, Bye, Tank, and sorry I woke you."

"No problem. Anytime, Blake," he said. With that, we both hung up.

I sighed and let my head fall against the headboard with a bang. "Ouch!" *Great, now I have a headache.*

Well, obviously Tank was not going to give me any of the information I needed about who was behind the kill order. *How else can I get the information?* If I was in Chicago, I could do some investigation, but I was in New Orleans. I needed someone who was there, who could do my work for me. *Whom can I trust?* Only one name popped into my mind. *Mark.* I flipped my phone open and dialed his number.

"He-hello?"

"Hey, Mark."

"Who is that?" I heard a woman's voice in the background.

"Tabitha, give me a second," Mark told his obnoxious girlfriend.

"Am I interrupting anything?" I asked.

"That's her, isn't it?" Tabitha angrily asked.

"Tabitha, can I please just have a second?"

"Fine; well, when you're done talking to Blake, your girlfriend will be waiting in the living room for you to apologize." I heard Tabitha slam the door on her way out of the bedroom.

"Damn, she sounds pissed," I joked into the phone.

"Blake, what do you want?"

"Can't I just call my best friend at one thirty-two in the morning?" I asked, glancing at the clock.

"No, you can't. What do you want?"

"A favor," I asked, as sweetly as I could.

"This couldn't wait until the morning?"

"Yeah, it probably could, but then I wouldn't have been able to piss off your girlfriend."

"Are you trying to convince me to *not* do you a favor?"

"You're right; I'm sorry for causing a conflict between you and the devil's minion."

"Whatever. What do you need?"

"Um, well, I need you to find out who gave Tank my kill order," I said, and waited for Mark's reply-which was to laugh. When I didn't join in his laughter, he stopped.

"You're serious."

"Yes, I am."

"You know they won't tell me. The controllers aren't allowed to tell us where they get the hits."

"I know, that's why I need you to *secretly* find out," I explained.

"Are you going to tell me why you need this information?"

"Nope." I waited for what seemed like a long time.

Finally Mark spoke. "OK, so let me get this straight. You want me to go against the controllers and find out the one secret they keep from us, but you will not tell me why?"

"Correct," I sighed, and continued. "You know I tell you everything, and I really want to tell you, but I can't. Not yet."

"OK, but you seriously owe me."

"Thanks, Mark. Now, go fix things with Hitler's mentor."

"Bye, Blake," Mark said, between laughing and hung up the phone.

I hung up my phone and set it on my nightstand before tucking myself into bed. I felt a weight lift off my shoulders, knowing Mark would do my searching for me. I closed my eyes and slowly drifted off to sleep.

Chapter 17

I WOKE UP FEELING pretty good. I had an option that didn't result in the death of my loved ones, and my best friend was helping me. I felt bad not telling him why I needed to know the source of the assignment, but the less he knew, the better. I was already putting him in enough danger by asking him to snoop around Tank. If he knew what was really going on, he would insist on coming to New Orleans, and I couldn't put him in the middle of me and the company.

I got dressed and went for my morning jog. I always felt rejuvenated after working out, so when I got back to the hotel, I didn't start the coffee pot. Instead, I hopped into the shower. Still energized, I decided to get completely dressed and do some errands.

I decided during my run that I couldn't fully count on this new plan to bail me out of my problem. I had to be prepared in case we needed to run from my company. I needed to go to the bank and withdraw some cash to keep on hand, in case we needed to leave quickly. I was just finishing straightening my hair when there was a knock at my door.

Confused, I slowly made my way to the door but not before picking up my gun. I peeked through the peep hole and saw Finn. I put my gun away and opened the door. He was leaning all of his weight against the door gripping both sides of the frame. A few strands of hair fell in front of his face as he stared at the floor. It was not hard to see that he was not himself.

"Finn, what's wrong?" I asked, unable to keep worry from my voice.

"Did you have anything to do with it?" He didn't look at me as he asked the question.

"What are you talking about?" He finally looked up at me and I could see pain behind his eyes. He quickly walked passed me into my room. I closed the door and stood by my bed. Quietly, I watched him pace the length of my room before he stopped in front of me.

"Did you have anything to do with it? Please just tell me. I have to know," he asked again.

"Finn, I don't know what you're talking about," I was getting aggravated and very worried. He stared at me for a second before speaking.

"Janey's dead."

I felt a stab in my heart as he said the two words. It felt like someone knocked the wind out of me, and I was unable to catch my breath. I knew my knees would not hold me much longer, so I sat down on the edge of my bed. I gave him a questioning look, so he elaborated.

"We found her a few hours ago, behind the house. Someone...shot her...in the head," he said, clearly having a difficult time putting it to words. I noticed his hands were shaking-or maybe I was shaking.

"Wait. I don't understand," I said, trying to make sense of those two words. *Janey's dead?* Suddenly I remembered the question he asked me earlier. I quickly looked up at him. "Finn, I swear, I had nothing to do with this. I promise. I could never..." I broke off my sentence. He nodded to me and turned around and gripped the top of my chair.

"I know you couldn't," he said softly. "I just...don't know what to do." I saw his knuckles turn white as he gripped the chair harder.

I didn't know what to do, either. I felt the tears beginning to form behind my eyes. So, like I had done hundreds of times, I pushed that pain and sadness to the back of my mind and focused on something else.

"What did the police say?" I asked.

"We didn't report it," he replied. "We are going to take care of this ourselves, and when we find the bastard who did this, we will not be turning him into the police." For the first time I could remember, Finn sounded dangerous.

I had killed many people and done some pretty bad things, not because I really wanted to, but because it was my job. I *wanted* to find the guy who killed Janey. I *wanted* to watch and participate in the "questioning." And I badly *wanted* to watch his face as the last light of life left his eyes.

I looked at Finn. I couldn't stand to see him in pain. I stood up and walked over to him. Softly, I placed my hand on his shoulder.

"Stop it," I told him.

He turned his head to look at me, confused.

"Stop it," I repeated. "Take all that hurt and pain you are feeling and push it out of your mind. None of that will help Janey. Instead, focus on your anger. That will help you bring her justice. Once she has that, then you can mourn her." He stared at me for a second.

"You sound like Courtney," he said, clearly not taking my advice. He sounded so upset.

"I know," I said, as I pulled him into a hug.

Finn had never been very good at hiding his emotions. Everyone knew when he was happy or sad. I held him and stroked the back of his head and his shoulders. As I hugged him, I thought about Janey. How could this happen? She was always the safe one of the group. She used to fuss at me for climbing the tree too high or doing anything she thought was too dangerous. She would develop elaborate plans for a kitchen break-in (which we never used, because we were not patient enough to wait for her to finish planning).

I remembered the video I had watched a few days back of her and Brooke arguing. I should have gone to see her. Now I would never see her again. I felt the tears forming behind my eyes, and again I tried to push them back, but this time I was unsuccessful. For the first time in years, a tear escaped my eyes. I squeezed Finn tighter as I felt the tears begin to make their journey down my cheeks. The situation had changed from me comforting Finn, to him comforting me.

He pulled his head back from my shoulder to look at me. He brought his hands up to hold my face. Softly, he brushed my tears away with his thumbs. My hands slid from his shoulders to rest on his chest. I looked into his eyes and saw so much pain behind them, and I knew that if I looked into a mirror, I would see the same in mine.

But his also held something else; behind those blue-green eyes I saw a spark of something, and I felt a wave of heat flow through my body. Slowly, he leaned his face toward to mine. It was obvious he was giving me enough time to pull away from him if I wanted to. But I didn't want to.

Softly, he placed his lips on mine and kissed me. It was one of the most, if not the most, gentle and sincere kisses I had ever had. I kissed him back as softly. After only a second, he pulled away and looked into my eyes. I saw that his were no longer filled with pain but the spark I saw was brighter. I smiled at him and he smiled back, sending a tingling sensation down my body. He leaned back toward me and kissed me again.

This kiss was much more passionate than the first. I opened my mouth to his, and the kiss grew more intense. I slid my hands up his chest and neck and into the back of his hair. His slid from my face to my waist, where they rested for a moment before he wrapped his arms around me and pulled me closer to him. I felt my blood racing through my body and thought my heart would beat out of my chest. His hands moved up my back before one made its way into my hair. I am not sure how long we were kissing, but when we broke apart, I noticed that he was breathing as heavily as I was.

He leaned forward and rested his forehead on the top of mine. He brushed the back of his fingers across my cheek before running them through my hair. I wanted more. I slid my hand up his neck and stroked his jaw with my thumb. I tilted my face to his but before I could search for his lips, he found mine. With a deep breath he drew me into him. I had to stretch up on my toes to completely wrap my arms around his neck. He held me so tightly that I was hardly standing.

As I held his head securely to mine, I heard a knock at the door. Both of our heads quickly turned to look at the door. I looked back at Finn, whose breathing had increased with mine.

"Expecting anyone?" he asked, as he slowly loosened his hold on me.

"No," I replied. Reluctantly, I slid from Finn's arms back to earth. I clumsily walked to the door, feeling like a baby deer learning to walk. I looked through the peep-hole. "What the-", I said, as I opened the door.

Chapter 18

"**N**ICOLE?" THERE STANDING in my doorway was the tall, thin, gorgeous, auburn assassin.

"Hey, Blake!" she yelled, giving me a hug which I didn't return. I was too shocked to move.

"What are you doing here?" I asked. She opened her mouth to answer when her eyes moved to Finn, who was now standing behind me. She lifted her eyebrow at me and smiled.

"Am I interrupting something?" *YES!* I just glared at her. She moved past me to stand a little too close to Finn. "Hi, I'm Nicole, a friend of Blake's." She held her hand out for Finn. He looked at me but politely shook her hand.

"Finn. Also a friend of Blake's," he said.

"Nice to meet you," Nicole said, as she walked past him to sit on the unused bed. I did not like the way she looked at him, but I couldn't blame her. He looked good. I was closing the door when I heard someone yelling down the hall.

"Damn, Nicole, do you need this much stuff?" I poked my head in the hall and saw Peter, aka Pack Rat, pushing a luggage cart loaded with five red suitcases, which I recognized as Nicole's, and one black bag, which I assumed was his.

He left the cart in the hall and walked past me into my room. "What's up, Blake?" he asked, as he plopped down on my bed. "Hey," he said to Finn, before turning to Nicole. "Really, you need five suitcases?" he asked her.

"I don't know what I am going to want to wear," Nicole explained to him. They argued back and forth, as if they had not just barged in my room and interrupted me and Finn. It was beginning to annoy me that they would not answer my questions.

"What are you guys doing here?" I asked firmly. Nicole stopped arguing to look at me and glanced at Finn.

"I think I should leave," Finn said behind me. I quickly spun on my heels to face him. The last thing I wanted was for him to go. I wanted Twiddle Dumb and Twiddle Dee to leave. "I should probably get back to the house," he explained. I looked in his eyes and saw pain beginning to make its way to the surface again.

"OK, I'll walk you out," I said, following him to the door.

"Nice to meet you," Finn called out to Nicole and Pack Rat.

"You too," they replied together.

We walked into the hall, and I left the door open a crack, because I didn't have my access card to get back inside the room. I leaned against the wall.

"Sorry about them," I said. "They are coworkers of mine. I had no idea they were coming."

"That's OK. I really should get back to the house. The others will be worrying about me, especially since Janey..." he didn't finish the sentence. I nodded my response. He was right. I knew Jake would be a disaster; after all, Janey was his twin. Brooke would be hysterical, and Courtney would be in full alert mode. She had always been so protective of us. "I'm sorry I accused you earlier," he said.

"No, it's OK. I unders-" but held up his hands to cut me off.

"It's not OK. I know you aren't capable of something like that, but I guess under the circumstances, I just needed to hear you say it."

The circumstances were that he had caught me breaking into his house with a gun. I told him that I would never hurt our family, and I meant it, but I was certainly capable of murder. It killed me that he believed I was not capable of it. I was not only capable of murder, but was guilty of it many times over. He stared at the floor again.

I placed my hand in his, and he looked up at me. "I promise we will find out who did this," I told him. He nodded to me and held my hand in both of his.

"I had better go. I'll call you," he said, before lifting my hand to his face and kissing my palm. "Bye."

"Bye," I said, as I watched him walk down the wall. I badly wanted to run to him, embrace him, and go back to his house to sort this whole thing out. As I contemplated that, I heard Nicole and Pack Rat arguing inside. I sighed and went back into my room, closing the door behind me.

"Damn, Blake, he is hot. Are you two...?" Nicole raised her eyebrows at me as she asked the question.

"What are you doing here?" I ignored her question and asked my own, with desperation in my voice.

"Tank didn't call you?" Nicole asked. Pack Rat was ignoring us and watching wrestling on my television.

"Does it look like Tank called me?"

"I guess not. Well, he called us late last night and told us to come down here to help you. He said you had this huge assignment and needed some assistance," she explained.

"I'm going to kill him," I mumbled under my breath.

"Is something wrong?" Nicole asked, concerned. I didn't feel like getting into it with her. The person I wanted to get into it with was in Chicago.

"Will you excuse me a second?" I asked, as I grabbed my cell phone and access card off the nightstand and walked out the room.

I flipped open my phone and called Tank. I didn't give him a chance to say "Tech support" before I yelled at him, "What the hell were you thinking?"

"Oh, hi, Blake, I was expecting a call from you," he said casually. That only made me angrier.

"Oh, so you intended to piss me off?" I stated, more than asked.

"Stop being a smart ass. I didn't do this to make you mad, I just knew it would."

"I asked you not to send anyone."

"Look, I've known you since you were in high school. I know something is going on that you are not telling me."

"So you sent people to spy on me, is that it?"

"No. I sent people to help you."

"I told you I do not need any help!"

"Blake," he sighed, "I care about you. I was good friends with your uncle, and not having a family of my own, I consider you a daughter."

"If I was really like a daughter to you, you would respect my wishes," I yelled. That seemed to make him mad.

"I do respect your wishes, but I also have to do what's best for you and the company. I thought I almost lost you when you were shot a few months ago, and I won't go through that again. I'm also your boss, and I have to make decisions on what's best for this job. You have six marks, which is a lot for anybody, no matter if they're as good as you. Nicole and Peter are both very good at what they do. Peter could break into the Pentagon if he wanted to, and Nicole has her own special ways of getting people to do what she wants."

"Yes, I'm fully aware of their qualifications," I replied, with my normal smart ass attitude.

"I've made my decision. I'm sorry you're upset about it but that's how it is," he said, ending the argument.

"Fine," I said, before hanging up the phone. Most people would not be able to or even consider talking to Tank like I just did. But like he said, I was like a daughter to him. I did respect him completely, but sometimes my temper took control. I walked back in my room and sat on the counter, facing Nicole and Pack Rat.

"I'm sorry," Nicole said to me. It was obvious she thought I was mad that he sent her. I didn't want to hurt her feelings.

"I'm mad he sent help when I told him I could handle this assignment, not mad he sent you. In fact, out of everybody, I'm glad he sent you," I said truthfully. I knew things didn't go well the last time Nicole and I worked together, but I trusted her and Pack Rat more than anyone else in the company, with the exception of Mark and Tank. That seemed to cheer her up. She sat up on the bed eagerly.

"So, who's the target?" she asked. I really didn't feel like getting into this right now.

"I've had a rough morning. I'm going to take a bath, and after we can go get dinner. I will explain the assignment then. Is that OK?" I asked. I would definitely have to leave Finn and the others out of my explanation.

"Yeah, that's cool." I turned to walk to the bathroom and stopped in front of the TV.

"Pack Rat, did you get a room?" He broke his staring match with the TV and looked at me.

"Yep," he answered. He had never been a man of many words.

"How did you get a room? I thought everything was booked for Mardi Gras," I told him.

"Simple, I hacked into the hotel's computer files and made a few changes." Someone was definitely going to be mad when they came to New Orleans, only to find their room reservations were lost.

I continued to the bathroom and filled the tub with hot water, dropping some bath salts in before lowering myself into the soothing water. I sighed as I submerged as much of myself as I could.

I closed my eyes and thought about the steamy kiss between me and Finn. I felt a fresh wave of heat flow through me that had nothing to do with the warm water I was sitting in. I smiled to myself, but it quickly faded when the two words he told me flashed across my mind. *Janey's dead.* I placed my face in my hands, and for the second time that day-and the second time in close to a decade-I cried.

Chapter 19

MY BATH-WATER COOLED before I was able to get my emotions under control. With my fair complexion, I knew my eyes would be red and my cheeks blotchy. I did not want to face the worried looks from Nicole and Pack Rat or their questions, so I turned on the shower. I stood there, letting the water beat against my back as I finally stopped sniffling. I washed my hair, got out of the shower, and began to dry off.

I wiped my hand across the mirror fogged by steam so I could get a glimpse of myself. My eyes were no longer red, so I could leave the hot bathroom without letting the others know I had been crying. I twisted my hair up behind my head and used a clip to keep it in place.

I opened my door and was greeted by the sounds of Nicole and Pack Rat arguing over which show they would watch. They cut off their arguing when I entered the room.

"Took long enough! You were in there for about an hour," Nicole told me.

"Yeah, sorry," I replied, as I sat on the edge of my bed.

"I'm starving. Where are we eating?" Pack Rat asked, diverting his attention from the TV to me.

I rubbed my forehead, trying to force out the headache I could feel forming. "There is a sandwich shop a few blocks from here. How does that sound?" I asked them.

"Good. Fine by me," they said at the same time.

We left the room and walked to the store/deli that Finn had taken me to the night before. I ordered a muffuletta and grabbed a glass Coke. Nicole and Pack Rat followed my lead and ordered the same. Once we had placed and paid for our orders, we took a seat at the same table Finn and I had used. The sandwich was just as delicious as the night before.

"This is so good. I almost forgot how amazing Louisiana food is," Pack Rat said, after his first bite.

"Oh, you've been here before?" I asked.

"I'm from here-well, not here, here. I was born and raised in Baton Rouge."

"I thought you were from Miami. Wow, this is delicious," Nicole said, digging into her muffuletta.

"I lived in Baton Rouge until I was twelve, when my dad got transferred to Miami."

"Oh, OK. So tell us," Nicole paused, trying to figure a way to state her question. "Why did our corporation send you here?" she asked me. She wanted to know about the assignment we were on, but she knew better than to talk openly about it in public.

"Well," I said, also trying to phrase this differently, "you know how our company usually sends me to fire someone?" I asked them both. They nodded their heads, understanding that "fire" meant "kill", so I continued. "This time I have to fire six people." I decided not to tell them that Janey was already dead, which meant we now only had five targets.

Nicole's eyes widened in surprise, and Pack Rat spoke. "That's crazy. The boss never sends us to fire that many people at one time."

"Yeah, but the really crazy part is that I don't know who I have to fire. I have to figure it out on my own," I said, before taking a sip of my Coke.

"That's insane," Nicole said, as she leaned back in her chair. "No wonder we were sent to help you."

When we finished eating, we went back to the hotel. I opened the door and sat on my bed. I pulled out the drawer and retrieved the kill order. I opened it to make sure that there wasn't anything written in it that told the others the real identities of the target and handed it to Pack Rat. He sat down next to me and looked over the order before handing it to Nicole. She opened it and paced the room as she read the little information that it contained. She closed it and sat on her bed.

"So the main target is the Mother, but who are these other people?" she asked.

"They are her entourage," I answered.

"Have you found out anything about who they are?" Pack Rat asked.

"Not really," I lied, as I rubbed my forehead. I had a bad headache.

"Well what have..." Pack Rat was saying but I cut him off.

"Look, I'm tired. I've had a rough day, and I'm sure you are probably tired from the flight, so let's go to bed. We can wake up early and start our stakeout, and I will tell you everything I have been doing," I said, not really intending to tell them everything I'd been doing-just the stuff that did not give away any names.

"OK," Nicole said. "I am kind of sleepy."

"Well, I guess I will see you in the morning," Pack Rat hesitantly said, as he walked out of our room.

I quickly threw on my pajamas, washed my face, brushed my teeth, and climbed into bed. Nicole took forever getting ready for bed. She washed her face with three different cleansers before applying an anti-aging lotion. She had to moisturize her arms and legs before finally climbing into her bed. No wonder her skin was perfect. She spent a lot of time each day making sure it was. I wished I would take care of myself the way Nicole did. Every now and then, I would decide to take care of my skin. I would buy expensive cleaners and face creams, but I would normally stop using them after a couple weeks.

"So the hottie who was here earlier, who is he?" Nicole asked, as she fluffed her pillow.

"He is a friend from a long time ago," I answered. I kept my eyes closed and my answer short. I was hoping she would notice that I was tired and let me sleep. I was wrong.

"How good of a friend?" Nicole asked, amused.

Nicole was one of those girls who gossiped with her friends about relationships and other things along that line. I was not one of those girls. I liked to keep my business private, and I worked hard to do so.

"Goodnight, Nicole," I said, refusing to get into the topic of Finn and me.

I didn't know exactly what to think myself. I knew that I cared a lot about him. If I never left the orphanage, things would have definitely happened between the two of us. We might have even gotten married. *Yikes!* I definitely wouldn't have become an assassin. But I did leave the orphanage. I did become an assassin. And I was definitely not married. I drifted off to sleep, thinking about Finn and the feel of his kiss on my lips.

The aroma of coffee woke me from my sleep. I opened my eyes and saw Nicole, sitting on her bed with her legs crossed. She was studying the kill order. I glanced at the clock next to my bed. It read ten till seven. I yawned and stretched my arms.

"Good morning," Nicole said, glancing at me. "I made coffee."

"Bless you," I said, as I crawled out of bed. I stumbled to the coffee pot and poured a cup. I went back to my bed and sat down with my back resting against the headboard. I pulled my knees up to my chest, wrapped my arms around my legs, and sipped my coffee.

"What time do you want to get started this morning?" Nicole asked.

"We could leave now. Call Pack Rat. I'm going to get dressed," I said, getting off my bed.

I grabbed a pair of jeans and a clean shirt and dressed in the bathroom. I walked back into the room and sat at the edge of my bed. Pack Rat appeared at our door a few minutes later.

The three of us left the hotel, and I drove us to the Mother's house. I parked the car and got comfortable in my seat; stakeouts always took too long. Every time we saw someone walking around the house, my heart stopped. I was terrified that the next person would be Finn, and Nicole and Pack Rat would recognize him. I explained how I broke into the house twice and what I found each time. I conveniently left out running into Finn and planting the camera and bug in their office. After a few hours, we were all beginning to annoy each other. Actually, they began to annoy me. Nicole and Pack Rat argued constantly about anything; most of the time I ignored them.

"That's ridiculous," Pack Rat said. "How could you think knives are better than guns?"

"They are smaller, easier to conceal, and you don't have to worry about bullets," Nicole explained.

"Yeah, but guns are more accurate and deadly," Pack Rat argued.

"You obviously don't know how to use a knife," Nicole snapped back.

"It's not rocket science. You stick the pointy end in the person," he joked

"No shit! But I can throw a knife more accurately than some can shoot."

I instantly thought about the job in Denver with Nicole. I remembered the deadly accuracy with which she planted a knife in the throat of a guard from a long distance away.

"Are you trying to tell me, that you are more deadly with a knife than I am with a gun?" Pack Rat said, laughing. "That's ridiculous."

"That's exactly what I'm saying," Nicole snapped.

"Blake, what do you think, gun or knife?" Pack Rat asked me. *Crap.* I had been hoping to avoid being dragged into their idiotic discussion.

"First of all, I think this is the stupidest argument I have ever heard. And secondly, I have seen Nicole with a knife and know that I would never question her ability with it. But for me, I prefer hand guns," I said.

"Ha! I win! Guns are better," Pack Rat teased.

"That is not what she said," Nicole argued back. I was beginning to feel a headache forming. I had to get out of there.

"Hey, how about we grab some lunch? I need to stretch my legs." I interrupted their ranting.

They nodded their agreement, so I drove to a nearby dinner. We ate lunch, and because I was not anxious to get back to the stakeout, I suggested we visit Garrett and get weapons for them.

We pulled up to Garrett's house and knocked on his door. When he cracked open the door, he saw me first, and a smile formed on his face.

"Oh, it's you, hi again," he said, as he fully opened the door. When he did that, his eyes took in Pack Rat behind me and finally Nicole. Like most people, his eyes stopped on Nicole. He opened his mouth to speak, but no sound came out.

"These are some friends of mine and Tank's," I explained, rolling my eyes at his reaction to Nicole. "They are in need of supplies."

"Anything I have is yours," he said, mesmerized. Pack Rat laughed at his comment.

"Great." I turned to Nicole and Pack Rat. "The room is the last door on the left. Go ahead and look around," I told them. "I need to get something from the car. Garrett, would you help me?"

"Sure," he said, pulling his eyes from Nicole. He followed me out to my car as the others walked to his supply room. I opened the trunk to retrieve the sound equipment Garrett had lent me. "How did the equipment work?" Garrett asked, as he picked up the main stereo.

"It worked great, thanks. I would prefer if you did not mention that I borrowed this to the others," I told him, as I picked up the cables and closed the trunk.

"No problem." He looked slightly confused at my request but agreed nonetheless.

We went back into his house and set the equipment in the corner of the room before joining Nicole and Pack Rat. Pack Rat was examining a 9mm. and Nicole was still looking around.

"Do you have any throwing knives?" Nicole asked. Pack Rat rolled his eyes but kept silent.

"No, I don't," Garrett answered, looking sad that he did not have what Nicole wanted, "but there is a store not too far from here that sells martial arts weapons. You could probably find what you want there."

Nicole walked around the room again until she picked up a small .380. Garrett turned to me, looking excited. "I have something you might want," he said, as he walked to the far side of the room. "Didn't you tell me that you just got a Llama .45?" he asked, as he pulled a gun off the shelf and brought it to me.

"This is nice," I said, examining the gun. "I will take it."

I got the address of the martial arts store from Garrett and we left with a few pistols.

We went back to the stakeout for a few hours then went back to the hotel. We walked into my room, and I pulled my cell phone out of my purse to call Tank and let him know we were in for the night. I was still angry with him, but he would call sooner or later, so I decided to beat him to it. I looked at my phone and noticed I had a message on my voicemail and a missed call from Finn. My heart beat faster as I waited to hear his message.

"Hey Blake, it's Finn. I wanted to let you know that we are having a funeral service for Janey tomorrow morning. It's going to be at the stables near the north side of Louis Armstrong Park at ten. It is only going to be our group." He paused. "I would really like you to be there, I know everyone would, but I understand if you don't want to come. Well, I guess I will talk to you later. Bye."

I hung up the phone without deleting the message.

Chapter 20

I DECIDED TO GO to the funeral, but I would hide from the others and watch from afar. I sent Nicole and Pack Rat to the martial arts store before they went to stakeout the Mother's house. I knew no one of consequence would be at the house while Nicole and Pack Rat were there, so I was not worried.

I got dressed in a gray skirt that stopped at my knees and a scoop neck black shirt that gathered in front. I finished the outfit with my stiletto black boots and my black and gray pea coat. As I had let Nicole and Pack Rat take my car, I had to hail a cab. The cab driver took me to the stables and I gave him a fifty dollar bill. I wanted the cab to wait for me, so if I wanted to I could leave in a hurry. He looked at me with surprised eyes. "And I will give you another fifty when I'm done here," I told the driver.

He agreed to wait for me, so I got out of the car and walked through the stable gate. Instead of walking straight through the stable yard, I went into my assassin stealth mode and sneaked around the gate to remain unseen. Walking along the wall of the horse stables and stopping at the edge, I peered around the corner and saw them.

They were standing in a semicircle around a small hole in the ground. Next to the hole was a small potted tree. Finn was on the end, wearing a blue dress shirt tucked into black pants. He was standing next to Jake. Jake was slightly taller than Finn but not as muscular. He had his hair cut short, and it was the color of his twin sister's, a sandy blond. He was wearing a black shirt tucked into black pants.

Standing on the other side of Jake was Brooke. Her black hair matched her black dress perfectly. The dress stopped a few inches above her knees and covered her shoulders. The neck line formed a V toward her chest. She had long sleeves that expanded as they moved toward her wrists. It was the type of dress that one would see in a display window, but very few people could pull it off. Brooke wore it well.

Beside Brooke was Courtney. She looked like she had not aged in the past ten years. She was slightly taller than me, with blond hair that covered a quarter of her back. She had perfect blue eyes and a full mouth that most men would stare at-if they were able to avoid staring at her full chest. She wore a black skirt that hugged her tiny waist and a gray button-up shirt. Like Brooke, she wore black high-heeled boots; and like Brooke, she looked beautiful. Closing the semicircle was a man I had never seen. He was a large, bald man, taller than Jake and more muscular than Finn. He wore gray pants and a black button-up shirt. He reminded me of Vin Diesel. I assumed he was the other man on the kill order, Lee Chauvin.

I watched as Jake stepped out of the semicircle and walked to the hole. I noticed for the first time that he held a small vase-like container in his hand. *Janey's urn?*

Jake opened the urn and sprinkled Janey's ashes into the hole. He turned and walked back to his place in line. Finn walked to the hole and picked up the shovel. He began filling the hole with dirt. He stopped and pulled the tree out of its pot and placed it into the hole. He held it while Jake took the shovel and dropped more dirt into the hole.

Jake handed the shovel to Brooke before going back to his place in the semicircle. Brooke stepped to the hole and shoveled some dirt into the hole. She handed off the shovel to Courtney. Courtney finished filling the hole. When she finished, she turned to face the others. She began speaking to them, but I was too far away to understand the words. I was only able to observe Courtney's facial expression. It was the first time I had ever seen that particular look on her face. She was totally defeated. She looked as if the world was crashing down, and she couldn't stop it.

When she was done with her eulogy, she walked over to Jake and hugged him. Brooke's shoulders shook as she cried into her hands. Finn went to her and tried to comfort her. He held her close as she cried into his shoulder. I could see the sorrow in his face as he spoke soothing words to her. He lifted his face and his eyes met mine. He stood there, staring at me, as Brooke held onto him as if her life depended on it.

I gave him a small smile, which he returned. He lifted a hand off of Brooke's back and held one finger up. He was telling me to give him a minute, and he would come to me. He did not want to leave Brooke in the condition she was in, and I agreed with him. I shook my head, declining his offer, and turned and walked back to the street where my cab waited.

I quickly jumped into the cab and told him I wanted to go to small café where I had found peace. I wiped a tear away from my cheek as we pulled to the curb in front of the café. I paid the driver the rest of the money I promised him and went to find a table. I ordered only a cup of coffee. I was not in the mood for dessert. I sat silently and watched the people walk down the sidewalk. I wasn't there long when I had that freaky feeling I was being watched. I didn't turn to see if someone was watching me or not; I knew someone was there. I waited for a second to be sure I was correct before leaning over and pushing the chair out next to me.

"Have a seat," I said, without turning. Finn appeared by my side and sat down.

"How did you know I was there?" he asked. I knew he would follow me, but I did not think he would arrive so soon. I also knew his cologne. I smiled in answer to his question and stared at my coffee. A waitress came to the table, and Finn ordered a cup of coffee.

"Why did you leave the others? They need you right now," I told Finn, keeping my voice low. I was not in the mood to be perky.

"They may not be the only ones," he said, trying to analyze my emotions.

"I'm fine," I answered him. "How are the others?"

"Jake is not doing too well. He hasn't spoken more than a few words. He reminds me of a zombie. Brooke is the complete opposite. Half the time she is furious, which you know how scary that can be." I did. There was little reasoning with her when she was angry. "When she is not terrorizing everyone, she is crying hysterically. Court has locked herself in her office, trying to figure out who killed Janey."

"How about you?" I asked Finn.

"I'm OK," he said, as he cracked his knuckles in his left hand. It was a habit he'd had since he was young. Every time he lied, he would crack his knuckles. I reached over and grabbed his hand, stopping him from cracking the rest of his knuckles.

"How are you, really?" I asked. He stirred his coffee and kept his eyes from mine. Just when I thought he was not going to answer my question, he spoke.

"It's my fault," he said, barely louder than a whisper.

"What? What do you mean, it's your fault?"

"I should have done something. I should have protected her."

"Did you know someone was going to shoot her?"

"No!" he answered, shocked I would even ask the question.

"Then how could you have stopped it from happening?"

"I don't know, but I should have! I promised her I would never let anything bad ever happen to her again, and I let her down. I should have-"

"Wait, what do you mean, again?" I said, cutting off his self-reprimand. He took a long time to answer. He sipped his coffee a few times before he spoke.

"After Janey and Jake got out of the orphanage, we were all living in a small, three-bedroom house. Janey and Brooke shared one room, Court had her own room, and Jake and I shared the last. It wasn't that bad of an arrangement.

"We all decided to go out to a bar we liked one night, but Janey went to a movie with her new boyfriend Frank instead. I left the bar early, because I had to wake up early for work the next morning. I walked down the hall, and as I passed the girls' room, I heard something." Finn paused and clenched his fist. "I looked in the room and saw Janey. She was crouched in the corner, crying. The front of her dress was ripped, and her lip was split and bleeding."

I didn't need Finn to tell me what that creep did to Janey. It was written all over Finn's face. I saw the muscles in Finn's jaw flex as he clenched his teeth together, like he always did when he was angry.

"I covered Janey with a blanket and called the others. They hurried back to the house, and Court and Brooke took her into the bathroom to clean her up. Jake and I were fuming. Court came out of the bathroom and told us what happened. I ran out of the house with Jake behind me and went searching for Frank.

"We found him at a local bar with a few of his friends. I knew Jake would kill him so I went to confront him instead. As I got closer, I heard Frank bragging about his conquest. He said some awful things about Janey. I snapped. I saw a beer bottle on a nearby table and grabbed it. I hit Frank as hard as I could and jumped on top of him. I just kept hitting him in the face. I didn't even feel his friends trying to pull me off of him. I don't know how long I was beating him, but the bouncer and a cop finally pulled me off of him. When they did, I saw the blood. It was everywhere. All over him and all down my arms." Finn was looking at his arms as if he was reliving the event. His hands began shaking, so he picked up his coffee to give them something to do. He cleared his throat and continued with his story.

"I was arrested and charged with attempted murder. I pleaded guilty and told the district attorney the full story. Because it was my first offense and Janey was evidence of the event, the DA pleaded down the charge to assault. I served eight months in prison." He was a little reluctant to tell me the last part.

"So, do you have any cool prison tattoos?" I asked after a brief silence, trying to lighten the mood. It worked.

"Only a swastika on my chest," he said, laughing.

"I love that movie!" I said. Edward Norton in American History X had a swastika tattooed on his chest. We were laughing when lightning flashed in the sky.

"It looks like I better grab a cab before it starts pouring," I said.

"Don't be silly. I'll drive you to the hotel," Finn said, as he dropped some cash on the table for our coffee.

After a little protest, I agreed to let Finn pay for the coffee and take me back to my room. We left the café, found his SUV, and headed back to the W.

"So, tell me something about you," Finn told me.

"Like what?" I asked.

"I don't care. I just want to know something, anything. How was high school? Do you like your job? Do you have a dog? I don't care."

"I don't have any pets," I answered, smiling.

"OK, that's something. Tell me something else."

"Um, high school was normal, I guess," I said, trying to think of something I could tell him without giving anything away about my current career choice.

"I bet you were pretty popular, huh?"

"No, I was kind of a loner," I answered. He looked at me, confused. So I elaborated. "At first, some of the 'cool' kids were nice to me, but that ended." When Finn required a more detailed explanation, I gave it to him.

"There was this guy, Jonathan, who was the quarterback and big shot on campus. He had girls all over him, and he could have whichever one he wanted. For some reason, he picked me. He made a crude comment to me; apparently it was supposed to be a compliment. I broke his nose." Finn began laughing and couldn't stop.

"Take the girl away from the fight, but you can't take the fight out of the girl," he said. I laughed at his comment with him.

Chapter 21

W E PULLED UP to the hotel, and Finn insisted on walking me to my door. He was such a gentleman that I thought he should have been born in the early 1900s. I opened my door and walked inside. I glanced out the window to see that it had started to rain as if the sky had suddenly decided to fill the bowl-shaped city.

"You can come inside, if you want to wait out the rain," I told Finn, who was still standing in my doorway.

"I don't know, you might break my nose," he said, with that wicked smile on his face.

"And when did the possibility of bodily harm keep you from doing something you wanted to do?" I replied, trying to mimic his smile.

"Good point," he said, as he walked into my room.

"Want a glass of water?" I asked, placing some ice cubes in two glasses.

"Sure." I filled the glasses and handed one to Finn, who sat in a chair at the small table. I leaned on the counter and sipped my water.

"I don't believe you ever told me about your relationship status?" I asked, grinning at him. Finn blushed slightly and looked away.

"I thought we talked about that," he said, trying to avoid the question.

"No, you told me about everyone else's relationship history, but not yours."

"What about yours? I don't remember you volunteering any information," Finn said, trying to turn the question on me.

"Oh, no, you don't. I asked you first," I told him.

He paused and looked at his glass of water. "Um, I dated a few girls, but it didn't work out," he said quickly.

"Why didn't it work out?" I asked.

He shrugged his shoulders before answering me. "I don't know."

"Were they not smart enough?" I inquired.

"No, they were smart, but..."

"Were they not pretty enough?" I began to badger him. I enjoyed annoying him.

"They were pretty, but..."

"Were they not nice enough?

"No, they were nice girls, it's just they weren't..."

"Weren't what?"

"They weren't you!" he exasperated. My heart stopped, but the butterflies went crazy. Finn stared at his glass of water for a few seconds. "Look, I'm not crazy. It's not like I've been waiting for you to come back. I dated some nice girls, but they never made me feel the way you always made me feel." Finn spoke without looking at me.

I could not believe what Finn had just said. I could not imagine that I had such an impact on him. I cared about him, too, and over the past ten years I had thought about him more times than I could count, but he made my feelings for him seem so insignificant. I stared at him.

Finn was beautiful. His blue shirt made his unique greenish-blue eyes brighter than normal. The black pants fit him better than the models who displayed them. The long, dark hair that fell in his eyes framed his perfect face. I needed to run my hands through that amazing dark hair.

I crossed the room and stood in front of him. I lifted his chin, so he would be forced to stop staring at his water and look into my eyes. When he did, something lit inside me. I leaned toward him and covered his mouth with mine. He kissed me back as intensely as I kissed him. I heard him set the glass of water down on the table before he wrapped his arms around my waist, pulling me closer to him. I opened my mouth slightly as Finn drew me into him.

He stood from the chair and moved one hand up to my face. He held my face and kissed me like he craved me. I returned his kiss with a hunger to match his own, as I ran my hands through his hair and down his neck. My fingers slid under the collar of his shirt before I brought my hands to the front and began to undo the buttons. He pulled his mouth away from mine but kept his lips close to me. He brushed them on my cheek.

"Blake." Finn said my name like he had been waiting a lifetime to say it.

"Mmm hmm," I tried to answer him, but I couldn't think of any words. A fire had broken out under my skin and consumed any thought that was not about Finn. "Blake, I need you to tell me to stop," he said, as his lips moved closer to my ear.   "What?" I asked confused by his request.

"I don't want to rush things with you and I don't think I can stop myself," he said, as he kissed my ear.

"And what makes you think I can stop myself?" I asked him, as I leaned into him and kissed his neck. I slowly moved my mouth down toward his collarbone. His fingers dug into my back as I moved my lips across his skin.

"Oh, forget it!" Finn exclaimed, as he lifted my face and kissed me deeply.

I was finding it hard to keep my heart from escaping my chest. I did not even realize we were moving until I felt my back pressed up against the wall. I went back to my previous task and worked my way through the buttons of his shirt. I slid the blue cloth off his shoulders, leaving him in a white undershirt.

Finn moved his lips along my chin toward my ear. When he hit the spot where my chin, ear, and neck met, I was unable to keep a moan from escaping. I felt him smile against my skin at the sound I made. He moved up to my ear. After a second, he moved back to the wonderful spot he had discovered. I fought the desire to moan as he deeply kissed the spot. I was unsuccessful in my attempt. I felt Finn smile again at his triumph.

"Oh, shut up," I told him. Finn laughed slightly against my skin, causing bumps to run along my arms.

"I like that sound," he told me, as he kissed his way down my neck. When he reached the base he continued his journey along my right shoulder. He gently slid the strap of my black shirt off my shoulder, giving him more places to kiss. I ran a hand into his hair as he journeyed across my skin. A sudden panic hit me.

"Wait," I said, reaching up to grab Finn's hand.

He stopped and looked up at me. "What's wrong?" He asked, breathing as heavily as I was.

"I have a scar," I told him, trying to catch my breath.

Finn began to laugh. I was so confused. *Why was he laughing? This is not funny.* The confusion must have shown on my face.

"You have no idea how beautiful you are, do you?" When I did not answer, he continued, "It's not just that you're gorgeous. You're sweet, funny, intelligent, and have this sexy confidence. I've thought you were amazing since I was ten years old. That is not going to change because of some scar, no matter how ugly you think it is." He slid the strap of my shirt back in place on my shoulder. "But if you are not comfortable with this, then I can wait," he said, taking a step back from me.

I looked into his eyes and saw only honesty. He was not giving me some line to get me into bed. He would have been happy just to hold me in his arms. His sincerity was a turn-on for me. I grabbed the bottom of my shirt, pulled it over my head, and let it fall to the floor. Finn's eyes never left mine to scan my body. "Are you sure?" he asked me.

I closed the distance between us and kissed him. I thought that was a better answer to his question than words. Finn's hands ran up my bare back and over my bra. I grabbed his undershirt and pulled it over his head. I gave my hands permission to move from his shoulders down his chest. He was more muscular than I realized. I knew he was in good shape, but his shirt hid his amazing body. He was shaped like a soccer player. I always liked soccer players. I could feel the lines of his strong muscles beneath smooth skin. I moved my hands around to feel the incredible curves of his back.

One of his hands traveled down my back, along my side, over my hip, and down my leg. His hand gripped the back of my knee and he lifted my leg and held it at his side. With one arm holding me securely around the waist and the other holding my leg he effortlessly lifted me off the floor.

Without any hesitation in his kissing, he carried me to my bed and softly laid me on the mattress. He climbed on the bed, keeping his lips on mine the entire time. Before I knew what happened, my bra fell to the floor. I loved the way his bare skin felt against mine. A slight sweat was breaking out on his body.

I allowed my fingers to trace the lines in his abdomen. I moved my hands along the muscles in his back as his mouth moved from mine to explore the rest of my uncovered body. His lips moved across my collarbone and down my right shoulder. He didn't hesitate as he found my scar. Softly, his kissed the part of me I thought was the ugliest. He kissed the scar for a moment before continuing his exploration. I found that the lower he moved, the harder it was for me to breathe. He had made it to my stomach when I heard a familiar sound. Both of our heads popped up in time to see the door open.

Chapter 22

FINN THREW HIMSELF on top on me to shield me from whoever was walking in the room. Unfortunately, he was not quick enough to pull the blanket around us before Nicole walked inside. She froze mid-stride when she saw us. She stared at us with her mouth agape. I was about to yell at her when someone walked in behind her.

"Well, well, well, what do we have here?" the tall man said at the sight of Finn and me.

"Mark? What are you doing here?" I asked, surprised to see my best friend, who was supposed to be in Chicago.

"Clearly not having as much fun as you are," he said, with a huge grin on his face. Mark and Nicole stood staring at us for a few awkward seconds.

"Well, get out!" I yelled at them. My yell startled Nicole, but she obeyed and ran out of the room, pulling a still grinning Mark behind her. As soon as the door closed I let my head fall back onto the pillow. Finn rested his forehead on my shoulder. We were both trying to catch our breath.

"You know, I am really beginning to dislike your friends," Finn said into my shoulder.

"Yeah, me too," I replied, causing Finn to chuckle. He lifted his head and looked at me with those beautiful eyes. I was really going to kill Mark and Nicole.

Finn sat up and ran his hands through his hair. He leaned over, picked up my discarded bra, and handed it to me. I took it from him, still clutching the blanket to my chest, and sat up to put it on when I realized he was looking at me.

"Turn around," I told him. Finn smiled at me and raised his eyebrows.

"Really, you're going to be modest now?"

I narrowed my eyes at him. "Yes, now turn around."

He laughed. "Yes, ma'am," he said, as he turned to let me dress.

He got off the bed and walked to the wall where we left our t-shirts. I pulled the blanket back up to cover myself as I watched him pull on his undershirt. *It's a shame to cover something that pretty.* Finn picked up the other shirts and walked back to the bed. He handed me my top and turned his back to me while I put my shirt back on. I stood up and straightened my skirt before Finn turned to face me. He smiled at me while he began buttoning his shirt from the bottom. I reached up and started fastening his top button.

"I can dress myself," he said, jokingly.

"Well, I helped take it off. It's only fair that I help put it back on," I replied.

He gave me that crooked, wicked smile I adored. "If that's the case, I should have put your bra back on for you." I gave him a sarcastic look before breaking into a smile.

"So who was that guy?" Finn asked.

"That's Mark. He's my best friend from Chicago," I answered.

"Oh, OK." I realized that I had not mentioned Mark to Finn yet. We had talked so little about my life.

"Would Jake be your best friend?" I asked.

"Yeah, I guess so."

"You don't sound very convincing."

"Well, some girl took that title a long time ago, and it's still hers if she wants it," he told me.

I took a few deep breaths before replying. "Why do you keep doing that?" I asked him.

"Doing what?" My question obviously confused him.

"You keep being all romantic and stuff," I answered.

He smiled again. "The guys you dated were never romantic?"

"Yeah, they were, but their comments were always a little cheesy. You pull it off better than they did."

"If you don't like it, I won't-"

"No, no, no, don't get me wrong. I like it. I just don't know how to respond to it."

He wrapped his arms around my waist. "I can think of a few ways," he said, kissing me. When he stopped, I laid my cheek against his chest and hugged him. I wanted to stay there for hours, but I had to deal with Mark and Nicole, who were waiting in the hall.

"I guess we should get this over with," I said. I knew Mark would enjoy this awkward scene a little too much. I tried to explain that to Finn, but I don't think he fully understood.

"They are your friends; it will be fine."

"Yeah, yeah," I mumbled, as I walked to the door. I caught my reflection in the mirror. My hair looked like I had just rolled out of bed. *That's appropriate.* I ran my hands through my hair, trying to get it to settle down.

"Stop, you're beautiful," Finn said from across the room. I turned to give him a cynical look.

"Remind me to give you a kiss for that," I said, as I walked to the door. I stopped by the table and picked up the glass of water Finn had discarded earlier. I took a sip as I swung the door open. I turned to walk back to Finn without looking into the hall.

"You know that the door is just going to close, and we're going to have to open it for them again?" Finn asked me, as I reached him. I handed him the water.

"Just wait," I said. The door was inches from closing when a hand reached out and grabbed it. Finn laughed as he took a sip of the water and handed it back to me.

Mark walked into the room with a huge grin on his face. He was followed by a very guilty-looking Nicole. I glared at Mark and his stupid smile. There were a few seconds of awkward silence, which Nicole broke.

"Blake, I'm so sorry. I had no idea that you and Finn were in here," she said. As she spoke, a flash of something crossed Mark's eyes but disappeared before I could figure out what it was. If I had not been glaring at Mark, I would have missed it. *What was that?*

"Let's just forget about it," I said, more to Mark than Nicole. His smile told me that it would not be that easy. I turned and introduced Finn to Mark, and they politely shook hands.

"So, I take it that you two are friends?" Mark asked Finn sarcastically.

"Actually, we met about thirty minutes ago at the hotel bar," Finn joked with Mark. It was obviously a lie, as Nicole knew who he was. Also, I was not the type to take guys I just met home with me.

"Oh, let me guess. You took one look at this sexy woman and was instantly hooked," Mark said to Finn, winking at me. *Oh great.* Mark intended to flirt obnoxiously with me in front of Finn. I guess this was payback for all the times I did that to him and Tabitha. I did not know how Finn would react to it. I hoped he would not be the jealous type and try to fight Mark.

"Yeah, it was those big green eyes that got me, among other things," Finn joked back. I let out an internal sigh at his response. I was thrilled that he wasn't letting Mark get to him. On the other hand, I was getting extremely uncomfortable with the talk about which of my features attracted them.

"Anyway!" I interrupted. "Mark, what are you doing here?"

"I tried to call you from the airport but you didn't answer, so I called Nicole," Mark answered, without answering the question.

"Oh, I forgot to take my phone off silent," I realized.

"I forgot to do that, too," Finn told me, as he pulled his phone out of his pocket. "Crap," he said, showing me his phone. It had four missed calls; one from Courtney and three from Brooke.

"What? Your girlfriend called?" Mark asked.

"Yeah, a couple of them," Finn joked before turning to me. "I better go, or they are going to freak out and hunt me down."

"Yeah, ok," I said. I did not want to see Finn go, but I understood. With Janey's death, the others were going to be paranoid. If Finn did not return home soon, I had no doubt that Courtney would send out a search party.

Finn said good-bye to Mark and Nicole before letting me lead him toward the door. "Don't worry, I will take good care of Blake for you," Mark called to Finn, as we left the room.

I closed the door behind me without worrying to grab a key. They had ruined my day, so they could get off their butts and let me back inside the room. Finn leaned against the wall in the hall and watched me as I leaned next to him.

"I'm sorry about Mark," I said. "He is trying to aggravate you because of me. It's kind of a payback thing." Finn gave me a look in question so I answered before he could ask.

"Well, Mark is dating this evil girl named Tabitha. She is horrible," I said, trying to find the right analogy of her. "You know that movie 'Children of the Corn'?" I went on. He nodded. "I think that movie was based on her childhood," I told him. Finn laughed at my analogy. "Anyway, I have been using our friendship to irritate her in hopes that it will drive a wedge or something like it between them," I explained. He nodded but showed little understanding. "Mark's my best friend and he is a good guy. He deserves someone better than her."

Finn didn't respond to my comment. I was hoping he wouldn't be like the previous few guys I dated and stress out about Mark and my friendship. "Is Mark going to be a problem?" I asked. I cared about Finn a lot, but I was not going to put up with insane jealousy.

"Is there anything between you two?" Finn asked.

"No, we are just friends," I answered.

"Well, then, there is no problem," he said, giving me a reassuring smile.

"Good," I said, leaning into Finn for a kiss.

After a few seconds of a great kiss, Finn pulled back from me. He suddenly looked shy and nervous. "Would you want to have dinner with me tomorrow?"

I wanted to kiss him again. He was nervous about asking me out, even after what had just happened between us. He was so cute.

"I don't know," I said, with a hint of flirtation. "I may have to work."

It was true. I needed to devote some time to figuring out what to do about my current situation. Somehow, I thought that the lives of Finn, Courtney, Brooke, and Jake outweighed my desire for a good meal. Plus, I now had Mark to deal with. I desperately wanted to say "yes" to him, but I did not need the distraction. Finn was definitely a distraction, a very sexy distraction.

"OK, I understand," he said, looking slightly defeated. He was trying to look like it was not a big deal, but I knew how he thought. Finn and I had been through a lot. We were each other's first kiss, and then what happened in the room a few minutes ago, but we had never been on a real date. He wanted to take me on a real date.

"Maybe I can," I said. "Could I call you tomorrow to let you know?" That cheered him up. It wasn't the answer he wanted, but the possibility of a "yes" had him smiling. He pulled me back to him and kissed me again. The kiss was cut short by the sound of his cell phone ringing. It was Brooke again.

"I better go," he told me. He gave me a final big hug and a quick kiss before turning to leave. He stopped and turned back to me. "By the way," he said, using his deep smooth voice that caused my heart to beat a little faster, "I think your scar is sexy." I blushed uncontrollably as he turned and walked down the hall.

Chapter 23

NICOLE LET ME back inside the hotel room. Mark was stretched across my bed, with his hands behind his head and his feet crossed. He looked a little too comfortable. I walked inside and sat down in the chair at the small table. Mark was staring at me with the same obnoxious grin he had been wearing since he and Nicole walked in on Finn and me. Nicole crawled on her bed and pulled her knees up to her chest. The three of us stared uncomfortably at each other, or it was more like the two of them stared uncomfortably at me.

"Fine, let's have it," I told them. I wanted to get this over with.

"What?" Mark asked, faking hurt. "I am just happy to finally know why you love your job so much." Nicole looked at me nervously to see how I would take Mark's joke. I rolled my eyes at his comment. I knew his remarks could get more invasive. "I was beginning to wonder why this assignment was taking you so long. I guess it's because you were lying down on the job," he quipped.

"Oh, come now, Mark, I think you can do better than that," I said. If he intended to make fun of me, he was going to have to try a little harder. Mark smiled at me.

"Can I ask a question?" Mark inquired. When I did not stop him, he asked it. "When did you start wearing black lace underwear?"

I froze. I was definitely wearing black lace panties. When Nicole and Mark walked in, Finn threw himself on top of me to shield my uncovered breasts, but I forgot about my skirt. It was twisted and slightly hiked up my thigh. *Crap!*

I could not believe this was happening. It was not as if Mark had never seen me in my underwear. I dated him for a few months, and things were pretty physical between us. However, it was completely different now, as I did not give him permission to see me that way. I was extremely embarrassed. Of course, I had to be a smartass and tell him to make better comments. *I need to learn to keep my mouth shut. Now I guess I need to add keeping the door locked to my list of things to remember.*

"If I can remember correctly, I believe you always preferred silk on your skin," he said. I knew I was turning red but tried to keep my face expressionless regardless. I looked at Nicole, who was biting her lip to keep from smiling.

"OK, you get one more," I said to Mark.

"Come on, just one?" he asked. My expression told him I was serious. "All right, let me think." Mark scratched his chin. He looked at Nicole for inspiration. It must have worked, because a grin crawled on his face. "I know you don't like to discuss your personal life, but please indulge me." I raised my eyebrows. "I was wondering who kisses better, him or me?"

I finally understood the grin. He was trying to impress Nicole, and he had always been a more-than-adequate kisser. He was expecting me to back that up. The truth would not help Mark's pursuit.

"You know you are a good kisser," I told him. He gave me his confident smile. It slowly faded.

"That's not an answer," he said.

"No, it's not," I said.

"Wait a second. Are you trying to say that he is better?"

"I didn't say that."

"So I am?" Mark was beginning to get frustrated.

"I didn't say that either."

"Oh, come on. I don't get it. I am definitely better-looking than he is." Mark never had a problem with self-confidence.

"Are you sure about that? Besides, what does that have to do with kissing," Nicole chimed in. She was taking advantage of the situation to tease Mark.

"You think he is good-looking?" he asked Nicole.

"Oh, yeah," she said.

As soon as the words escaped her mouth she looked at me and gave me an apologetic smile. I guess she thought I would get jealous. I smiled at her to reassure her that I was not upset. How could I be? Finn was hot, and it would be insane to think she did not notice. Besides, it wasn't as if Nicole flirted with him. She would not do that to me. Mark looked disappointed. His plan had backfired.

"Mark, what are you doing here?" I asked. He perked up a little.

"What? Can't a guy visit his best friend from time to time?" he asked defensively.

I wasn't going to let him get away with that bull-shit answer. I glared at him and waited for a different response. "OK, Tabitha broke up with me," he said, in a sad voice. "I needed to get away, and I knew my best friend was here."

He was full of crap. He was trying to get sympathy but I knew better. There was no way he was heartbroken over Tabitha. Apparently Nicole did not think the same way I did.

"Aw, Mark, I'm sorry to hear that," she said to him. I could not believe she was falling for that, but I didn't rat Mark out. I knew he liked her and was fairly sure that she liked him as well.

There was a knock at the door, and I was grateful for the break in the conversation. I ran to the door and opened it for Pack Rat, and we rejoined the others.

"You missed the fun," Mark told Pack Rat, as we sat down. *Oh, great. I thought we were off that subject.* Pack Rat looked at Mark, confused, but it was Nicole who responded.

"We walked in on Blake and Finn," she explained. She was clearly not nervous about upsetting me anymore. I sighed and leaned back in my chair as she explained everything that had transpired to Pack Rat. Once the talk of Finn and my recent activities died down, I joined the conversation.

"What do you want to eat for dinner?" Pack Rat asked us.

"One of the desk clerks told me about a good sushi restaurant nearby," Nicole recommended.

"That sounds good, but can we call in the order?" I asked. I was in no mood to dine in. As Mark had no objections, we placed an order. Mark complained about jet lag, so Nicole and Pack Rat offered to pick up the food.

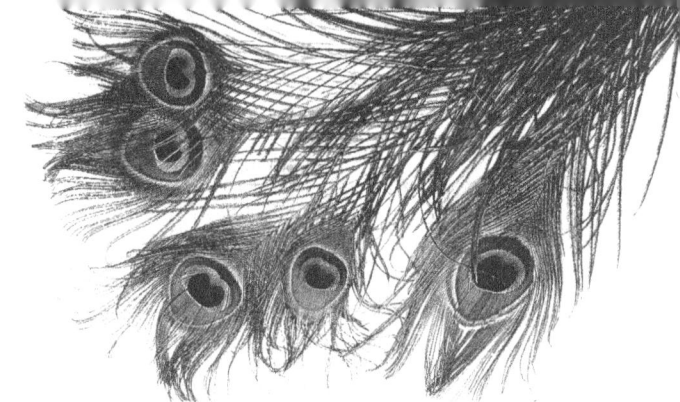

Chapter 24

ICOLE AND PACK Rat left the hotel room to pick up our sushi. As soon as the door closed behind them, Mark turned to me.

"So, Finn is the target," he said. It was not a question. He said it as if it was common knowledge, like the sky was blue or Lucille Ball was the greatest female comedian who ever lived. OK, so maybe the last part wasn't common knowledge, but it should be.

"What?" I said. "Why would you think-" I started to deny Mark's statement, but he cut me off.

"Come on, Blake. I have known you too long for you to lie to me." When I didn't respond, Mark continued to talk. He liked to talk. "I have known you for seven years. In all that time, I have never seen you hesitate or question a job until now. That tells me there is something about this job or the target that has you doubting the assignment. Then I come here and find you, let's say 'indisposed' with the boy from your orphanage. It fits that he is the reason you have problems with completing the assignment."

"'indisposed' with the boy from your orphanage." That was what flashed across Mark's eyes. Recognition. He recognized Finn's name.

"Yeah, you talked about your orphanage friends, and I listened, sometimes," he said, the last part with a smile. He knew I would argue with the statement that he listened. That was one of the problems in our relationship. He only listened to what he wanted to hear.

"Yeah, OK, Finn is one of the targets." I knew there was no point to argue. Mark knew me too well for that. I got up from my chair and threw myself dramatically on Nicole's bed. "I don't know what to do!" I yelled into her pillow.

"You said he is one of the targets. Who are the others?"

"All the other kids from the orphanage," I answered.

"Wow, no wonder you seem stressed. So here are your options: you could kill them," I shook my head at the first option. "OK, you could take on the company," I gave a sarcastic laugh at the second, "or, you could listen to what I found out for you," Mark said. My head popped off the pillow.

"I completely forgot! Did you find out who gave Tank the kill order?"

"I know you forgot, plus you were a little distracted." Mark gave his sly smile. He was never going to let go the fact that he found me in bed with someone. "And to answer your question, sort of."

"What do you mean, 'sort of'?"

Mark got up from the bed and walked over to my computer. He began typing something and turned the laptop toward me. I left Nicole's bed and joined him at the table.

"The order was sent from this address," he said, as I looked at the screen. It was completely black, with a small log in box in the center. It required a username and a password to gain access.

"What does this gain access to?" I asked. Mark shrugged his shoulders in response.

"All I could find was this address. I tried to hack into the server, but that is not my best skill, and I assumed you didn't want me to ask someone to help."

I sighed. I was not very good with computers either. My assassin training consisted mainly of learning the fastest way to stop someone's blood from pumping through their veins.

I began typing on the keyboard. I was trying the few things I knew about hacking and finding that they did not work very well. I felt a headache coming on. I leaned back in my chair and ran my fingers through my hair in frustration. I felt like I was so close to the source of my problems but unable to reach it. If I could find out who wanted Court and the others dead, then I might be able to do something about keeping them alive. As it was, I stood little chance.

After a few more minutes, Mark began to laugh. "What?" I asked in frustration.

"Oh, nothing; it's just that between the two of us, we have killed more people than the mafia, some under situations that seemed utterly impossible, but a simple computer is our unbeatable opponent." I snorted my agreement. "That was one thing about Tabitha, she was good at the things I couldn't do," Mark said.

"What really happened with her?" I asked. I was sure they had broken up. Mark would not lie about something that could be easily proven-but I seriously doubted that he was heartbroken.

"I got tired of her crap. Every time I went somewhere without her, she thought I was running off to meet another girl. I don't put up with insane jealousy," he said.

"I told you she was psycho." Mark nodded his agreement and I went back to computer hacking.

"What are you going to do about Finn?"

"What do you mean, what am I going to do about him?" I was confused by the question.

"Are you going to tell him *all* about you?" I had been thinking about doing that but didn't know how he would take the news.

"I don't know. I want to, but he...," I could not finish my sentence. I did not know how to express the fear of Finn's rejection to my ex-boyfriend, who had never been rejected before.

"Maybe you don't have to," Mark said. "Maybe you should hang out with him and do a little investigating. If this computer hacking thing doesn't work out, you are going to need to figure out something else. If we are lucky, you may be able to find out why someone would want them dead and go from there."

I thought about that as I went back to work on the login page. That was not a bad idea, but it felt wrong to spy on Finn and the others. *Hopefully I can crack this computer, and I won't have to worry about it.*

I was not working too long before Pack Rat and Nicole arrived with our food. We ate our sushi and before I knew it, the topic of conversation shifted back to my embarrassing situation that happened earlier that day. Finally I had enough and left the table.

"Where are you going?" Mark asked. I pulled my boots off on my way to the shower.

"I'm getting naked. That way Pack Rat won't feel left out and we can stop talking about it," I told them. Pack Rat's eyes lit up as he swiveled around in his chair, so he could get a good view of me.

"Are you serious?" he asked, with too much excitement in his voice.

"No, I'm going to take a shower. I expect you boys to be gone by the time I get out," I said, as I closed the door to the bathroom. *Like I would ever strip out of my clothes in front of them. Are they crazy?*

By the time I got out of the shower, the boys had indeed left for their room. I sighed with relief when I saw they were not still occupying my bed. I had enough for one day and did not feel like answering anymore questions about my love life.

Unfortunately, I did not consider Nicole. She was sitting on her bed with her legs crossed. I climbed into bed and adjusted my pillow. I had just closed my eyes when Nicole thought it would be a good time to chat.

"So, tell me about Finn," she said, excited, as if we were in high school discussing who we wanted to ask us to the prom.

"No."

"Aw, come on, Blake. I never get good gossip, and don't try to tell me he is just a friend." When I did not answer, she sighed and crawled under the blanket. "Fine, but this is not over," she said, as she turned out the bedside lamp.

Chapter 25

THE NEXT MORNING I woke up early so I could get a quick run in before the others harassed me. I got dressed quietly, trying not to wake Nicole, but was unsuccessful. As she was awake, she decided to join me in my run. We left the hotel and ran a few blocks.

"So I take it you're not going to talk about Finn," Nicole asked, as we rounded a corner. I had to hand it to the girl, she was persistent.

"Nope."

"Fine, what about Mark?" Nicole asked, between breaths.

"What about him?"

"Is there anything between the two of you?"

"No," I answered honestly. I was getting annoyed with answering that question.

"Why did you two break up?"

"We weren't right for each other. No big thing. We just decided to be friends." Nicole was quiet for a couple blocks. I could almost hear the wheels in her head turning. "Mark is a really good guy," I told her.

"Yeah?"

"Yes, and I think he may have a thing for you." A smile formed on her face as we turned around and headed back to the hotel. We talked about Mark the rest of the way back, and I was thankful that her mind had drifted from Finn and me. I had found a topic Nicole liked better than my love life-hers.

After our showers, Nicole and I met the boys for breakfast. I noticed a definite spike in Nicole's flirtation with Mark. I was happy for him. I finally approved of a girl for Mark. After breakfast, all of us went to Garrett's house to get Mark a weapon. Garrett got instantly excited to see Nicole. I had a feeling he was smitten with her. *Big surprise.* After loading up on guns and ammo, we left to go back to the hotel to map out the rest of our day.

I intended on spending the entire day devoted to my laptop and the website Mark had given me. But I did not know how to keep Nicole and Pack Rat busy so they wouldn't know what I was doing. I thought about sending them on a stakeout but did not want to risk them identifying Finn, especially if I decided to go to dinner with him. They would definitely see him leave the house to pick me up if they were staked outside. I needed a distraction. *Mark.*

I asked Nicole to give Mark a tour of the city. I told her it would help with the assignment if everyone knew their way around. I could have told her it was because I wanted to stay in and contact the ghost of Marilyn Monroe with my Ouija board, and she wouldn't have noticed. All she heard was alone time with Mark. Pack Rat wasn't that difficult. I sat him down in front of the television and told him I was doing some online research on the Mother.

I worked on the computer until I felt like I was going to pull my hair out. *How people do this every day, I will never know.* Pack Rat might as well have not been in the room for the amount of noise he made. He was completely engulfed in some weird shopping channel. I looked up to see a set of metal army soldiers representing the ones from the Civil War. They were supposed to be collector's items. I would not have been surprised to see Pack Rat order them.

Mark and Nicole walked into the room breaking my concentration from the computer. Mark plopped down beside me and leaned in close. "Get anything?" He whispered. One look at my face told him I did not. "You need a break; call Finn," he said.

I had a huge headache and looked like crap from staring at the screen all dang day long. *Maybe, I do need some personal time.* "Besides, maybe you will learn something about our problem," Mark whispered.

After giving it some thought, I decided to take Finn up on his offer of dinner. After I called him, I quickly took a shower and got dressed. I was ready before he arrived, so I sat back down in front of the computer. Nicole and Pack Rat ran to the drug store to get me some ibuprofen, so I didn't have to worry about them. I was so focused on the task at hand that I did not even realized Finn had arrived until he was standing in front of me. I assumed Mark let him inside the room.

"Hey, Blake," Finn said, bending down to kiss my cheek, as I was still in my chair. "What are you working on?"

"Oh, just some work stuff," I said, closing my laptop.

"You two go ahead, I will finish up here," Mark said, taking my laptop from me. I picked up my favorite brown jacket and my purse and followed Finn to the door. Mark grabbed my arm and pulled me back. I asked Finn to give me a second. "What?" I asked Mark.

"I am going to send the other two on a stakeout later. Nicole mentioned something about not working enough on this assignment. She is going to get suspicious soon."

"Yeah, OK. I'll call them away from the stakeout once Finn drops me off, so they won't see Finn arrive at his house later."

Once our plan to keep Nicole and Pack Rat from discovering the truth was set, I joined Finn in the hall. "Everything ok?" he asked, as we walked to his car.

"Oh, yeah, Mark had a quick work question." It wasn't a complete lie. After Finn loaded me into his SUV, we pulled away from the hotel.

"So where are you taking me?" I asked Finn.

"Dinner, and then we will see," he said, with that wicked grin on his face that I loved.

Now that I wasn't worried about work, I got to look at him. He was wearing nice dark jeans and a black buttoned shirt. I could smell his cologne, and it took all of my strength to keep my hands off of him.

"You smell amazing," I told him.

"Brooke made me wear it. She said it was necessary in hooking a girl," he said, with the same grin.

"Wait, Brooke knows you're with me?" I was about to panic. I did not think I was ready to see everyone quite yet.

"No, she got me this cologne a few weeks ago. But she does think that I have a secret girlfriend and has been bugging me about it." I let out a sigh of relief as we pulled into the parking lot of the restaurant.

Finn opened my door for me without my protest. As it was a date, I was going to allow him to behave like a gentleman without any harassment. We walked into the crowded restaurant, and I was certain we would not be able to get a table. There were people piled in the waiting room. Finn walked up to the bar instead of the hostess stand. The bartender ran over and greeted Finn like they were old friends.

"Hey, Luke, this is Blake," Finn introduced us. "Luke is the best bartender/manager in New Orleans."

"And people wonder why you are my favorite customers. Where is Brooke?" Luke asked. That made more sense. I doubted that Finn and the others were his favorite customers because of the compliments they gave. It was probably because Brooke was beautiful and a huge flirt.

"She is at home. I didn't think it would be wise to bring her on my date," Finn told Luke, who gave me a smile that made me blush.

"Do you want to sit at the bar, or would you like me to find you a romantic table?" Luke asked.

"A table would be great, but you're busy; you don't mind getting us one?" Finn asked.

"Not at all, just wait here for a second, and I will be right back."

Luke wasn't kidding. We waited for about a minute and a half before he showed us to a table. *He must really like Brooke to rush us to the front of the waiting list like that.*

We sat down, and I had hardly looked at the menu before the waiter came to take our drink order. I decide to let Finn order for me and he ordered a couple glasses of beer that I did not recognize. He told me it was from a local brewery, which I was happy about.

"Good, I wanted to try something I haven't had before," I told him. Apparently that was something Finn wanted to hear, because a huge grin stretched across his face. He reached over and took my menu from me.

"Hey, I haven't figured out what I was going to order," I protested.

"Don't worry; I will make sure it is something good."

I was not used to being treated like that. Having a guy order for me seemed so old fashioned-which I was not, but for some reason I liked it. The waiter came back to the table with our drinks and to ask if we were ready to order.

"Yes, we will have the blackened alligator for an appetizer and a seafood platter. Can you make the seafood platter half fried and half grilled?" he asked the waiter, who nodded and rushed off to place our order.

"Alligator? You are kidding me."

"Nope. You said you wanted to try something new." I could have guessed those words would come back to bite me in the ass.

"So, I answered your question. Now it is time for you to answer the relationship question."

I took a sip of my beer to postpone the answer. "Nothing too interesting to tell. I dated a few guys, but that never lasted long."

"How long was your longest relationship?" *Great.* Finn is going to think I'm weird, because my longest relationship hardly lasted through one of the four seasons.

"Let me think…it would probably be Mark. He lasted about three months." Finn looked at me, confused and slightly shocked.

"Wait. Mark? Mark from the hotel, Mark?"

"Yeah, didn't I tell you we dated?"

"No, you said that you were just friends," he said.

"We are just friends. Friends who once dated, that's all," I assured him. Finn didn't argue with me about Mark. I don't know if it was because he believed me, or if it was because our alligator arrived.

He picked up his fork and stabbed a piece. He dipped it into the sauce provided and held it up to my face. I gave him a skeptical look but took the bite off his fork. It was delicious. It tasted similar to chicken, with only a slight difference in texture.

"This is really good," I told him, picking up my fork and digging into the appetizer. He smiled and took a bite.

"So I have another question." Finn leaned back in his chair. *Oh great, more questions.* "How did you get that sexy scar?"

I hadn't been expecting that question or expecting to blush at it. I couldn't tell him the whole truth, but maybe I could work around it. I really did not want to lie to him.

"Well, Nicole and I went to a bar a few months back. Someone was trying to kill some guy. A gunfight broke out. Everyone was running for the door, and more people began shooting. I got in the way." I spoke as if it was no big deal.

Technically, I did not lie. We did go to a bar, although we were the ones trying to kill the guy. A gunfight did break out, which I started, causing everyone to run for the door. And I did technically get in the way of some guy trying to kill Nicole. So officially I did not lie.

"Shit, that's terrible! Did they ever catch the guys that started it?"

"Nope." Still not a lie, but I was beginning to get nervous with all these questions. Luckily for me, the waiter brought our entre to the table, ending the gunshot wound conversation.

He brought the seafood platter, which I discovered was shrimp, crawfish, catfish, oysters, crab au gratin, soft shell crab, and a seafood stuffed potato. It was a lot of food.

Finn picked up a spare plate, put a little of everything on it, and placed it in front of me. I was a little nervous about the food. I did not normally eat a lot of seafood, with the exception of sushi. I picked up a piece that looked harmless and tasted it.

"OK, it's official. Louisiana has the best food!" I said to Finn, who laughed.

"I'm so glad you like it," he said, before placing a piece of shrimp in his mouth. "We were all talking about you yesterday."

"You were?" I asked, a little nervous.

"Court brought up the time you broke into the cafeteria at the orphanage and stole that cheesecake," he said, smiling. "Brooke was supposed to be your lookout, but she got *distracted* by Eddie's lips, and Ms. Roberts caught you digging a fork into her new birthday cheesecake. She was pissed."

"Yeah, I got detention because Brooke wanted to make out with her new boyfriend. If I can remember correctly, you egged Ms. Roberts' office, so she would send you to detention with me," I said, with a sly smile before taking a bite of potato. Finn blushed and looked down at his food to hide it, but it didn't work.

We reminisced about all the pranks we used to pull on Ms. Roberts, who was the head of our orphanage, while we finished off the meal. I was amazed we were able to eat it all. The waiter came back to clear the plates and asked if we wanted dessert.

"I am completely stuffed," I said, but Finn smiled that wicked smile at me.

"What do you have?" Finn asked the waiter.

"Bread pudding, double chocolate cake, lemon pie, chocolate cheesecake, apple..."

"Chocolate cheesecake," Finn said, cutting off the waiter's speech. I glared at Finn but he smiled at me. "What? I know you like cheesecake."

"Yeah, but I don't know how I am going to be able to eat it. I'm full!" Finn smiled at me.

It did not take long for the waiter to arrive with our dessert. I seriously doubted I could eat a single bite. He placed the cheesecake, along with two spoons, in the center of the table. The cheesecake had a chocolate crust and chocolate swirled throughout the cream cheese filing. It looked fantastic.

I picked up a spoon and scooped a small bit of cheesecake into my mouth. I moaned at the taste of it. It was even better than it looked. I looked across the table to see Finn watching my expression as I swallowed the dessert. He had not touched his spoon and it did not look like he had any intention of eating the chocolate goodness that was between us.

"How is it?" he asked. I scooped more cheesecake into my spoon and leaned across the table. I held the spoon in front of his mouth until he gave in and took the bite. "Wow, that is really good."

I smiled my agreement and took another bite of the dessert as Finn picked up his spoon to join me. I had just placed the spoon in my mouth when I heard a voice behind me.

"Finn? Is that you?" The voice was too familiar. I didn't turn around; instead, I looked at Finn who hung his head down and shook it back and forth. I didn't know if I was ready for this, but I was about to find out.

"Hi, I'm Brooke," she said, approaching me from behind. I turned to greet her, and she froze. Her mouth dropped open as she stared at me.

"Blake!" She screamed like an excited cheerleader and ran to me.

I barely had time to stand out of my chair before she slammed into me. I hugged her back as tightly as she held me. People all around the restaurant turned to see what the commotion was. I didn't care. I could not stop smiling. As much as it terrified me to have Finn and the others find out who I really was, I was so happy to see them again.

Brooke pulled back from me but kept a firm hold on my shoulders. "What are you doing here? Oh, I don't care. I'm so happy to see you," she screamed, as she hugged me again. Laughing, I finally pulled myself out of her arms.

"It's good to see you too, Brooke," I said, unable to keep myself from smiling. The tall, gorgeous, army-looking guy I saw her making out with on the hidden camera walked up to stand behind her.

"What are you doing here, Brooke?" Finn asked, not hiding his aggravation at her walking in on our date. She turned and gave him a mean look.

"Luke called me and asked where you met this new girl, so I came here to check her out for myself. How could you not tell me it was Blake?" Brooke was fuming.

An angry Brooke was not the most pleasant person, to put it mildly. She could be outright mean when she wanted to be. I guessed that Finn was in for a rough time for hiding me.

"That's my fault," I told Brooke. "I wanted to surprise you." She glared at me for a second, but the look was quickly replaced by a smile.

"OK, you're off the hook," she said, as she sat down at one of the two empty seats at our table. She motioned for the guy behind her to join us, which he did without comment. "Joshua, I would like you to meet Blake Morgan."

He shook my hand politely and turned to do the same to Finn. Finn reluctantly took his hand before he turned to Brooke.

"You know you're not supposed to date the recruits, right?" Finn told her.

"Right, like we all haven't done it...besides, I'm not sure I want to talk to you right now," Brooke said, whipping her hair at him and facing me. Finn threw his hands into the air and let them fall on the table.

"So, what are you doing in New Orleans?" Brooke asked me.

Crap! I had not thought of an answer yet. I was trying to think of something when Finn spoke for me.

"She is here for Mardi Gras," he said, smiling at me. Bless him, I would not have thought of something that good in time.

"Great! It's amazing! You're going to love it, and you can come with us," Brooke said, as she picked up Finn's spoon and ate a bite of our dessert. "This is delicious."

"Yeah, that's why we ordered it," Finn told her, giving her a smartass look, which she ignored and proceeded to finish off the cheesecake. I could not stop smiling. It felt like the old days, listening to Brooke and Finn argue.

"Finn, pay the bill so we can go," Brooke told him, as she pulled me to my feet. "I cannot wait till Courtney, Jake, and Jan-" she cut herself off.

"I heard about Janey," I told Brooke. "I am so sorry."

"Me too."

Finn had managed to flag down our waiter and pay the bill in time to follow us as Brooke pulled me out of the restaurant. She had her arm locked through mine and was refusing to let me go. The second we stepped out of the building, I wished we hadn't. I saw my rented silver Acura parked across the lot. The doors flew open and Nicole and Pack Rat stepped out, looking nervous and angry. *Crap! Crap! Crap!*

Nicole and Pack Rat must have been on the stakeout when Brooke left the house. They would have followed her here. Now they probably thought I was discovered and captured.

I discreetly waved them off before pulling my arm out of Brooke's. Finn walked up behind me and placed a hand on my lower back to lead me to his SUV.

"Where are you going?" Brooke asked us.

"Well, you interrupted our dinner, and I was thinking of taking Blake to get a drink somewhere," Finn told Brooke, who gave him a dirty look. She was not going to let him take me anywhere without her. She would follow us. She could be stubborn but so could Finn, so I decided to step in before they killed each other.

"We can go back to your house," I told Finn. "Besides, I would really love to see Court and Jake."

"Are you sure?"

"Yes, I'm sure."

"Ok, we will meet you at the house," Finn told Brooke, before leading me to his vehicle. He opened the door for me, and I quickly jumped in and pulled out my cell phone. Holding it down by my side so no one would see my actions, I texted Nicole.

I'm fine. Stay Back

Finn climbed in the SUV and turned to face me. "I'm so sorry. I had no idea Brooke would show up, and-" I covered his mouth with a finger to stop his apology.

"It's fine. I'm really glad to see her and excited about seeing the others." I leaned across the car and gave him a soft kiss on the cheek. "Thanks for dinner."

"You're welcome," he said, as we pulled out of the parking lot and followed Brooke's black convertible back to the house. I casually pulled down my visor and opened the mirror. I pretended to check my lip gloss but looked to see if the silver Acura was behind us. It was.

"You look great," Finn said, closing the mirror as we pulled up to his gate. The guard waved us through, and we drove up to the front of his house.

Chapter 26

FINN OPENED MY door for me, and I got out of the SUV. He placed a hand on my lower back and led me to the front door of the house, where Brooke and Joshua were waiting. I had not lied to Finn; I was excited to see Courtney and Jake, but I was nervous as well. It had been close to ten years since I last saw them, and a part of me was scared they would not like me anymore. It was a childish thought, but they were the only family I had left, and I had changed over the years. They may no longer like me.

We climbed the steps to the front door. Brooke was talking to her boy of the moment. She pulled him down to her and kissed him passionately. Brooke had no qualms about public displays of affection.

"Leave your door unlocked tonight," she told him, before he turned and left the three of us alone. She smiled at me as she pulled out her cell phone. "Jake, meet me at Court's office," she said into the speaker, as she opened the door. "Because I said so, that's why." She hung up the phone and rolled her eyes before looking at me. "You ready?" I felt like screaming *No!* but nodded instead.

We followed Brooke through the door and into a giant foyer that had three hallways branching from it. "Can I take your coat?" Finn asked, from behind me.

I nodded, and he pulled the coat off my shoulders. After removing his own coat, he hung them in a closet by the door. Brooke led us down the hall directly across from the front door. She was practically skipping as she turned down a hall to our left. Once we made it to the end of that hall, we turned right down another. *This place is a maze.* Brooke finally stopped at a door at the end of the hall. She looked as if she was about to explode with excitement. She knocked on the door but did not wait for a reply. She slightly opened the door and stuck her head inside.

"Hey, I got something to show you," she told the room's occupant. My heart was racing as she opened the door and walked into the room. The only thing that calmed my nerves was Finn's hand resting at my back. I took a deep breath, followed Brooke, and stepped inside the room.

The room had a big red couch and two recliners situated around a glass coffee table. The office was lined with bookcases filled to the max. There was also a giant flat screen TV in the upper corner. At the back of the room was a large mahogany desk where a beautiful blond sat. She looked at me with big blue eyes and her full lips formed a smile on her face. She leaned back in her chair.

"Blake Annabel Morgan."

"Hey, Court," I said, as Finn pushed inside the room and stood beside me. Courtney rose from her chair and crossed the room. When she reached me, she pulled me into her arms and firmly hugged me. I felt the emotions bubbling inside me rise to rest behind my eyes. I shut them tightly to keep from crying. I was so happy. There was a reason Courtney was called the Mother. She raised us at the orphanage. Many people would say that Ms. Roberts raised us, but that was not true. Courtney took care of us. She protected us. She loved us. We considered her our mother, and hugging her felt like I was returning home.

She pulled away from me but kept her arms on my shoulders. I could not help but smile, looking into her eyes. She pulled me to the couch and sat me down, and Brooke took the seat on the other side of me. Finn sat down in one of the recliners and watched us, smiling.

"Blake, it is so good to see you! How have you been?" Courtney asked.

"I've been good. You look good, Court." I smiled. She did look good. She was twenty-eight years old and was beauty personified. She would have given Barbie a run for her money.

"What have you been up to? What brings you to New Orleans?" I was going to stick with the story that I was there for Mardi Gras, but before I could get the lie out, Brooke spoke up.

"She is on vacation for Mardi Gras. I found her with Finn," she said, glaring at him, "at Luke's restaurant."

"Ah, now it makes sense," Courtney said, looking at Finn. "She is the reason you have been abnormally cheerful the past few days."

Finn's cheeks turned pink as he looked away. Suddenly the door behind Courtney's desk opened. A large, muscular, attractive bald man walked through, carrying a couple of files. "Hey, sweetie, come here for a second," Courtney said to the man, without looking over her shoulder to see who it was.

The man dropped the files on her desk and walked to the couch, where he stood behind Courtney. He placed one of his large hands on Courtney's shoulder. "Blake, this is my boyfriend Lee. Lee, this is the infamous Blake Morgan." I laughed, as I reached to shake his hand.

"Blake, I have heard a lot about you," he said, as one of his hands swallowed mine.

"All good things, I hope."

"Mostly," he said, with a smirk on his face.

He was an attractive man. He would have to be, to catch Courtney's eye. He was all muscle. I doubted if he had any fat on his entire body. I opened my mouth to comment on his 'mostly' when the main door to the office opened. I turned to see a tall skinny man walk through the door. He had light brown hair, and his face held a sad expression.

"What's so important?" Jake asked, without looking around the room.

"Hi, Jake," I said, standing from the sofa. He looked at me, confused.

"Blake?" Once it soaked in that it really was me standing in front of him, he grabbed me and hugged me hard. I patted his back, trying to get him to ease up on his grip.

"I heard about Janey," I said, rubbing his back. He hugged me tighter, but I did not care. He needed to be comforted. When he finally pulled away from me, I saw tears in his eyes.

"She loved you, too," he told me, causing tears to begin forming behind my eyes. I smiled and blinked them away. We sat down and picked up the conversation again.

"I take it that Joshua accompanied you to spy on Finn?" Courtney asked Brooke, who looked surprised by the comment. "Did you really think no one knew you two were fooling around?"

"I was careful not to let you find out," Brooke told Courtney.

"Not careful enough, sweetie," she said, smiling at Brooke. "Just be careful with him. We made the rule not to date the recruits because sometimes they don't take a breakup well."

She glanced between both Brooke and Finn. Obviously something had happened in the past involving those two and some recruits. I was going to have to remember to ask Finn about that one.

"And plus," Courtney said, patting Lee's hand, "sometimes they won't go away." Lee bent down and kissed her cheek.

"Nope, you're stuck with me," Lee told her. She smiled and winked at me.

"So, tell me, Blake. What have you been doing these past ten years?" Courtney asked.

Murdering people, and you? I looked at Finn. He knew I did not want to answer this question. He had asked me the same thing, but I couldn't give Courtney the same response. Finn may not have liked the fact that I didn't wish to talk about my job or the past ten years but he accepted it. I didn't think Jake would care too much but he would not be the problem. Brooke would be too curious to leave the question unanswered, and Courtney was used to people telling her what she wanted to know. I had to tell them something, so I lied.

"After college, I started working for a consulting agency."

"Really? What kind of consulting?"

"We are hired when large companies need to downsize. What happens is a struggling company contacts us, and we look over their personnel. After examining everything, we tell them who needs to be fired."

"I see," Courtney said. "I bet people hate to see you coming," she joked. *Yeah, because typically when someone sees me coming, it is with a .45 pointed at their head.*

I looked at Finn, who gave me a small smile. He knew I had lied. He had always been able to tell when I was lying-plus, if what I said was true, there would be no reason for me to keep my life a secret from him.

My phone beeped, indicating that I had a text message. I picked up my phone and flipped it open. It was from Mark. "Excuse me, it's one of the friends I'm here with," I said, as I read the text.

Nicole is freaking out. You need to come back soon.

I sighed before I realized everyone was looking at me waiting to know what my friend wanted. *Oh, he is just letting me know that one of the trained killers that I am here with is a little upset. She would like to storm your house, killing all of you, because she thinks that I am being held here against my will. I* had to tell them something but the truth was out. "They are wondering what time all the Mardi Gras stuff starts."

"We are going at nine in the morning. You have to come with us!" Brooke exclaimed.

"Sounds good. I'm telling them right now," I said, as I replied to Mark's text.

I'm fine. Keep them back. I will be back later.

I was not ready to leave the house yet. I knew once I got home, I would have to give some explanation of why I was at the house with potential targets to Nicole and Pack Rat. And why Finn knew who they were-for that matter, how I knew the person they were tailing. I had no idea what I was going to say.

I leaned back against the couch, and the conversation turned from questions about the present to jokes about our past. We sat there reminiscing on old times and all the pranks we used to pull on Ms. Roberts. I was crying from laughing so hard at some of the stories. Finally our laughter died away, and I felt my eye lids getting heavy. I looked at my wrist to see what time it was. *I keep forgetting I don't have my watch.*

"What time is it?" I asked anyone who would answer.

Finn looked at his watch and answered. "Twelve-oh-five." I had no idea it was so late.

"Wow, time flew by. I feel lost without my watch," I said, rubbing my bare wrist.

Jake looked at Brooke, who then exchanged looks with Finn and Courtney. I had the feeling they were talking through expressions. Courtney nodded to Jake, who got up and walked out of the room.

"What's going on?" I asked them. Finn smiled at me without saying anything.

It only took a few seconds for Jake to return with a box in his hand. Finn sat up and placed his elbows on his knees. Jake handed me the box and sat back in his chair, mirroring Finn's position.

I opened the box and pulled out a wrist watch. It was silver with a mother of pearl dial and sapphires set around the edge of the circle face. It was gorgeous. I looked up at the others. "What's this?"

"It was Janey's," Courtney said, as she took the watch from me and looked at it. She turned it over so I could see the inscription on the back.

We are so proud of you and wish you nothing but the best.
Love, Your Family.

"We gave it to her when she graduated from nursing school," Brooke explained.

Courtney took my hand and slid the watch into place before securely fastening it. I looked around the room. "I can't take this," I said, noticing how shaky my voice sounded.

"We want you to have it. We all have something of hers that meant a lot to us. Janey loved it. She wore it every day. You were here sister, too. You should have it." Courtney squeezed my hand. I looked at Finn, who gave me a sad smile. I turned to Jake.

"Take it, Blake. I think she would have wanted you to have it," he told me. I did not trust my voice to answer, so I nodded. Courtney stroked the back of my hair, soothing me.

"Well, we better call it a night if you four are going to go to the parade in the morning," Courtney told Brooke, Jake, Finn, and me.

"You're not coming?" I asked.

"No, I have a lot of work to do. But will I see you later?" she asked. I nodded as we all made our way to the door.

I hugged everyone good-bye, but Brooke held on longer than the others. "Be good to Finn," she whispered in my ear. "We never forgot you, but Finn never let you go."

I pulled away from her and looked into her dark eyes. There were few times I could remember when Brooke was completely serious. That was one of those times. "Plus, if you hurt him, I'm going to have to kick your ass." She added a smile to the last part, proving that she was unable to stay serious for long.

I returned her smile and reassured Courtney I would see her again before I left for Chicago. I was certain that was a promise I would keep. I had to find a way to keep her safe from the assassins trying to kill her. Jake went to his room to sleep, and Brooke scurried off to Joshua's bed for something other than sleep.

Finn grabbed our coats from the closet and helped me put on mine before leading me outside. He helped me into the SUV, and we pulled away from his house.

Chapter 27

I STARED AT THE watch on my wrist as Finn pulled the SUV onto the street. *Janey wore this watch.* I stroked the sapphires, feeling more connected to her somehow. I could feel Finn looking at me.

"Could we go somewhere?" I asked him, without looking away from the watch. "Someplace quiet."

"OK," Finn said, turning down an unmarked street.

I had to think of what I was going to tell Nicole and Pack Rat about tonight, and I was not ready to take their questions yet. After a few minutes of silence, the SUV slowed to a stop. I looked up to see Lake Pontchartrain. Ordinarily this was not the most beautiful lake in the country, being somewhat dirty from the Mississippi River that poured muddy water collected throughout the country into it. But that night it was beautiful. The moonlight played across the water's surface with a background of lights from various boats and buildings.

Finn got out of the car and walked around to my side. He opened the door and offered his hand to me. I accepted it, and he helped me out of the vehicle. The warmth of his skin surged through my hand and into my arm, causing my pulse to jump excitedly.

He laced his fingers through mine as he led me to the bank of the lake. We stopped at a tree, where Finn removed his coat and spread it on the ground against the tree's trunk. I took my jacket off as well and did the same. Finn sat down on our coats and leaned against the tree. He held out his hand and I sat down beside him. He wrapped his arm around my waist and pulled me to him, so that my back was pressed against his chest. I sighed as I let my head rest on his shoulder.

We watched the moonlight ripple across the lake in silence. Being with Finn was comfortable, yet incredibly nerve-racking. I felt so safe with him that we did not need to talk at all times. I could just rest my head against him and be completely content in his presence. But at the same time, that presence sent shivers down my spine. That sensation caused me to not only want to rest my head on his shoulder but to let my desire take control of my actions. It was a battle between my need to be comforted and my basic desire to run my hands over Finn's chest.

He took my hand in his and flipped it over. With the other hand, he stroked my palm with his fingertips. Slowly, he moved his fingertips up my wrist and across my lower arm. A hot tingling sensation shot throughout my body as his fingers danced across my skin. He moved his fingers up to my shoulder and trailed them back down my arm.

He continued this for some time and the sensation that was shooting through my body became soothing. I turned my head and nuzzled my face into his neck. He kissed my forehead before resting his cheek on my hair. He moved his fingers to my left arm and restarted the path he took on my right. When he made it to my wrist he stopped. He lifted my wrist and looked at Janey's watch.

"I remember when we gave this to her. She was so excited."

"Are you sure I should have this?" I asked, cautiously. I wanted to keep the watch. It was my only physical connection to Janey. I had my memories of her but no other connection. I needed the connection the watch provided. But the watch was obviously expensive, and I had nothing to do with giving it to her. I felt like I had no right to it.

"Yeah, Jake is right. She would want you to have it."

"It must have been expensive," I said, looking at all the jewels.

"Yeah, we each put up some money. Janey never bought anything nice for herself, and we wanted to spoil her."

I stared out at the lake as Finn's fingers returned to their task, and I was soon feeling even more relaxed. I closed my eyes and listened to the sound of the waves as I inhaled Finn's scent. The combination of his touch, scent, and the sound of the lake caused me to drift off to sleep.

"Blake, wake up." I heard Finn's voice but refused to open my eyes. "Blake?"

He rubbed my shoulder, gently trying to wake me. Lips touched my forehead stirring me. I forced my eyes open and looked up at him. "We fell asleep," he told me, shifting his weight from behind me. I glanced at the watch on my wrist.

"Crap, it's almost three in the morning," I said, sitting up straight. Finn stood and took my hands. He pulled me to my feet and picked up our jackets. "I have got to get back to the hotel."

We jumped in the car and I noticed I had several texted messages from Nicole. *Crap, Crap, Crap.*

We pulled up to the hotel, and I still had no idea what I was going to tell Nicole and Pack Rat. Finn walked me to my room and hugged me tightly. "I'm sorry tonight didn't go the way I had planned," he said.

"I had fun. I'm really glad we went back to your house."

"I didn't think that our first date would include everyone else we know," he said softly, brushing his lips across my cheek. I rubbed his back as I felt my pulse quickening.

"And what exactly did you have planned?"

Finn pulled back from me and looked at me. He was wearing that wicked grin I loved so much. He leaned forward and placed his lips on mine. He slid a hand behind my neck holding my face to his. He deepened the kiss completely claiming my mouth. I could feel my heart beating rapidly in my chest.

I returned the kiss as intensely as he gave it. My hands found their way into his thick, amazing hair. I knotted my hands behind his head, holding him tight. I needed his kiss. I put everything I had in that kiss. He wrapped an arm around my back and pulled me firmly against his chest. I loved the way my body seemed to fit against his perfectly. We kissed for a long time, and when we broke apart for air, we were both breathing heavily.

"That is somewhat close to what I had planned for tonight," Finn said, grinning. I smiled back before giving him another kiss. "So, are you really going to come with us to the parade tomorrow?" he asked, as he ran a hand up and down my side.

"Yeah, I want to find out what all the fuss is about Mardi Gras. Could I bring the others?" I asked, motioning to my room.

"You can bring whoever you want, as long as you bring these," he said, sweeping his thumb across my lower lip. I resisted the urge to pull his finger into my mouth. Finn tilted my chin up and kissed me again.

"OK," I said breathless. "I guess I will see you in the morning then."

Finn didn't let go of me. Instead, he pulled me closer and claimed my mouth one more time before releasing me. He gave me a quick kiss on the tip on my nose before turning to leave. I leaned back against the door to catch my breath before I entered my room.

I walked quietly, hoping Nicole would be asleep. Why I thought I would get out of the talk that easy, I don't know. Nicole was sitting on her bed with her legs crossed beneath her. Mark was sitting beside her, and Pack Rat was stretched out across my bed. I glanced at Mark, who gave me a sympathetic look. I turned my attention to Pack Rat and Nicole. She looked furious.

"Where the hell have you been?" Nicole was fuming, but when I looked in her eyes I saw concern mixed with her rage. I sat down on the end of my bed next to Pack Rat's feet.

"Well, are you going to explain why the people we were tailing ended up at the same restaurant you were at? And why they seemed to know you? Oh, and why you went back into the house where the six people we are supposed to kill live?" She was yelling by the time she asked the last question.

I hate when people asked multiple questions at once. I guess it is because, when trying to get information out of people, I have found if helps to ask one question at a time. And to use violence. I, however, did not think it would be a good idea to point this out to the assassin whose anger was directed at me.

"OK." I said, trying to calm Nicole. I looked at Mark, searching for help but he had none. I would have to tell the truth, or at least part of the truth. "Did I ever tell you about my childhood?" I asked Nicole and Pack Rat.

"Don't try to change the subject," Nicole said.

"I'm not-listen. I grew up in an orphanage." Nicole looked at me. Her anger was dying and being replaced with compassion. I ignored her expression and continued. "There was a group of kids I grew close to. We became a family. Finn was one." I let that sink in before getting back to my story. "The girl you followed was another." I decided not to tell them about Jake and Courtney yet.

"Why didn't you tell us about Finn?"

I rubbed my hands across my eyes and took a deep breath. "I didn't want to get him involved with this." I knew that was impossible, since his name was on the kill order.

"They live at the house? Do they know who the Mother is?" Pack Rat asked. He was normally a laid-back, unfocused guy, but when he set his mind on something, it became one-tracked. It would be my luck that he was focused on this.

"I don't know," I lied. "I was hoping they could lead me to the Mother."

After a second of silence, Nicole drew in a deep breath. "You scared the crap out of me," Nicole told me. "I thought they had figured out who you were and grabbed you. Well, I guess this is a good thing. We have a way into the house and a possible lead to the identity of our targets."

"Yeah, that's what I was thinking." I looked at Mark, who showed no expression. I wanted to yell at him for not helping me, but I guess he did not want the others to know that he knows more than they do. "I am going to work that angle with Finn and the others but under no circumstances are they to be harmed." I added a little force behind my voice to make the last part a threat. It must have worked, because they agreed.

"All right, let's get some sleep. Tomorrow I'm going with Finn and some others to Mardi Gras. He invited all of you along if you want to come."

They all seemed excited about it, so we called it a night. The boys left and I crawled in bed. The second I turned out the light, Nicole decided it was time to gossip.

"So, you have some serious feelings for Finn, don't you?"

I sighed. I did not feel like getting into my relationship with Finn at that moment. It was four in the morning and I was ready to sleep. But I had a feeling Nicole would not let this go until she got answers.

"Finn and I had a thing a long time ago."

"Yeah, well it looks like you two have a thing again," she said, and I could hear the smile in her voice.

"What do you want me to say? Yeah, I like him. Are you happy now?"

"You like him a lot." It wasn't a question. "And yes, I am happy now. Oh, it's so romantic. A rekindled love from your childhood." I rolled my eyes at her.

"Let's get some sleep." For once she did as I requested, and we slept.

Chapter 28

I WOKE UP AFTER four and a half hours of sleep. It was not enough, but seeing as I told Finn and Brooke I would meet them at nine, I had to get moving. Nicole was already getting ready, so I jumped in the shower and got dressed as fast as I could.

The boys joined us as I was straightening my hair. I knew the colors of Mardi Gras are green, gold, and purple, so I picked a green shirt from my luggage and threw it on. It was a simple green tee but it matched my eyes perfectly. Nicole was wearing a purple shirt with a gold design. She looked perfect, as usual.

The boys did not care about colors. Mark was wearing black, and Pack Rat had on blue. We did not have time for them to change, so I decided not to tell them about the color theme. I grabbed my favorite brown leather jacket and stuffed my cell phone, money, ID, and room key in the pockets of my jeans, and we left the hotel.

People swarmed the streets. We had to weave through the crowds to get to the sandwich shop where we were supposed to meet the others. I was amazed there were so many people out this early.

I heard Brooke before I saw her. She ran to me and almost knocked me over as she hugged me. She was wearing a fitted purple shirt with an intricate gold Mardi Gras mask on the lower left side and fitted designer jeans. She would have given Nicole a run for her money on the best-dressed award.

She led us to the others. I instantly met Finn's eyes. He was leaning against the shop, holding half of a sandwich. He had on dark jeans that made his muscular legs stand out and a dark purple shirt that hugged his shoulders. Jake was beside him in a green shirt, looking bored. Joshua walked out of the shop as we approached. I introduced everyone to each other as I made my way to Finn. He hugged me tightly and kissed my cheek.

"Good morning," he said. I pulled his hand toward me and took a bite of his breakfast sandwich. It was delicious, as all food in Louisiana had proven to be. "Have you eaten?"

"No, we were running late," I told him, as I took a sip of the coffee I brought with me. Finn handed me his sandwich, insisting that I eat it. I did not argue with him for long. I was tired and hungry, but the sandwich and coffee solved that problem.

Brooke hooked her arm through mine and pulled me away from Finn. "Let's go, people. I want a Bloody Mary, now."

Brooke was incredibly bossy for such a tiny person. In truth, she was my height, maybe slightly shorter at about five feet three inches, but when she spoke people took notice. We let her lead us down the sidewalk toward a bar. I noticed that many people on the street were already drunk. *It is nine-thirty in the morning. This is crazy.* I had a feeling that the day would get even weirder.

We made it to the crowded sports bar and worked our way to the bar. Finn offered to get the drinks, and Brooke ran off to secure a table. I looked around and noticed all the tables were occupied, but I doubted that would stop her.

Jake and I went with Finn to help carry drinks. Finn caught the bartender's attention and ordered eight Bloody Marys. I passed the first three back to Jake, and he left to carry them to the table. Finn paid for the drinks but wrapped an arm around my waist, keeping me from following Jake. He leaned down and softly kissed me. I had never been a big fan of public displays of affection, but I thought the kiss ended a little too soon. I enjoyed kissing him and didn't care who knew it.

We worked our way out of the crowd and saw that Brooke had indeed been able to secure a large table in the corner of the bar. We talked and joked as we drank our Bloody Marys. I was thrilled that all of my friends seemed to get along. The only one who remained quiet was Joshua, and I figured that was because he was intimidated by Finn and Jake. Boys tended to be nervous around a girlfriend's big brothers.

As we joked, I felt Finn slide his hand down my thigh and wrap his fingers around my knee and leave them there. I hooked my arm through his and leaned into him. I looked up to see Nicole watching me with a huge grin on her face. She seemed to be enjoying what was going on between Finn and me more than I was. Well, maybe not more but at least she enjoyed it a lot.

"Shit. Finn." I heard Brooke say on the other side of me.

Finn and I turned to look at her, and she motioned to the door. I did not see anything unusual, so I looked back at her. She had an angry look on her face, which was never a good thing. I looked at Finn, whose face became as serious as hers. Confused, I looked back at the door and saw a bunch of people walking into the bar.

One was a tall, muscular man with dark hair, a strong chin, a slightly hooked nose, and dark eyes. He was attractive, but the girl next to him drew the attention. She also had dark hair, but hers reached her shoulders. She had delicate features and a straighter nose but the same dark eyes. The similarities in those eyes told me they were related. I turned back to Finn.

"What's going on?" I asked. He pulled his hand away from my knee and set it on the table.

"You remember Courtney saying we had rules about dating the recruits?" he asked me. I nodded. "Well, those people aren't the reason we made the rules but a good example of why we have them."

"You dated her?" I asked. Suddenly, my distaste for her grew. I knew it was stupid to be jealous of a girl he used to date, but I could not help myself.

"Yes. And Brooke dated her brother. Neither ended very well." I looked at Jake, who confirmed what Finn said. "Let's just get out of here. I don't want there to be a scene."

I agreed with Finn. Brooke looked like she was ready to cause one. I looked across the table and met Mark's eyes. He had been watching the conversation between us and was now on full alert. A few seconds later, I heard a husky voice behind me.

"Well, well. What do we have here?" We all turned to face the man standing behind us. "How are you doing, Brooke?" he asked.

"What the hell are you doing here, Kevin?" Brooke asked, with an edge to her voice.

"Just stopped by to get a drink," Kevin answered.

Finn turned and stood in front of him. I began to worry. Finn had always been extremely protective of us, and he clearly did not like this man. He must have hurt Brooke. Finn turned to me and placed a hand under my elbow, gently pulling me out of my chair.

"Let's go," Finn told us. The rest of our crew stood as well. I noticed a large group of people moving to stand behind Kevin. I did a quick head count. Fourteen people-and only a handful were girls-against our eight. Not great odds, but some of us were trained killers.

"You don't have to run off," Kevin said to Finn. "I just wanted to stop by and say hello." There was nothing in his voice that indicated his intentions were innocent. "So Joshua, I see you are Brooke's new toy nowadays." Joshua remained silent but moved to Brooke's side.

"Leave her alone, Kevin," Finn told him. His voice had reached a threatening level.

Kevin stared at Finn for a second before his eyes drifted to me. He gave me a wicked smile that was nowhere as cute and teasing as Finn's. His was truly wicked.

"I don't believe I have had the pleasure," he said to me, as his eyes scanned my body. I returned his body scan.

"That doesn't surprise me," I said, with an amused look.

Kevin laughed at my comment. "Feisty, I like that."

Finn tried to pull me behind him, but I held my ground. The girl I saw earlier walked up to us and stood by her brother's side, placing her directly in front of me. I searched her face, hoping to find some imperfection but was unable to do so. She had flawless skin to match her eyes.

"Hello, Finn," she said, a hint of anger in her voice. Clearly what happened between these people was bad, and it was not too long ago.

"Crystal," Finn acknowledged her, but glared at Kevin.

I placed a hand on Finn's arm in attempt to calm him. Crystal noticed my move, and her eyes narrowed on me.

"You must be Finn's new distraction. Can I give you a word of advice?" she asked me, but did not wait for an answer. "Don't get too attached. He's still hung up on some slut from his childhood."

I smiled at her before turning to Brooke. "I hardly think I would be classified as a slut. Do you think so?"

Brooke returned my smile before I looked back at Crystal. Her facial expression changed from arrogant to angry as she realized what I said.

"*You* are the girl from Michigan?" I raised my eyebrows and my smile answered her question. "Huh," she said, scanning my body. Hers was not the same scan as her brother's. His was sexual, where as hers was analytical. "Always thought you would be prettier."

Finn wrapped his arm around my waist. She saw the move and did not like it. Apparently she was not over the break-up. She gave me a wicked smile, similar to her brother's. "If you are from Michigan, I guess you knew Janey."

That one comment made half of our group tense up. I felt the blood begin to rush through my veins.

"Watch it, Crystal," Brooke growled, but Crystal's eyes never left mine.

"Where is the old prude?" Crystal asked. I clenched my fist. I knew Brooke, Finn, and Jake were doing the same.

"Crystal, don't you remember hearing about her?" Kevin innocently asked his sister.

My blood was racing. I could feel my pulse beat through my clenched fingers. I knew if I looked down, my knuckles would be white under the tension. I was furious. I wanted to hurt these people. I had never attacked out of anger; I had only ever fought because it was my job or out of self-defense. I wanted to beat the shit out of this girl.

"Oh, yeah, I remember hearing that someone finally put the old girl out of her misery." The second Crystal spit out the last word, I snapped.

I lunged at her and wrapped a hand around her throat. I shoved her against the wall as hard as I could and heard a thump when her head hit the brick, but it wasn't hard enough to render her unconscious.

The second I moved, all hell broke loose. Kevin ran at me to pull me off of his sister, but Finn was there. He caught Kevin around his chest and threw him away from me. Crystal sent blows to my ribs but I ignored the pain and punched her repeatedly in the face. I wanted to kill her and was perfectly capable of doing it.

Crystal coughed, due to either my hand at her throat cutting off her oxygen or blood pouring from her broken nose and busted lips into her mouth, or maybe both. The cough sprayed blood on my face and shirt. The blood hitting my face caused me to snap out of my red haze and see what I was doing. True, I did not like the girl, but I could not kill her.

I let go of her throat, and she fell to the ground. I turned my attention to the fight that had broken out in the bar. Finn was fighting Kevin and another man. He was dodging blow after blow and delivering some pretty hard hits. *Man, he could move fast.*

Brooke was kicking some girl in the stomach. I yelled for Mark. He turned and looked at me. I mouthed the words "No Killing" to him, and he nodded before relaying the message to the other assassins.

A girl jumped on Brooke's back, knocking her to the ground. I moved to help, but a man appeared at my side, reaching for my throat. Before I could react, a beer bottle flew inches in front of my face and hit the man in his forehead. He fell back hard. I turned and saw Nicole give me a quick wink. She really could throw.

The guy jumped back up and ran at me. He tried to back hand me across the face, but I easily ducked out of the way. I threw a fist in his chin, and he staggered back a few steps. That really made him mad. He threw a left at me, which I dodged and easily grabbed his wrist. Implementing my favorite move, I hit the back of his elbow as hard as I could and heard the distinct sound of cartilage breaking. He fell to his knees, screaming and clutching his broken elbow to his chest.

I pulled the girl off of Brooke and threw her at a guy rushing towards me. The man threw the girl away before continuing toward me. He did not get very close before Finn grabbed him around the neck and slammed him to the ground. I moved back to help Joshua fight off two men when a hand grabbed my shoulder. I turned and threw a punch. Finn caught my fist with one hand. *Oh, crap, I almost hit Finn.*

"We need to leave," he said. I looked around at the pandemonium that had erupted. Many people were fighting. Not just our group and Kevin and Crystal's group were involved. I looked to the left and saw three guys attacking Jake. One held him in a full nelson while the others punched him in the ribs.

"You go get Jake; I'll round up the others."

Finn nodded and ran to help Jake. Mark and Pack Rat were taking care of the people attacking Joshua, so I grabbed his shirt sleeve. "Go get Brooke," I yelled at him.

We both looked at Brooke. She was straddled on top of Crystal and punching her repeatedly in the face. Crystal's face was hardly recognizable from all the blows Brooke and I had given her. Blood was flowing from her face to pool around her body. She was going to look really bad the next day.

Brooke was now wearing Crystal's blood on her sleeves. I looked down to notice I was wearing the same modifications to my outfit. Joshua wrapped his arms around Brooke's waist and lifted her off Crystal. She was still kicking and throwing punches in mid air. Finn appeared by my side with a beat-up Jake. Once we had everyone we started with, Finn led the way out of the bar, stopping occasionally to throw people out of our path.

Chapter 29

FINN GRABBED MY hand as he pulled me out of the bar. We pushed people out of our way as we ran down the crowded street. I saw police officers rushing toward us. They obviously were called in due to the massive bar brawl I had started.

Finn must have seen them, too, because he jerked me down an alley. I looked behind us, relieved to see the rest of our group was following close behind me. We ran down street after street and alley after alley.

Once we were several blocks away from the bar, we slowed to a walk and turned down a dark abandoned alleyway. Our group had safely secluded ourselves, so we stopped to rest. Finn pulled me in front of him and tilted my face so he could examine me.

"Are you all right?" he asked, as he turned my face to the side. His eyes widened when he saw the blood on my face, hands, and arms. "You're bleeding," he said, as he quickly pulled his shirt over his head leaving him in a white undershirt.

He intended to press his shirt to my wounds, but I did not have any wounds. I was covered in the guy whose elbow I'd broken and Crystal's blood. There was so much on my hands and jacket that the only logical explanation would be that I was bleeding.

"Finn," I said, holding up my hands to stop him from ruining his shirt. "This isn't my blood. I'm fine."

He paused for a moment, then went on to wipe the blood away from my face and hands with his shirt. He let out a sigh of relief when he realized I was unharmed. He held my face and kissed me quickly.

"Is everybody OK?" I asked the rest of our group.

Brooke was wiping blood away from her busted lip with a sleeve. Jake was crouching against a brick wall, holding his side, but otherwise he looked all right. Joshua looked frazzled but did not have a spot of blood on him. My assassins did not have a hair out of place.

I shrugged my leather jacket off and sat down on a nearby stoop. "I'm sorry, guys; I shouldn't have lost my temper."

"Don't worry about it. If you wouldn't have hit that bitch, I would have." Brooke looked down at her shirt, which had blood on the sleeves. "Well, great, now my shirt is ruined. I can't go anywhere dressed like this."

"I'll run to the store and get us some clothes," Finn suggested.

Brooke raised her eyebrows and looked at him. "Right, like I am going to let *you* buy my clothes," she said sarcastically.

"I can go with him," Nicole offered. Brooke looked Nicole up and down. Nicole's fashion sense must have passed, because Brooke agreed to let her pick out a shirt for her. "I guess I will pick up something boring for you," Nicole told me.

"What does that mean?" I said. Nicole raised her eyebrows and looked at my shirt. I followed her gaze to my plain green top, which was now littered with dark spots. "OK, maybe my clothes aren't the most exciting, but they work for me." Nicole smiled and let Finn lead her to the clothing store.

I leaned my head against the wall as I listened to Brooke complain about Crystal. I used Finn's sweater to wipe the blood off my hands and face as we waited for Nicole and Finn to return with our shirts.

It took about half an hour for them to return. Finn was wearing a green sweater that hugged his shoulders drawing attention to his muscular chest. Nicole reached into her shopping bag, pulled out a shirt, and tossed it to Brooke.

Brooke turned her back to us and pulled off her shirt and replaced it with the new one. It was purple, with long sleeves. It had cutouts at the corners of the shoulders and was tight enough to draw male attention to her chest. Brooke looked down at her shirt before nodding her approval.

Nicole reached in the bag and pulled a white shirt out and tossed it to me. I followed Brooke's action and turned my back to the others before putting on the new shirt. It had short sleeves and a V neckline. Purple and green lines swirled around the bottom of the shirt. "Not bad," I said to Nicole. She was grinning at me like an idiot.

"Wait, there is something else," Finn said, reaching into the bag.

He pulled out a square jewelry box. It was not long and skinny, like the kinds that hold bracelets, nor was it small and square, indicating a ring. It was large and square. That only left a necklace or earrings. He opened it and handed it to me.

It was a white gold chain with a small Mardi Gras mask attached to it. The mask was lined in emeralds that matched the green in my shirt perfectly. I stared at the necklace without speaking. "Do you like it?"

I looked from the necklace to him then back to the necklace. "What is this?" I asked Finn. I was not accustomed to getting gifts and did not know how to take that one.

"I saw it and immediately thought of you. It reminded me of your eyes," he said, with that grin that causes my knees to turn to jelly.

"This must have been expensive. I can't accept this," I handed the necklace back to Finn.

"It wasn't that much. Besides, I like to spoil," he said, as he pulled the necklace from the box. "Now, turn around."

I did as he said and held my hair up so he could fasten the chain. The mask rested against my chest and I noticed he was right. It matched my eyes even better than the green in the shirt. It was beautiful.

"Finn, I don't-"

"You aren't very good at the whole gift thing, are you?" he asked. I didn't answer. "I saw it and thought you would like it. That's it." He brushed a thumb across my cheek.

I looked down at the necklace and back at him. "I love it, thank you." I leaned up and kissed him softly. At that moment, I did not care that the others were watching us. I deepened the kiss, and by the time I pulled back, Finn was breathing as if he had just run a mile. I smiled at his response to my kiss.

Finn laced his fingers through mine, and we left the alley. We walked to a nearby restaurant, where Brooke and I went to the restroom to make sure we had all the blood off our bodies. I washed the blood off my jacket before putting it back on. We rejoined the others and ate a late lunch of burgers, fries, and beer. We left the restaurant but continued drinking as we walked the streets of New Orleans.

By nightfall, we were feeling pretty good. We found a spot where we could watch the parade. As the parade of floats passed by us, people went crazy. They were yelling at the people on the floats, begging for them to throw beads. People were dressed in amazingly colorful, sometimes humorous, costumes. I saw people wearing masks on their faces similar to the one around my neck.

After the first few floats passed, I could not help but join in with the crowd surrounding me. I was reaching for beads and snatching them out of Finn's grip. He laughed and teasingly fought me for the plastic jewels. By the time the parade had ended, I was a fan of Mardi Gras. I understood the excitement. It was the ultimate party.

We walked down Bourbon Street with the rest of the people looking for a great night out. People were pressed against each other, trying to make their way through the crowded street. One man walked up to Brooke and asked her what she would do for the unique fleur-de-lis beads around his neck. Brooke asked what he would do for her beads. The man answered by dropping his pants. We gasped before laughing and running away from the guy. People where hanging off balconies, throwing beads to anyone who would flash them, which surprisingly was a lot of people.

We stepped inside a bar, and Brooke pulled Nicole and me to the dance floor. As we danced, a man walked up behind me and wrapped an arm around my waist, pulling me against him. I spun around to look at the man harassing me. He was tall, with blond hair, and looked too young to have the drink he was spilling on me.

"What the hell are you doing?" I asked, as I pushed him away from me.

"I want to dance with you," he said, pulling me by the hand back toward him. I broke his grip on my hand.

"Yeah, I don't think so, Baby Huey. Why don't you go find the other Mouseketeers and leave the grownups alone?" I turned my back to him and rejoined my girls, who were laughing at me.

Moments later, a hand wrapped around my waist again. I spun around to yell at the teenager but met Finn's gaze. He gave me a quick kiss on the forehead and handed me my drink. His kiss had my hormones responding appropriately.

Mark and Joshua showed up to deliver drinks to the other girls. I wrapped an arm around Finn's neck as we began to dance. Mark and Nicole escaped off the dance floor as Brooke and Joshua joined Jake and Pack Rat at the bar. I pressed my body close to Finn, and the dance continued through the next song.

After a few moments, Brooke pulled us apart and handed Finn and me a shot. His was a light brown liquid that I immediately recognized as my nemesis, whiskey. Thankfully, Brooke's and my shots were a clear liquid. We toasted our drinks before taking the shots. *My favorite, tequila.*

Brooke took the glasses from us and returned to the bar. I turned my attention back to Finn. He smiled and leaned down to kiss me. I pulled my head away from his.

"I don't think so, not after you just took a *whiskey* shot." I let the way I pronounced *whiskey* indicate my feelings for the beverage. He smiled and reached in his pocket and pulled out a piece of gum. He popped it in his mouth and chewed quickly.

"Better?" he asked, as he leaned forward. I nodded quickly before his lips claimed mine. I could taste the peppermint on his tongue and welcomed the flavor. Before he pulled away, I quickly stole the gum from his mouth. When he realized what I had done, he smiled. "I would have given you a piece if you asked."

"What's the fun in that?" I asked, with a smile.

Finn only laughed and pulled me to him for another dance. Sweat was beginning to run down my spine as we continued dancing.

I heard Finn laughing in my ear. I pulled back and looked at him. He nodded toward the wall, and I turned to see what he was looking at. Nicole and Mark were dancing. Only their bodies weren't moving, just their tongues. They were kissing like their lives depended on it. I laughed with Finn.

"It's about time," I said.

"You're not jealous?" Finn asked in my ear. I turned around and wrapped my arms around his neck. He was wearing a smile that was teasing, but he also looked slightly worried about my answer.

"Now why on earth would I be jealous?" I leaned forward and lightly kissed his neck.

Finn tightened his grip around my waist and leaned down to claim my mouth. Desire rushed through my body as I pressed myself against him. I wished we were alone someplace where we could explore and extend the kiss further, but I realized I would have to settle for an intense, heart-pounding, pulse racing kiss.

We danced for a moment more before joining the others. Pack Rat was talking to a cute blond girl at the end of the bar, and Jake, Brooke, and Joshua were joking next to them. Finn ordered me a drink as I ordered a round of shots. We took more shots throughout our stay at the bar. When we left the bar, I was laughing and flirting with Finn like a maniac. I always became more sociable when I had liquor in me. It wasn't long before the night faded into darkness.

Chapter 30

I WOKE UP TO the sound of drums in my head. I raised my hand and tried to rub the pounding that had settled behind my eyes. The mattress moved slightly beneath me before lips brushed my forehead.

"Good morning," said a deep, sexy voice.

I opened my eyes and saw Finn smiling at me. I groaned and pulled the covers back over my head. I had to look as bad as I felt. The smell of alcohol was drifting from my pores. I did not want him to see me like this.

Finn laughed and pulled the covers away from my face. He smelled wonderful. A fresh scent drifted off his body that screamed of scented soap and delicious aftershave. I smiled at him and decided to keep my lips pursed together. Morning breath after a night of drinking could be a bitch. I rubbed my stomach and realized I was wearing a large cotton t-shirt. Not only did I have no clue as to how I ended up in this shirt, but the boxer shorts I was wearing was a mystery as well.

Suddenly a bolt of fear shot through me. *Did I have sex with Finn and not remember it?* It wasn't the idea of sleeping with Finn that made me nervous. I would have already if it wasn't for Nicole and Mark barging in on us back at the hotel. It was the thought of not remembering the first time I was with him that had my stomach rolling.

"Did we...?" I asked, covering my mouth to keep my breath from hitting him.

He smiled at me. "You don't remember?" *Oh, great, we did.* I shook my head. "No, we didn't," he said. I let out a silent sigh of relief until I saw Finn's grin. His smirk told me he wasn't telling me something, that there was more to the story. I narrowed my eyes at him and gave my best questioning look.

"Well," he paused for a second, "you weren't very happy with the decision to *postpone* activities last night."

Oh, no. I pulled the covers back over my head. I knew from experience how forceful I could be when I was intoxicated. If Finn turned me down, I would be quite upset. I probably yelled at him or made another of my smart-ass comments. I am always a very pleasant person. *Right.*

I guess I should have been happy that Finn did not take advantage of my drunken state, but embarrassment took precedence over relief. Again Finn pulled the blanket off of me and smiled.

"Brooke put some clothes for you in the bathroom across the hall. There is also an extra toothbrush next to the sink. I set a glass of water and some ibuprofen on the counter for you. Make yourself at home. I will be downstairs when you're ready." He kissed me on the forehead again before leaving the room.

I stayed where I was for a few moments and looked at Finn's room. I was in a large bed across from a closet. I turned my head to see bookshelves lined the wall. He had an assortment of classic novels on the shelf. I smiled as I noticed that wedged between Moby Dick and Dracula, was a worn copy of Huckleberry Finn. By the look of it, I assumed it was the same copy from his childhood.

I pulled myself out of bed and made my way across the hall. I immediately took a few ibuprofens, chasing them with the water provided. After brushing my teeth, I decided on a shower. I felt a hundred times better after I had shampooed the bar smoke out of my hair and was clean. I dried off and put on the clothes Brooke had lent me. She was my size, so the jeans and t-shirt fit nicely. I towel-dried my hair quickly before discarding it into the used towel basket. I left the bathroom and walked down the stairs to find the others.

The bottom of the stairs opened to a living room containing an extra-large couch, three recliners, and a giant flat-screen television. Sitting at the end of the couch was Finn. I walked over to the couch and fell down beside him. He wrapped an arm around my shoulders and pulled me into him. I pulled my knees up to my chest and turned my body so I was cuddled up beside him.

He bent his head down and softly brushed his lips over mine. I wrapped my hand around the back of his neck to keep him from pulling his lips from mine. When the soft kiss ended, I rested my head on his shoulder.

"Thanks for taking care of me last night," I told him.

"My pleasure." I could feel his chest rise and fall under my hand and resisted the impulse to let that hand roam his body.

"What happened last night? The last thing I remember was leaving the club."

Finn pulled his head back to look at me. "Which club?"

My eyes widened. "We went to more than one?" Finn laughed at my response.

"You had fun," he said, which was all I was going to get out of him.

He rubbed my shoulders as he lifted the remote to change channels on the TV. Brooke walked in seconds later.

"Thought I heard voices in here. Good morning, Pepper," she told me, as she walked over to sit in a recliner. I gave her a confused look at her greeting. "Oh, I'm sorry," she said, "do you prefer Salt?" I was still confused.

Finn looked at Brooke with an amused expression. "She doesn't remember last night." Brooke chuckled, as I looked back and forth between the two.

"What happened?" I asked, somewhat scared to hear the answer.

"You karaoked-wait, no, performed 'None of Your Business' by Salt and Pepper last night," Brooke said, as she laughed enthusiastically.

My eyes widened in disbelief, or perhaps more in embarrassment. I thought back to the previous night but was drawing a blank. The only karaoke bar I knew of on Bourbon Street was the one I had stopped at on my first day in New Orleans. Suddenly, a hazy image of the bar appeared in my mind. And the scene of me on stage facing a sea of drunk faces came in focus. I turned and buried my head in Finn's chest. "No, no, no," I mumbled into his shirt.

I felt the rumble of his laughter deep down in his chest. "It wasn't that bad, you didn't miss a word," he said, trying to make me feel better. It didn't work.

"I can't believe you let me do that," I said, slapping his shoulder. It wasn't a hard hit, more of a teasing slap.

"Hey!" he said, laughing. "I didn't know what you were doing. I went to the bar for drinks, and the next thing I knew, you were on-stage, rapping."

Brooke and Finn went on for a few more minutes about my 90s performance. I was mortified. I had to change the subject. "Where are the others?"

"Who knows were Court is, Jake is exercising, and Mark and Nicole are still asleep in Brooke's room," Finn explained.

I raised my eyebrows. "Really, Mark and Nicole slept together?" I hated gossip when it is about my business, but I loved hearing about other people's private lives. I was hypocritical like that, and I was OK with it.

"Don't get too excited," Brooke said. "They were too drunk for anything other than sleep. I went in there about two hours ago to get clothes for you to wear-you're welcome for that, by the way. And they were both sound asleep, still in their clothes from last night."

I ignored the jab at my manners. "Where is Pack Rat?"

"He left with some blond. Nicole tried to call him last night, but he didn't answer. That reminds me, your phone is upstairs. I charged it for you. I'll go get it," Finn said, as he got off the couch and ran up to his room. He had just gotten out of hearing range when Brooke turned to me.

"So, what happened between you two last night?" she asked, with a sparkle in her eye from the prospect of good gossip.

"What song did I sing last night?" I asked innocently.

"None of Your Business."

"Exactly," I said, grinning.

Brooke did not appreciate my joke, or the fact that I wasn't going to give her the answer she wanted. Before she could argue with me, Finn appeared. He saw the disappointed and annoyed look on Brooke's face. "You didn't ask her, did you?"

"Yes, I did," she said, as she glared at me, "but she won't tell me, either."

Finn walked to my side and handed my phone to me. I flipped the phone open and saw I had four missed calls. All of them were from Tank. *Crap.* My face must have given away my enthusiasm about my missed calls, because Finn looked at me. "What's wrong?"

"My boss called. Is there somewhere I can call him back?" I did not need to add "in private," because Finn understood. He knew anything work-related was a secret I refused to share.

"Yeah, you can stay here. Brooke and I were just going to make breakfast." Brooke looked at him with a look that said her making breakfast was news to her. But when he didn't back down from his statement, she gave in and followed him to the kitchen.

I dialed Tank's number, and he answered after the first ring. "Where the hell have you been?" he yelled into the phone. "I tried to call all of you, and no one answered. I was about to send some people to New Orleans to look for you."

"Sorry, Tank," and I really was. "We got caught up in the whole Mardi Gras thing."

"That is no excuse," he paused, before letting out a sigh. "How is everything going?" I heard papers rustling and heard his assistant, Sarah, tell him something. He was obviously busy.

"Everything is going well; I think we are close to figuring this thing out." I did not like lying to him, but I had no choice in the matter.

"Good. Now, please be a good little assassin and check in with me daily," Tank said, before he hung up the phone. I sighed and leaned my head against a pillow.

I had just closed my eyes to rest them when I heard a door open at the far end of the room. I looked up to see Courtney walk in and sit in a recliner opposite me. "Looks like you had fun last night."

"Yeah, just wish I could remember it," I said, smiling at her.

Finn walked in through the other entrance and sat down next to me but not before handing me a cup of hot, wonderful coffee. I could have kissed him at that moment. "Bless you," I said, taking a sip.

We heard the stairs creaking and looked up to see Mark and Nicole walk into the room. They were wearing borrowed clothes as well and looked as if they showered recently. Nicole sat down on the opposite end of the couch, and Mark fell down in a recliner. I introduced them to Courtney. They politely greeted her and closed their eyes. Apparently they were hurting more than I was.

Finn began to fill Courtney in on our activities last night. I listened intently, hoping to remember something. No such luck. Talk of last night ended when a man rushed into the room and stopped in front of Courtney.

"Excuse me, ma'am, Robert was practicing weapons handling and cut his leg. He is bleeding pretty badly, and Lee sent me to get help." He was shifting his weight from one leg to the other, clearly anxious about either his hurt friend or talking to Courtney. I guessed it was Courtney. She emitted power and superiority.

Courtney sighed and looked at Finn. "Please go see what's going on." Finn nodded before following the man out of the room. Courtney shook her head at me. "Always something going on around here."

I leaned my elbows on my knees and wrapped my hands around my coffee mug, letting the warmth of the coffee melt my fingers.

"Court? How is the hunt for Janey's killer going?" I asked, keeping my voice low. I was not comfortable talking about her death yet.

"I have a couple leads," she said, with the same emotion I was feeling. I nodded my head.

"Would it be OK if I saw her room?" I asked.

Courtney studied my eyes for a moment. I saw a look of sympathy in them. She understood my desire to feel connected to Janey. She and the others had spent the last ten years with her, whereas I had not. I wanted to see something of who she became, what kind of person she was.

"Of course. Top of the stairs, last door on the right."

I stood and walked up the stairs. I reached her room and took a deep breath to steady my nerves before opening the door.

Her room had a layout similar to Finn's. A large bed was pushed up against one wall, and a desk was against the other. I walked to the desk and looked at the papers scattered on top of it. I knew I should be examining the room for clues as to either her killer or why someone would want these people dead, but all I could think was that everything in this room was connected to Janey.

I walked into her closet and ran my hands over her small collection of blouses. She was a modest person, and her wardrobe showed it. I moved to her dresser and examined the things on it. Where most people had perfume or jewelry, Janey had a stethoscope. She was more concerned with helping others than herself.

I left her closet and moved to her bed, picking up her pillow as I sat on the end. I buried my face in the fluffy cotton and tried to keep the sting away from my eyes. I inhaled deeply to push the tears back and caught Janey's scent. It was a jasmine smell. I recognized the smell. It was from the shampoo I had used. It must have belonged to her.

I heard a knock and looked up to find Courtney standing in the doorway. She walked in and sat next to me, took the pillow from my hands, and set it in her lap. She gently smoothed out the wrinkles in the pillow-case, and I saw a couple of wet spots from my tears.

"Brooke has been sleeping in here every night," she told me, without looking away from the pillow.

"I thought she had been staying with Joshua the last few nights?"

Courtney shook her head. "No, she visits him in his room but always comes back here to sleep. I came here last night to check on her and could hear her crying." Courtney shook her head as if she was trying to shake a memory. "I don't know what to do to help her."

I watched her hands move from side to side over the pillow. I did not have an answer for her. I had no idea how to help Brooke-or Courtney, for that matter. Courtney had always been the strong one of the group. I had never seen her in a vulnerable state before, and witnessing it now unnerved me. Seeing Courtney upset made Janey's death more real, more permanent. We sat there in silence. What was there to say?

"Breakfast is ready!" Brooke yelled, from downstairs. I was amazed at the amount of volume that girl had. We did not move from our spot. "I cooked, so you better get your asses down here and eat it!"

Courtney and I laughed as we got to our feet and left the room. I turned and gave the room one last look before turning out the lights and closing the door.

Chapter 31

W E WALKED DOWN the stairs to find a massive breakfast awaiting us in the living room. Brooke had a tray of different types of omelets and waffles sitting on the coffee table. Jake was sitting on the couch, scarfing down a cheese omelet. He looked up as we walked in. "What's up, Salt?" *I was never going to live my karaoke performance down.*

I rolled my eyes at him and picked up a plate. After deciding on a vegetable omelet, I sat down next to Jake and began eating.

I was halfway through with my breakfast when Finn joined us. He finished off the waffles, and I helped myself to another cup of coffee. Once everyone had finished eating, Finn offered us a ride back to the hotel. I needed to find Pack Rat. I assumed he was at the hotel, so that would be a good place to start looking as he refused to answer his cell phone.

After I said good-bye to the others, we let Finn lead us to his vehicle. I was glad he led the way out of the house. That place was a maze. It would have taken me some time to find my way out. Finn opened the passenger side door for me, and I noticed Mark followed his example for Nicole. I smiled and withheld the laugh bubbling up inside of me. Mark was not the door-opening type. He was a great guy, but old fashioned manners-he did not have.

Once we were on the road, Finn reached across the seat and took my hand, lacing his fingers through mine. A smile tugged my lips as I held his hand in my lap. Finn parked in front of the hotel as usual. The bellmen still thought he was a police officer, so they did not object to his parking.

The four of us walked to my room, and Nicole and Mark quickly walked inside, but Finn pulled my hand back to keep me in the hall. I turned to see why he hesitated about entering my room, and his mouth covered mine. It was a hard, thorough kiss that had my body responding. I wrapped my arms around his neck as his arms circled my waist. Heat rushed through my body, like it always did when Finn touched me. With this kiss came desire and need. I pushed him back against the wall and let my hands roam down his chest. My fingers slide under his shirt and glided along his stomach.

"What are you doing?" he asked, slightly amused. I could feel his breath against my lips.

"This seems to be the only place we can be alone," I whispered, letting my voice drop to a seductive pitch.

It turned out I was wrong. Whistling echoed down the hall, drawing our attention. Pack Rat appeared around the corner, heading to his room. "And where the hell have you been?" I asked, keeping my body pressed against Finn's.

"Spent the night at a friend's house," Pack Rat answered, with a sly grin. Well, good for him. *At least someone is getting some action around here.* "Well, I'm going to my room for a shower." Pack Rat left us alone as he walked down the hall.

I leaned my forehead on Finn's shoulder taking in his warmth and scent. Wrapped in his arms was the most comfortable and safe I had felt in a long time. I would have loved to stay there for hours, but unfortunately that was not possible. I had work to do. "I better get inside," I said. Finn groaned a protest before he dropped a kiss on my lips.

"Call me later?" he asked. I nodded and stole another kiss before turning to enter my room.

Nicole was sitting with her legs crossed beneath her, and Mark was lying beside her. Both of them had serious looks on their faces, which worried me. *This scene is way too familiar.*

"Tell me the truth," Nicole said, as I walked to my bed. I gave her my confused expression. "You have known who the targets were the whole time."

I sat down and rubbed my hand across my eyes. Nicole was not asking a question. She knew who the Mother was. She had figured it out and wanted confirmation.

"How did you figure it out?" I asked. I was tired, tired from hiding the truth from her, tired from keeping it from Pack Rat and Tank, tired of secluding my life from Finn. Hell, I was just plain old tired.

"I knew there was something you were not telling me. But it all became clear this morning, when we met Courtney." Nicole did not sound as angry as I thought she would. She spoke as if it was just regular business, which I guess to her it was.

"I can't do it, Nicole. I won't kill her, or any of them. And I will not allow anything to happen to them. They are my family." I looked at her in the eyes and gave her my most serious look. She nodded and looked away.

"So, what are we going to do?" she asked, after a slight hesitation. I raised my eyebrows at her.

"What do you mean, we?"

"I'm with you Blake. I want to help. I owe you that much for saving my life."

"No, you don't understand what is at risk. We may have to go up against Tank."

"We like Tank, don't get us wrong, but you have our loyalty," Mark said to me, as he wrapped a hand around Nicole's knee.

"So, what's the plan, boss?" Nicole asked again, with more enthusiasm in her voice.

I knew it would not be possible to keep her away from helping me, so I caved. Besides, I could use the help. I was relieved that I could trust her. She was my friend, and a dedicated one at that.

"We need to find out who hired us, who wants them dead. Mark was able to get a web address belonging to the person who sent the kill order to Tank, but we haven't been able to hack in yet," I explained.

Nicole looked at Mark. "You knew about this the whole time?"

"Blake is my best friend. She needed help, so here I am. Why? Are you jealous?" Mark asked and squeezed her knee.

Nicole laughed and squirmed away from him. I was immediately uncomfortable with witnessing their teasing. I cleared my throat, and they got the hint. They settled down and focused their attention back on the problem.

"Let me see the computer," Nicole said, with confidence. I had no idea she knew how to hack. My expression must have shown my disbelief. "What? You don't think I'm smart enough to hack into a web site? You know, I'm really getting tired of this shit. Yes, I'm pretty, I know that. People have been telling me that since I was twelve years old-but I am capable of doing something other than seducing a man!" she snapped.

I think Nicole needs a therapy session with Dr. Harris. I did not respond to her outburst. I just got up and brought the computer to Nicole, who took it and began to work. She was definitely capable. I was having a hard time following her as she worked her way through the computer.

"Are you going to tell Pack Rat?" Nicole asked, as she worked on the computer.

I did not want to tell too many people but he was the only one here who did not know. I had no idea how much longer I could keep it from him.

"He's not a stupid guy; he'll figure it out. You might as well tell him now." She was right. I needed to tell him. I nodded at Mark. He leaned across Nicole, picked up the phone, and called Pack Rat.

A few minutes later, Pack Rat walked into our room. His hair was wet from the shower, but he still had the glow from the previous night. "What's up?" he asked, as he plopped down next to me.

I turned to him. "I know who the targets are."

"Great."

I looked at Mark and Nicole for a second before addressing Pack Rat again.

"It's complicated." I hesitated. "Finn, Brooke, and Jake are on the list which also includes the others from my childhood." I left off Courtney's name, because he did not know who she was. His eyes widened slightly.

"I see. So, you don't think you can do it?" I shook my head. "OK, I will take care of it for you," he said sympathetically. He made it sound like he was doing me a favor by killing my loved ones.

"No. I do not want them dead, Peter. I won't let anyone hurt them. I will stop anyone who tries, even you." Pack Rat looked from me to Mark then Nicole.

"What are you planning to do?" he asked skeptically. "I doubt Tank offered to drop the kill order."

He was right. Even if I did tell Tank about Courtney and the others, he would not cancel the job. Tank always got the job done.

"Tank doesn't know yet."

Pack Rat examined me for a moment before he rubbed his eyes. "I'm sorry, Blake. I would love to help you, but I can't. I won't go up against Tank and the company. There is too much at risk."

I nodded my head. I understood his reasoning. Chances were that if we went up against Tank, we would all die. I couldn't ask him to risk his life for people he did not know.

"I'm going to pack my bags," he said, as he stood to leave.

Before he took a step, Mark jumped up in front of him. "I'm sorry, Pack Rat, but we can't let you leave."

Mark placed himself between Pack Rat and the door. The two stared at each other with deadly intent. The only way Mark would let him by was if Pack Rat killed him. I really did not want that to happen. I doubted Pack Rat could do it, but I didn't want to take a chance.

"Mark, let him go," I said.

Mark looked at me like I had lost my mind. He clearly thought Pack Rat would spill the beans and ruin any chance we had of keeping this from Tank. "Pack Rat, would you do me a favor?" He did not respond so I continued. "Please don't tell Tank. Give me some time to figure this out."

"Tank is going to want to know why I returned home before the mission was over."

"I'll call him and say that you were recognized, and your continuing presence threatened the job." Pack Rat looked at me with a look of indecision. "Please."

He sighed. "OK. I won't tell him."

Mark stepped aside and let Pack Rat leave. When the door closed behind him, I leaned back on the bed and covered my eyes.

"I'm sorry, Blake. I really thought he would help us," Nicole said.

I did not respond. Instead I stood, grabbed my cell phone, and called Tank. I told him that Pack Rat was spotted trying to break into the house and that he jeopardized the hit so I sent him home. Tank offered to send another person to New Orleans but I refused. After a few minutes of arguing, Tank agreed to give me a few more days to finish the job. I walked back to my bed and watched Nicole work.

After an hour, she sighed and leaned back against the headboard. "We need a better computer system, and I could use a little help. This is more complicated than I thought it would be." She closed her eyes. Slowly a smile tugged at her lips. "I know just the place. Let's go."

We pulled up to Garrett's house and walked to his door. He answered after the second knock. He opened the door, and his eyes immediately got caught on Nicole. She may be able to do other things besides look beautiful, but her looks were the most effective.

"We have a job for you," I said, as I handed him a bag. He opened it and looked inside.

"How much is this?"

"Five thousand dollars. We need your hacking ability." He looked back in the bag.

"I take it this is to be kept off the record," he said, stepping aside to let us in the house. I nodded. The last thing I needed was for Tank to find out what I was up to.

Chapter 32

I SAT ON GARRETT'S couch with Mark. We were not very useful in computer situations. I drummed my fingers nervously on the coffee table as I watched Nicole and Garrett work on their computers. I hated not being able to do anything. The feeling of having no control over events was not something I was used to or happy about. The only sound to be heard was the tapping of computer keys and the occasional sigh of frustration. I glanced at Mark, and he looked as unhappy as I felt. His face was set in an expression of annoyance, and he rubbed his forehead with one hand.

"What's wrong?" I asked him.

"I have a killer headache, and your finger tapping is not helping," he growled. *My, my, someone is grumpy.*

I placed my hand in my lap and began twiddling my thumbs. My nervous energy was keeping me from holding still. I was ready to find out what that website said.

My phone rang; the vibration in my pocket caused me to jump. Mark looked at me like I was going crazy. An unknown number flashed on my screen. I normally did not answer the phone if it was a number I didn't know. I fought with the desire to let my voicemail pick up the call and my need for something to do. My boredom won, and I flipped open the phone. "Hello?"

"Hey, Blake. It's Courtney."

"Oh, hey, Court. What's up?"

"Not much, I got your number out of Finn's cell phone. Hope you don't mind."

"Of course not."

"Good. Well, I was wondering if you had dinner plans. I haven't had the chance to spend much time with you and was calling to see if you wanted to have dinner with us tonight."

"Um," I looked around the room. I mouthed the words "Dinner tonight?" at Mark.

"Go ahead. We will call you when we find something," he whispered.

"OK, yeah, I would love to have dinner," I told Courtney.

"Great! How does seven o'clock sound?"

"Awesome, see you at seven," I said, and hung up the phone.

I leaned my head back against the couch. It seemed like half a day had gone by with us on that couch, instead of the two hours that had actually passed since Courtney's phone call. I looked down at the new watch on my wrist. It read six o'clock. I blew out a breath of frustration and boredom.

"Just go," Mark blurted out.

"What?"

"You are driving me crazy! You keep tapping on everything and moving around. You can't stay still for one minute. Just watching you makes me anxious."

"Wow, I'm sorry," I said sarcastically. "The last thing I want in life is to make you uncomfortable."

I stood up and walked across the room to end the argument before it got too heated. Mark and I had a tendency to bicker when stuck in the same space together for too long. That was one of the reasons we had decided to end our relationship. I sat at the kitchen table and waited until my watch read a quarter to seven.

"Call me when you find something?" I asked the people in the room. Nicole gave me a thumbs up without turning her head away from the computer. I walked toward the door and slapped Mark on the forehead as I ran past him on my way out of the house. It wasn't a hard slap, just a pat that I knew would annoy him.

I drove to the house and made it there right on time. I pulled up to the gate and rolled down my window for the guard. "Name?"

"Blake Morgan," I said politely through the window. He checked the clipboard and looked up at me. "Go on through, Ms. Morgan," he said, before returning to the guard house and pushing a button that opened the gate.

I parked my car next to Brooke's convertible and walked to the front door. I was walking up the steps when a group of guys ran around the corner of the house. They were running in organized lines, with one man leading them. My heart skipped a beat when I recognized Finn.

He was wearing jogging shorts, and sweat from his hair was dripping down on his face and his bare chest. He turned his head and met my eyes. He smiled and slowed down to run beside another man. He spoke briefly to the man before turning toward me. The other runners continued around the house. Finn jogged up the steps and stopped in front of me. His chest rose and fell as he breathed heavily from the exercise. He leaned close to hug me and I pushed a finger in his chest to hold him back. "Oh, no you don't," I said teasingly.

"What?"

"You are all sweaty, and I'm clean," I said, stepping back from him as he took a step closer.

I really did not mind the fact that he was sweating. I actually liked the way he looked, but I wanted to be the reason he was sweating.

I was determined to hold my ground and keep him at bay. I did not want to go to dinner smelling like sweat. Finn realized I was not going to give in so he stopped walking toward me. Hoverer, he did not back up so his body was still close to mine. The only thing separating the two of us was my hand pushing a finger in his chest. He gave me the smile that made my knees turn to rubber.

"So, what brings you to my doorstep?"

"Court didn't tell you? I am here for dinner."

"No, she did not," he said, with a hint of surprise.

"You don't want me here?" I asked flirtatiously.

"No, I'm thrilled you're here. I just wish Court would have told me, so I would have been dressed and ready for you." He smiled. I gave him a flirtatious smile back.

"I doubt you could ever be ready for me," I said, dropping my voice down to a pitch that would have made adult phone service operators envious.

A wicked smile tugged the corners of his lips. "Oh really?"

He leaned his face toward mine, but I side stepped his attack and quickly stepped into the house before he could reach for me. One of the runners was making his way to the steps to speak with Finn, so I knew he wouldn't follow me into the house. I winked at him before turning and making my way down the hall toward the living area I remembered from that morning.

Chapter 33

I ENTERED THE LIVING room and found Courtney, Brooke, and Lee lounging around the room. They all looked up at me with a look of confusion. All except Courtney. I guess she did not tell anyone I was coming to dinner. Brooke's statement confirmed that thought. "Blake, what the hell are you doing here?"

"Here for dinner. Guess Court didn't tell anyone," I said. Brooke gave Courtney an angry.

"So, I am not allowed to have a friend over for dinner in my own house?" Courtney asked Brooke, before looking at me. "Glad you made it. Have a seat."

I did as she suggested and sat next to Brooke. We were talking about nothing in particular when Finn ran into the room.

"Thanks for the heads up, Court," he said, as he stopped beside the couch. She ignored the comment. "I'm going to hop in the shower," he said, more to me than anyone else.

"That's a good idea," I said, with a grin. He did not smell bad; I was just giving him a hard time. He smiled back and ran up the stairs, taking them two at a time. We went back to our conversation.

Jake walked in from the other side of the room. "Dinner's ready. Blake? What brings you here?"

"Court invited her here without letting anyone know she was coming," Brooke said, with an angry tone.

Courtney threw her hands in the air in frustration. She stood up, and we followed her out of the living room. She led us through the cafeteria. It was a large room, with many long tables and benches on either side of them. The room resembled the cafeteria at my high school. We crossed the room and walked into a smaller dining area. It had one large dinner table, with ten chairs placed around it. Expensive china tableware was set at each place, and exotic paintings hung on the walls. It was a nice, romantic room.

Jake poured everyone a glass of red wine. No one sat down; instead, we stood around the table talking. A few minutes later, the door opened, and Finn walked in the room. His hair was wet from the shower, and he was dressed in jeans and a cotton pull over shirt. He walked over to me and stood a foot in front of me.

"Better," I said, taking in his attire. He leaned forward and gave me a quick kiss.

"Yum, I guess we are having Merlot with dinner," he said, as he pulled his head away from me. I stared into his face as he smiled at me.

"That's impressive," Brooke said. "You knew what kind of wine we were drinking just from kissing her?" He nodded and tried to look arrogant.

I wasn't fooled. I stared at him and grinned. "The wine bottle is sitting on the table."

Finn grinned back. "Yeah, that helped."

I shook my head and turned to the table. Finn held out my chair for me, and I sat down. He took the spot next to me and wrapped his hand around my knee. After everyone was seated, the door opened, and two army looking guys walked into the room carrying a tray of food. Pork tenderloins, mashed potatoes, and green beans were set in front of us. We served ourselves and talked as we ate. Both the meal and conversation were excellent.

Finn swallowed his mashed potatoes and washed it down with wine. "Oh, Brooke, I almost forgot. Joshua said he will drop by your room when he is finished working out, if that's all right."

Brooke blew out a deep breath and rolled her eyes. I smiled at her but did not comment on her reaction to Finn's message. However, Courtney did. "What? Tired of him already?"

"He is just so...so nice," Brooke said, by way of explanation.

"Oh, I know exactly what you mean," I said sarcastically. "I hate when a guy is nice to me. It is such a turn off." Finn and Jake laughed, but Brooke glared at me.

"You know what I mean. He is *too* nice. He's always worried about my feelings and stuff. It's annoying."

"That's why I treat you like shit," Jake said. "It means I care."

Lee and Courtney choked back a laugh. This was what I missed so much about my childhood. We argued like a family. We were a family. Brooke hit Jake in the shoulder, which made him laugh harder.

"So, I heard you handled yourself pretty well against the Malones," Courtney told me, once the laughter died down. I gave her a confused look. "Brooke said you wiped the floor with Crystal and Kevin Malone."

"Oh, them," I said, slightly embarrassed. Finn rubbed my leg comfortingly. "I guess I did all right."

"You kicked their asses!" Brooke exclaimed before taking a sip of wine. I shrugged my shoulders.

Courtney studied me from across the table. "Did Finn tell you what it is we do here?"

I shook my head. "We don't really talk about work stuff."

Jake suppressed a laugh. "I bet you don't."

Courtney smiled but continued. "We train potential recruits for the CIA." I frowned at her. "The CIA finds recruits and sends them to us. We train them physically, then send them back to the CIA to finish their training in intelligence."

I leaned back in my chair and stared at her. She lifted her glass and took a sip of wine before scooping up some mashed potatoes with her fork. I looked at everyone at the table before drawing my attention back to Courtney. "You're serious?"

She nodded. "Jake teaches weapons handling, Finn and Lee teach unarmed combat and conditioning, and Brooke...well, I'm not really sure what Brooke does."

Brooke turned to her, offended. "I...I do schedules, plan diets, boost morale." Jake choked on his wine when she mentioned morale. Brooke gave him an evil stare.

"Anyway," Courtney continued, "we need someone to teach combat to the female recruits. There are different techniques girls need to know when fighting, and let's face it, guys can't teach what they don't know. So...I'm asking you to stay here. Besides, you belong here, with your family."

I set my wineglass on the table. I had no idea what to say. Courtney was offering me a job. A job I would be very good at. A job that would keep me in New Orleans with my family.

"Just think about it," Courtney said. I nodded.

Finn rubbed my knee, and I looked at him. He was looking at me with anticipation. He assumed I was going to take the job without a second thought.

"Blake, you would be awesome at this job. The way you fought was incredible. I bet you could even kick Finn's ass," Brooke said.

Finn laughed low in his throat. I turned and glared at him. He didn't think I could do it. I was always being underestimated, and it was beginning to piss me off.

"There is no way she would beat Finn in a fight," Jake argued with Brooke.

"I bet you two weeks of shift scheduling that she kicks his butt."

"You're on." Jake and Brooke shook hands.

"Hold on guys, I'm not fighting Blake," Finn said.

"Think of it as sparring," I said to him. Brooke's eyes lit up with anticipation. Finn's showed shock.

"You want to fight me?"

Yes, I did. The fact that he thought he could beat me fueled the anger I had from Courtney's offer. It wasn't the offer that made me angry, it was that look on Finn's face. He had known she was going to ask me the question before she asked it. I would have appreciated a heads up from him. I nodded.

"No, I'm not fighting you."

"Why not?" I asked. "Afraid you will lose?"

He grinned. "I don't want you to be angry with me when I win." He was teasing me now. That only furthered my desire to fight him. I hated being patronized.

"Brooke, set up the mats," I said. Brooke jumped out of her chair, and she and Jake ran out the door. I stood and followed them to the gym.

Chapter 34

BROOKE LED US into the gymnasium, which was a room split into three sections. The middle section was a basketball court. On one side of the court was a weight lifting area filled with the latest equipment. And on the other side, mats were positioned along the wall where recruits could practice fighting. Brooke escorted me to the mats and helped me put on the boxing gloves, along with the protective footwear. I hated the footwear; it was boxing gloves for your feet. They were annoying and uncomfortable, but I would appreciate them if I got kicked in the head. Brooke laced up the gloves as she spoke. "Finn has a weak left knee."

I rolled my eyes at her. I did not want to injure him, just beat the ego out of his head. Once both of us were laced up and ready, we stepped onto the mats. The others retreated to the bleachers to watch the fight. Brooke and Jake sat anxiously on the first row. Courtney sat behind them and leaned back into Lee's legs, as if he was a recliner.

"You sure you want to do this?" Finn asked, as he shook out his arms in preparation. It looked like he thought we were only going to play and not really spar.

"Absolutely. I'm mad at you," I said, stepping close to him. "I think it would help to hit something."

As I said it, I struck out and punched his left shoulder. It was not a hard hit. I wanted him to fight, and he did not look like he would take this seriously.

"Why are you mad at me? I haven't even hit you yet." He easily dodged my second blow.

I stopped fighting and stood in front of him, letting my hands fall by my sides and looked him in the eyes. "Did you know Courtney was going to ask me to stay?" I asked him in a low voice, so the others would not be able to hear the question.

"I thought she might," he answered, as if it was no big deal. That angered me even more.

"Why didn't you give me a heads up?" He shrugged a reply. That was it.

I lunged forward and threw a hard punch at his face. He swatted it away an inch before it hit his nose. He gave me a confused look. *Surprise, I really intend to fight.* I threw another punch that he had to jump back to avoid. The fight was on.

He threw a punch at my shoulder, which I easily ducked, then swooped to the ground and tried to swipe his feet out from under him. He jumped over my feet, and I was up before he landed. I sent a cross, he dodged, and then I brought a heel up and connected with his stomach. He backed away quickly before attacking faster than I thought he could.

I dodged blow after blow and sent some punches of my own. He dodged them as well. Occasionally punches would connect, but nothing that would knock either of us off our feet. One of his punches made its way past my defenses and struck my shoulder, but it was not at full force. I remained on my feet and saw he left his right side open. It would be an easy hit. Too easy. I looked into his eyes and saw that it was purposefully left open. I refused to take the hit. He would not let me win this fight, not if I had anything to do with it. He realized I would not take the hit and resumed fighting.

Sweat began to slip down my spine as the battle progressed. Finn struck out with his left hand. It was a familiar punch that I had seen thousands of times. Like the others, I responded the same way and slipped into the movements that were as natural to me as breathing. I grabbed his wrist with one hand and prepared to attack his elbow with the other. Before I could strike, I remembered that this was Finn and I did not want to cause serious damage. Instead of breaking his arm, I spun around to his back and punched the back of both knees. This move causes your opponent to fall to his knees, where you can grab his head and swiftly break his neck. Although I did not intend to break his neck, if I could position my hands in place, the fight would be over.

However, instead of falling to his knees, Finn fell straight to his back. The move surprised me, and that instant of surprise was what he needed. He reached above his head and grabbed my ankles. He swiftly yanked my feet out from under me, and I hit the ground hard. Before I could get off my back, Finn crawled on me placing a knee on either side of my upper thighs to keep them together and sat on my legs. He grabbed my hands and pinned them next to my head. The fight was over. I lost. *Damn it.*

"I didn't tell you about the offer, because I wanted to give Court a chance to convince you. I thought she could do a better job with that than I could. I'm sorry; I just want you to stay." Finn was breathing as heavily as I was. It was a damn good work out.   I heard Jake cheering from the bleachers and Brooke shouting "Best two out of three?"

Finn's hands loosened around my wrist, but I didn't move them. I lay there and looked into his eyes. I wanted him to bend down and kiss me, but before he could, Jake was pulling him up by the shoulders. Courtney walked over and offered me a hand. I took it and let her help me to my feet.

"Brooke was right, you can fight," Courtney told me, as she walked me back to the bleachers, where my purse and boots waited. I sat down and pulled the gloves off my feet and hands. Brooke was arguing with Jake about a technicality of the bet, so Finn left them to walk over to where we sat.

"Court, can you give us a minute?" he asked her.

She looked from his face to mine. I dropped my gaze and pulled my boots back on. I'm sure she could sense the tension between the two of us.

"Sure," she said, before leaving to join my arguing friends.

Finn sat down next to me. For a moment he did not speak. "You know how I feel about you, right?" he finally said, turning to look at me. I stared back at him. I really did not want to have the relationship talk right now, and in front of the others. "Blake, I l-"

"No, you don't." I interrupted him before he could tell me he loved me. It was too soon. I had only been in New Orleans for a couple weeks. That was not enough time to develop those types of feeling for one another. Was it?

"Yes, I do," he firmly stated.

"No, you are in love with the girl I was ten years ago."

"What's wrong with that?"

"She doesn't exist anymore." I looked at him for a second before dropping my eyes. "I am not the same person I was in Michigan. You couldn't feel that way, not if you knew the real me, what I have become." I stared at my hands.

"I am trying. But you won't let me!" he sighed, and lowered his voice. "I am not asking for you to tell me everything. But you won't tell me anything. Every time we talk about you, you change the subject. How am I supposed to know you, if-"

"If you knew the real me, you wouldn't..." I studied my palm, "you wouldn't look at me the same way. I don't think I can handle that."

"Blake," he said. I looked up in his eyes. "Do you really have that little faith in me?"

I didn't answer right away. "No, I have that little faith in me," I said softly.

I knew that if I told Finn the truth about what I had become, he would disapprove. Finn was a good man. He did not believe in hurting others. He was a protector. He would be appalled by my chosen profession. A trained killer does not deserve someone that good. I did not deserve someone that good.

"You're planning on leaving." It wasn't a question.

"I don't know." I didn't know. I had no idea how this job was going to turn out. We both may be dead by the end of it, and if not, I didn't know if he would want me after he found out the truth about my life.

"I don't know if I can handle you leaving again," he said softly. "Last time, it...I don't think I can do it again." He reached out and took my hand in his.

"Then maybe we should stop this, before it gets too-" I began. Finn suddenly pulled me to him and kissed me hard. His hand wrapped around the back of my neck to hold my face to his. He kissed me as if had craved it, as if he would die if he didn't kiss me. He told me everything he was feeling in that kiss. He needed that kiss, needed me. He pulled away from me and looked in my eyes.

"Please don't ever say that again. The only worse thing than having you leave is having you here and not being able to touch you."

My phone chose that moment to ring. I wanted to ignore it. This conversation seemed more important than whoever was on the other end. I sighed and reached in my purse and found my phone.

I flipped the cell open. "Get your ass over here now," Mark's voice said in my ear.

"You're in?" I asked.

"Oh, yeah." I closed my eyes and turned off the phone.

"You're leaving?" Finn said to my hand.

"Yeah."

Finn took a deep breath and stood up. I followed his lead and gathered my things. I walked to the others and thanked them for dinner. Courtney gave me a concerned look but did not ask any questions. She could tell I did not want to talk. I hugged everyone and left the room with Finn on my heels. "I'll walk you to your car."

I didn't argue. He was a good man, and yes, he deserved better. I had kept my life from him for my own selfish reasons. I was afraid he would reject me. Maybe he would, but he at least deserved to know the truth. I owed him that much.

He probably would never want to see me again, but then again, who knew? If things ended because I was too afraid to try, I would regret if for as long as I lived. In my line of work, that may not be long, but I didn't want to risk it. I had to come clean.

We reached my car, and he opened the door for me. I stood in front of him. "I have to go to work, but when I'm finished, we need to talk," I told him. He was looking at the car door, not me. "I will tell you everything and answer any questions you have."

Finn turned to me. "Any questions?" he asked. I reached up and kissed him softly.

"Any questions you have," I repeated. He smiled.

Soon he would know everything. Part of me was incredibly nervous about how he would react, but another part was relieved. I was tired of hiding things from him. I was tired of not knowing how he would take that fact that I was an assassin. At least soon, I would know and could go from there. I got in the car and drove off to Garrett's house.

Chapter 35

I DID NOT BOTHER knocking on Garrett's door. I went straight inside and found the other two positioned around Garrett's computer. Mark looked at me when I approached. He shook his head and stepped aside, so I could see the monitor. The computer showed something that looked similar to the kill order. "The Mother" ran top and center on the screen, with a blank square where her picture should be. Next to the square was the name section. It, too, was blank, along with age, weight, height, and hair color. It contained all the questions one would fill out for a driver's license. The only question with an answer was address. It was the same address I had. There were a few differences between the site and my kill order. The main difference being the symbol on the top left of the screen.

My stomach dropped. I recognized the symbol. It was a circle with a bald eagle in the center. Around the edge of the seal were the words "National Security Agency."

"What the hell?" I asked, looking at the others. *What did the NSA have to do with the hit? They were the ones who hired us?*

"Why would they hire us? Surely they have trained people who could do the job," I asked Mark.

He did not reply. He bit his thumbnail, like he always did when he was in serious thought. I turned back to the screen. "Scroll down," I told Nicole.

She did as I asked. At the bottom of the screen were the words "Project Phonoi." *What the hell is Project Phonoi?* Beneath the project was the name: Agent Nicolas Powell. The symbol, the project name, and the agent's name were the only differences between what was on the screen and the paper Tank gave me.

I turned and looked at Mark and Nicole before I began to pace around the room. Mark had sent Garrett away when he saw we were dealing with the NSA. He was trying to keep him from getting too involved with this.

I tried to think of some possibilities for why the government would want Courtney killed. Nothing. It had to have something to do with the training she was administering for the CIA. Right? I had to find out. It was the only way I could think of to possibly keep the people I loved alive. Find the reason they want her dead, and maybe I could change their minds. I had thought about killing the person who hired us, but seeing as that person was the US government, I did not think that was a possibility.

"Nicole, can you book a flight for me to Washington DC?" Nicole gave me a concerned look but turned to the computer.

"Why do you want to go there?" Mark asked.

"I need to talk to this Agent Powell. Maybe he can tell me why they want to kill Courtney."

"Are you serious? You can't walk up to a government official and confess you're an assassin and ask why he hired you."

"I know that, Mark. But we need answers and this guy will have them. What else am I supposed to do?" Mark did not have an answer for me.

"I can book flights for the three of us leaving at ten-forty-five. We are going to Fort Meade. The NSA is in Maryland not DC." Nicole said.

I looked at my watch. It read ten o'clock. That would put me arriving in Maryland at around one-thirty in the morning. If that was the earliest I could get, it would have to do. "That's good, but I'm going alone."

They turned and looked at me. They looked surprised and concerned. "No, we are coming with you," Nicole stated.

I shook my head. "I have something else for you."

I told them everything Courtney told me about working for the CIA. I left out the job offer. That was something I had to decide for myself, and I doubted my friends could be impartial enough to help me make a decision that could result in my moving hundreds of miles away from them.

"So what do you want us to do?" Mark asked.

"Court and the gang seemed to have angered the Malone siblings. Go and question them. Find out if they are just upset about being dumped, or if there is something else going on."

"The people you beat the hell out of yesterday?" I nodded. *Was it really only yesterday? It seems like days ago.* "I don't think they will be too eager to talk to us."

"Make them talk."

Nicole nodded. "Be careful in Maryland."

I smiled at her. "I'm always careful."

Mark laughed at me. Clearly, he thought I was not nearly careful enough. I could have brought up the near deaths he had encountered due to his carelessness but decided to stay silent; I didn't have the energy for an argument. Instead, I grabbed my purse. After promising to call them when I landed, I left for the airport.

Chapter 36

I DID NOT HAVE time to drop by my hotel room to get a sweater, not if I wanted to make it to my flight on time. All I had on was my designer t-shirt and my light leather jacket; so, upon arrival, I was greeted by Baltimore, Maryland's less-than-friendly February air. I hurried into a nearby tourist shop and bought a sweater with a picture of the Baltimore Ravens's mascot on the front. *Brooke and Nicole would die if they saw me in this.* It was not the most fashionable thing I had ever bought, but it was warm.

I took a cab to a hotel and rented a room. I tried to get a few hours of sleep but was unable to do so; I was too anxious about the questions I needed answered to relax. At eight o'clock in the morning, I took a quick shower and left the hotel.

A cab drove me to the border of Fort Meade. I didn't know how tight security would be on the military base so I didn't want to test my luck. Instead, I waited on a bench in a nearby park. I had time to kill before I needed to contact Agent Powell, so I pulled my phone out of my purse and called Mark.

"How is the questioning of the siblings going?" I asked.

"Not so great. You really did a number on Crystal. She has a broken nose, a black eye, and a few cracked ribs. She is somewhat reluctant to help us."

"Surprise, surprise. I thought you would be able to handle a challenge. Guess I was wrong," I teased.

"Oh, don't worry. We will get your answers. Nicole has proven to be quite efficient at making men talk," he said, with amusement in his voice. I heard a man scream in the background. Apparently torturing Kevin was how they were getting him to talk. "I have to admit, it's kind of a turn-on." Mark lowered his voice.

"I heard that," Nicole called out.

"That's weird, Mark," I told him. He never had a fetish for the rough stuff when we were dating, much to my relief.

He laughed at me. "You would not think it was weird if you saw how this girl handles a blade." I had seen her handle a blade and had not gotten any special feelings about it, but hey, maybe it was a guy thing. "Have you talked to the agent yet?"

"Nope, I was waiting a while to make sure he was in the office."

"Call when you hear something."

"Will do," I said, and hung up the phone.

I looked down at my watch. I decided to wait until 9:30 to contact Agent Powell. My watch read 9:40. I called the front desk of the NSA headquarters and a woman answered.

"Can you please connect me to Agent Powell?" I asked.

"May I ask who's calling?"

"Rebecca Johansson," I answered.

"One moment," she said. She put me on hold. I waited patiently, knowing they were probably trying to trace my cell phone for security purposes. *Good luck with that.* I listened to music fit only for elevator or for phone services, and after a few moments, the music stopped, and a man answered.

"Agent Powell," he said by way of greeting.

"Hello, Agent Powell. I was wondering if you could spare a few moments of your time."

"Ms. Johansson? Why do I get the feeling that is not your real name?" he asked. *Probably because my phone refused to be traced.*

I had no intention of giving him my real name. "You can call me..." I glanced around searching for inspiration then looked down at my sweater, "... Ms. Raven."

"If you have no intention of telling me your name, this chat is over," he told me, in a grumpy voice. Clearly, Agent Powell was not a morning person.

"I have information on The Mother."

Silence followed my statement. "I have no idea what you are talking about."

"I think you do."

"Very well, I will play along, what do you know?"

"I don't think so. I want to meet in person. Six Flags Theme Park in thirty minutes, and I would prefer that you came alone."

"I have no idea who you are, and you want me to trust you enough to meet you alone? That's not going to happen."

"Fine, bring a weapon if you like."

I did not care if he came armed or not, despite the fact that I did not have my gun. I was a trained killer who could kill easily with my hands if a problem should occur.

"OK, you have a deal. I will be at there in thirty minutes," he told me, before hanging up. I found a cab and instructed him to take me to the theme park. I bought a ticket and went through the gates. Twenty minutes after I arrived, a man in a suit walked through the gates. The business suit alone was enough of an indicator that he was the man I was waiting for. He walked around, searching for someone. He placed his hands on his hips, and I walked up behind him.

"Powell?"

He spun around quickly and looked at me. He had dark hair with streaks of white at the temples and dark eyes. Going by his hair, I guessed he was in his late fifties. He was a very ordinary man, the kind of man one would meet and instantly forget. His eyes scanned my body, as if he was evaluating me.

"Ms. Raven, I presume." I nodded and walked along with a crowd headed for a huge red rollercoaster. Powell quickly fell in step behind me. "You have information for me?"

"I do, but first I need some information," I said, as I faced him. He raised his eyebrows at me. "Why are you so interested in her?"

"If you have the information I need, you would know that answer."

"I know more about this woman than you could imagine. I still want to know your reason."

His eyes narrowed at me. "Do you work for her?"

"No, I do not."

"Are you aware of her criminal activities?" I stared at him. Surely he was joking. Courtney was not a criminal. My expression must have told him what I was thinking. "She is one of the biggest arms distributors in the world."

"What?" I almost laughed at the thought. "Surely you are mistaken."

"No, we have been trying to get her for some time. She has been selling weapons to unfriendly countries."

"That's why you want her dead. You think she is a weapons dealer."

"Who said I wanted her dead?" *Shit.*

I can't believe I let that slip. I did not intend on telling him I knew about the hit. Understanding appeared on his face. "You're Tank's girl." It wasn't a question. He folded his arms over his chest.

"What is Project Phonoi?"

Agent Powell turned and walked away from the crowd and toward a more secluded area. He motioned for me to follow him, so I did. "About thirty years ago, the NSA was trying to arrest a terrorist but was unable to get enough evidence to arrest him. We could hardly find him, and we needed to get him off the streets before something bad happened. So we started Project Phonoi. It was named after the Greek spirits of killing, murder, and slaughter." He looked at me. "That's you."

"I don't understand. Are you telling me you put out a contract on this guy?"

"So to speak, yes. What the project really did, was create a company to take care of any problems like the one with that terrorist."

"Is that company the same one I work for?" He nodded. An ache began to form between my eyes. I rubbed my forehead. This was not making any sense to me. "So, all the contracts that we get are..."

"...people we cannot convict? Or who are too dangerous to the country to leave alive? Yes."

Holy crap. Everything I had known about my job just went up in flames. I was a hit man for the government. I thought back on all my assignments. They were all people who were involved in illegal activities. *Shit.* Somehow, I thought knowing the people I killed were bad guys would make me feel better, but it did not. I felt like I was being used.

"So, what do you know about The Mother?"

I looked at him, and it all hit me. The government was determined to get Courtney one way or another. They were so desperate to stop her from doing what they thought she was doing that they hired me to kill her. I would not be able to talk Agent Powell out of this contract. "I have to go," I said.

"Wait. I answered your questions, now it's time to answer mine."

"No. I need to think." I began to pace back and forth. "I have to go."

I couldn't talk to him about Courtney. I knew I could not stop them from trying to kill her, but I would not give them information that would help them accomplish it. My heart began to beat faster in my chest, and I was taking sharper breaths. I felt an anxiety attack approaching. I had to get away from him.

I turned from him and ran as fast as my legs would carry me. Agent Powell yelled after me; he may have even chased me. I didn't turn to look, and he didn't catch me. I did not know what else to do, so I ran.

I moved through the crowds and soon found myself running through the park. I didn't hesitate as I ran around families having picnics. I heard them yell something at me but didn't care. The only time I stopped was to catch a kid who I had bumped into while cutting across the line waiting to ride *Elmer's* Around the World in 80 seconds.

I ran until my legs would not hold me anymore. I fell to my knees and rested in a corner in Gotham City. I breathed deeply through my mouth, trying to regain stability in my lungs and my head. My mind was spinning with what he told me. I looked at my surroundings. Kids of all ages, along with their exhausted parents, were waiting to ride *Batman* themed rides. I could hear their screams as they twisted and flipped along the rollercoaster tracks.

I got to my feet and carefully made my way to the exit. I didn't know if Agent Powell was still in the park searching for me. Eventually, I made it out of the amusement park and called a cab. I gave the driver my destination, the airport. I needed to talk to Courtney. I had to find out the truth. I had to tell her the truth about me. Together, I knew we would be able to fix this.

I booked the first flight to New Orleans I could get. The only flight I could book connected in Atlanta, and I would arrive in New Orleans at 11:49 p.m. Anxiety took over my body as I waited for my flight. I knew I had told Mark I would call him after talking to Agent Powell, but I did not feel like explaining things to him. I could hardly wrap my head around it myself. I would wait until I arrived in New Orleans to call him. Maybe by then it would make more sense to me.

I skipped lunch, knowing I wouldn't be able to eat anyway. I circled the airport several times and went into every shop they had. By six o'clock, I had the airport memorized. My flight was uneventful, and I landed in New Orleans on time. After I got into my car, I picked up my phone and called Mark. The voicemail picked up.

"The shit has hit the fan! Our whole damned company works for the government. They think Court is some type of arms distributor. I'm on my way to her house now to straighten this shit out, and I'll call you when I know something." I hung up the phone and headed to find Courtney and the others.

Chapter 37

MY STOMACH WAS tied up in knots by the time I reached the house. I stopped at the gate and rolled my window down for the guard. Before I could give my name, the guard waved me through. It was the same guard who was on duty when I arrived the day before for dinner. I guess he remembered me.

I pulled through the gate and parked next to Jake's Jeep. I was incredibly nervous about the talk I would have with everyone. I was going to tell them all about my career and the real reason I was in New Orleans. I would finally know how Finn would react to the knowledge that I was an assassin. After I dropped that bombshell on them, I would have to ask Courtney about the accusations Agent Powell made about her. This was going to be a long night, but by the end of it, I would have the answers I needed. I climbed out of my car and walked to the front door.

"Blake?" Lee said, as he tapped me on the shoulder and scared me half to death. I nearly jumped out of my skin. It was past midnight, and I did not expect to run into anybody outside. Not many people had ever been able to sneak up on me; it helped that I was distracted by the anxiety I was feeling. I guess I was more nervous than I thought.

"I'm sorry. I didn't mean to scare you," he said.

"That's all right."

"What brings you back this late?" he asked, as he walked beside me toward the front door.

"I need to talk to Court and the others. Are they in bed yet?"

"I doubt it. Jake had the early shift, so he may be asleep, but I doubt the others are. Just go on in," he told me, stopping behind me. "I have some things to do out here or I would escort you."

"Thanks." I turned and reached for the door.

Before I could grab the door-knob, an arm wrapped around my waist from behind me. Lee lifted me off my feet and placed a handkerchief over my face. I inhaled a sweet but sharp odor. *Chloroform. Shit.*

Lee was trying to sedate me. I had no idea why but I was determined to break free of his grip and find out. I placed my feet on the wall and kicked back as hard as I could. The force of the kick sent us back until he encountered one of the wooden posts on either side the stairs. The post at his back kept him from falling down. His hold on me did not falter one bit. My fighting actually made him squeeze me tighter. If my kick had been able to throw him a foot to the right, he would have fallen down the stairs, giving me a better chance of escape.

"Stay still," Lee whispered in my ear. My vision was becoming more distorted. *I hate chloroform!* I would not go down that easy. I elbowed him as hard as I could in the stomach. He let out a yelp but did not loosen his grip on me. The chloroform took effect, and my dizziness turned to complete blackness.

I woke up confused. It was as if my mind was in a fog. Slowly, the memory of being chloroformed came back to me. It was not the first time I had come in contact with chloroform, but normally I was on the other side of the blackout.

I opened my eyes. My hair fell around my face, and I was looking down at my lap. I realized I was seated in a chair instead of lying down. I tried to lift a hand to pull the hair out of my face but the pain in my wrist quickly told me my hands were tied behind my back. It was a plastic tie that bound my wrist, the same kind police officers used in raids when they did not have enough handcuffs. The tie was too tight, and the plastic cut into my wrist.

I looked around the room, trying to figure out where I was being held. I was seated in a wooden chair, and my feet were not tied. *I guess that's a plus.* I saw shelves of various types of yard equipment to my left. I turned my head and saw there were plenty of spare sparring mats behind me and a small metal closet. I was in a storage room of some kind.

I heard something moving in the shadow to my right. I snapped my head toward the sound and saw a rat scurrying across the concrete floor. Panic caused me to take a sharp breath. I hated rats. I considered them disgusting, disease-infested rodents who just looked evil. I heard another sound to my left and turned to look. What I saw was much larger and scarier than a rat. Lee was sitting in the shadows watching me.

"What the hell is going on?" I yelled at him.

Lee did not answer, he just smiled at me. I twisted my wrist in attempt to slip free but only managed to cause the plastic to cut deeper. There was no chance of me escaping the tie; it was too damn tight. I knew I would be bleeding soon if it was not removed.

The door directly in front of me opened. Courtney walked through with Finn, Brooke, and Jake close behind. *Were they all behind this kidnapping?* Courtney's face was cold and emotionless. Finn saw me and his cool expression dropped. "What the hell?"

My thoughts exactly. He ran to my side and knelt beside me. He pulled out a pocket-knife with his initials engraved in the blade and moved to cut the tie at my wrist. I blew out a breath of relief. Finn would rescue me from whatever the hell was going on. He was on my side.

"Finn, wait." Courtney told him. He looked at her, and I saw confusion and anger in his eyes, but he pulled the knife away. Brooke and Jake had similar confused looks on their faces.

"Court, what's going on? And why am I tied?" I was trying to remain calm.

"Do you want to tell them, or should I?" Courtney asked me. I had no idea what she was talking about, so I did not answer.

"Very well." She turned and faced the others. "Blake is an assassin." I stopped breathing. I had intended to tell them, but tied up was not the way I wanted to do it.

Finn let out a laugh next to me. I couldn't look at him. That gesture alone told him she was right. When his laughter stopped, I risked a glance and saw the uncertainty growing on his face. "You're serious?" he asked Courtney, but kept his eyes on me.

"Yes, and she is here to kill us." I did not know what to do. She was right. That's why I was in New Orleans. I knew I should say something but what would I say.

"It's not like that," I said. *Oh, good, that will explain everything.*

"She killed Janey," Courtney told them.

I jerked my head up. *What did she just say?* I looked at everyone in the shed. Jake's eyes were no longer holding confusion, it was all anger. He made an aggressive step toward me, but Finn caught him before he could reach me.

"No, I did not kill her," I told them. No one replied. I turned to the one ally I was hoping I still had in the room. "Finn, you have to believe me. I didn't kill Janey."

I could practically hear Finn's thoughts. I could see him running through the events of the last few weeks, starting with my sudden appearance in his home, concealing a pistol. All the pieces of the puzzle would fall in place: my refusal to discuss work and my knowledge of hand to hand combat.

"You said the family was not in danger," he said calmly. His face had gone cold again. This was not looking good. "You lied. You were sent here to kill us?"

He looked down at me in disgust. His expression cut deeper than the plastic at my wrist. It felt as if someone had punched me in the stomach, and I couldn't catch my breath. Seeing the anger and hatred on his face caused tears to form behind my eyes. That was what I was hoping to avoid. That face was the reason I did not want to tell him the truth about me. My fear was becoming my reality.

"Let me explain," I said.

I could hear my voice shake. Finn looked away from me and shook his head. He turned and walked out of the shed. I opened my mouth to call after him but no sound came out. I didn't know what to say. I was disgusted with myself for not telling him sooner, but this was the reason I had not.

"Let's go," Courtney told Brooke and Jake. Brooke was now crying and Jake looked like he was ready to kill me, literally. "Lee, stay here until I know what to do with her." Courtney led the other two out of the shed slamming the door closed behind them.

I blinked the tears away from my eyes. I refused to let Lee see me upset. I ignored him as he leaned against the wall. I had nothing to say to him. I had to find a way to convince Courtney I was innocent. If she believed it, the rest would also; at least, I hoped so.

I closed my eyes, and Finn's face appeared in my mind. His anger and disappointment was frozen in my head. I tried to explain everything to him, but he wouldn't listen. He did not even give me a chance to explain. He left me alone and tied to a chair. The physical pain from my restraints weren't what hurt. What really hurt was the look on his face. That image alone broke my heart.

Chapter 38

LEE AND I did not talk for what felt like hours. Since my hands were tied behind my back, I had no way to look at my watch and see how long I sat there. I did not try to fill the time gap by talking to Lee. He was not the one I wanted to talk to. Finn probably never wanted to see me again, and I did not blame him. I did not handle the situation well. I should have been honest with him from the start. All of this was my fault.

The door in front of me opened. The sound caused me to look up, and I saw Courtney enter the room. Lee found a wooden chair and set it in front of me. Courtney sat down and looked in my eyes.

"Court, I did not kill Janey," I said. I had to make her believe that. Somehow I would.

"I know," she said softly.

"I would never hurt her. I... What did you say?"

"I know you did not kill Janey," she told me. I let out a sigh of relief. But that was cut short when I realized Courtney was still staring at me, instead of removing the tie at my hands. Something was not right.

"How do you know I didn't kill Janey?"

"How is Agent Powell?" She ignored my question and asked her own. I did not answer her. There was a look in her face that unsettled my nerves. It reminded me of a cat who was playing with the mouse it intended to have as dinner. "Oh, don't look so surprised. Your friend Garrett told Lee what you were up to."

I looked at Lee, who had an evil look on his face. I had no doubt in my mind that Garrett did not willingly tell him why I was going to Maryland. Courtney knew Agent Powell. Or at least knew of him. *Could he be right? Was she really the person he said she was?*

"It's true. You really are a weapons dealer." I did not make the statement a question. I did not need her to respond to know it was true. Her expression gave it away.

"Did you really think I would be working for the government? Come on, Blake, out of everyone, I thought you would know better," she said. Her voice was steady and calm. It sounded as if she had this conversation everyday; like it was no big deal.

I shook my head. "Do the others know?"

"Are you kidding me? Of course they don't know. Finn and Janey are too *moral* to do something like that." She said the word like it was a disease. "No, they don't know. They believe that we are really training CIA agents, instead of training my 'henchmen,' so to speak."

Courtney gave a wicked smile at her triumph in deceit, and Lee let out a tinny laugh. "Between you and me," Court said, leaning closer to me, like she was about to tell me some great secret, "that's the real trick. Obtaining and selling firearms to different terrorist groups can be difficult, but to condition people to be so completely devoted to you that they will believe anything you say-now, that's masterful."

She leaned back in her chair and watched my facial reactions. Courtney was not the person I thought she was. She was a terrorist. She treated all of us like pawns in her quest for money and power. Everything slowly clicked into place.

"You killed Janey," I said, looking her straight in the eye.

"Janey was an unfortunate circumstance that had to be dealt with."

"You bitch!" I yelled.

The words had barely left my mouth when Lee stepped in front of me and hit me hard. The back of his hand struck my mouth, and the copper taste of blood hit my tongue. I licked my lips and felt a cut in the corner of my mouth.

"You're an assassin. You've killed more people than I have, probably, and you think I'm the bad guy." Courtney said. I did not respond. "It was nothing personal. Janey found some documents she should not have and confronted me about it. I had to eliminate her before she could tell the others what I was doing."

She had killed Janey to keep her precious secret; I had no doubt that she would kill me too. I had nothing to lose. "I guess watching your father butcher you mother in front of your eyes messed you up more than I thought. That asshole destroyed your ability to feel."

Something in her eyes flickered for a second. "How did you know about my father?"

"You taught me how to spy when I was young. I guess you were a good teacher."

She looked at me for a moment. "My father was a great man."

What? He made Courtney watch as he brutally killed her mother and she was calling him a great man?

"My mother was a pathetic excuse of a human being. She was weak. My father knew what he wanted, and he took it. And because of her, he will spend the rest of his life in prison." Courtney was fuming. Anger flared in her eyes. *Courtney is bat shit crazy.*

"Wow, you're a fucking psycho." That might not have been the right thing to say. Lee hit me again, but this time he closed his fist. The blow knocked me over and I fell on my side.

Courtney motioned for Lee to pull me off the cement floor and put me back how I had been. Lee walked over to me and lifted me up by my arms. When I was standing in front of him, I kicked him in the groin as hard as I could. My hands might have been tied but I was not going down without a fight. Lee grabbed himself and fell to his knees. I turn to Courtney in time to briefly see her before her fist hit my cheek.

It felt like the right side of my face was going to explode. I have been hit in the face before, several times in fact, but never had it felt like that. I fell face-first to the floor. I did not dare to move yet. I felt warm liquid dripping from my cheek-bone down my face.

Large hands grabbed my upper arms tightly and hauled me back to my chair. Lee was not careful in how he handled me. I would probably have bruises in the shape of hands on my arms. I looked at Courtney in astonishment. *How had she been able to hit so hard?* I glanced at her hand and found my answer. She was wearing brass knuckles. *That would do it.*

"Blake, this really has been fun, but I have to go. But before I do, I want to know something. Who else knows about my chosen career?" Courtney was seated in her chair again.

I looked away from her. She wanted to know so she could eliminate them too. Mark and Nicole knew too much and were in danger. There was no way in hell I was going to tell her which of my friends to kill. Lee grabbed my hair and yanked my head back so I would have to look at Courtney. "Go to hell," I told her.

"I'm sure I will." She had an evil smile. "Lee, find out the answer to my question, won't you, baby? I have to go console the others. They are really upset about Blake's betrayal." She smiled at me. "Don't worry, Blake, I will see you later. Lee, have fun." With that, she exited the shed and left me alone with Lee and his questioning.

Chapter 39

WHEN I TORTURED people for information, I always tried to be civil at first; I did not think Lee would share my technique. It turned out that I was completely correct about how the questioning was going to go.

The door had not even shut before Lee hit me. His blow to the face sent me flying from my chair, again. He pulled me to my feet but was careful not to directly face me. I guess he learned from my first kick, and he did not want that to happen again.

He punched me hard in the stomach. All the breath was knocked out of me, and I struggled to catch it. Lee took hold of my shirt and threw me at the wall where I collided with a bunch of shelves.

"You know, when you're torturing people for information, it usually helps to ask a question," I told him. He was going about this all wrong, and I felt the need to help him-or was it the need to be a smart ass?

That comment warranted another punch to my face. "Believe me, I have not begun torturing you yet-but if you have an answer to Courtney's question, I would be happy to hear it."

"Nope, not yet," I said, while I struggled to push myself up. I was on my knees, with my head resting on the floor when Lee decided to kick me. I was in the perfect position for it. His foot caught my ribs and threw me to my back. I coughed at the pain and was relieved when blood did not pour out of my mouth.

I was, however, leaving puddles of blood on various spots of the cement floor. My face was burning from where Courtney's brass knuckles had hit. Blood was dripping down my cheek and spilling on my t-shirt and jacket. After a few more blows, I was lying on the floor, motionless. My entire body hurt. I tried to push myself to my knees but decided against it when my ribs screamed in protest.

"Anything you want to say?" Lee asked, as he leaned in close for an answer.

"Yeah, when I kicked you a while ago, I didn't feel anything. Does Courtney have your balls in a jar or something?" I asked. Tank had always told me that my mouth would get me into trouble someday. I was beginning to believe him.

Lee picked me up by the back of my jacket and threw me as hard as he could into the wall. My hands were still bound behind my back, so I was not able to brace myself before I hit the bricks. I closed my eyes and gritted my teeth in preparation for the impact.

The right side of my face hit first. My cheek-bone, which Courtney had already split open, collided with the bricks, followed by the rest of my body. I slid down the wall to the floor and let my forehead rest on the cold cement. I opened my eyes and saw red. Pools of blood were forming beneath my face from the wound on my right cheek. The taste of pennies filled my mouth to the point where I parted my lips to breathe and saw a line of blood pour out.

I heard Lee walk to my side. He squatted down to my side. He grabbed my jacket and pulled it down my arms. I was too hurt and exhausted to fight him. My hands were tied, so the jacket bunched at my wrist. Next, I heard the sound of steel being pulled from a sheath. *Oh, crap!*

Lee set the flat of the blade against my cheek so I would know what he had. The cold blade was a relief against my burning face. "Now the fun begins," he said.

He held my left arm firmly in one hand. With the other hand, he slowly pushed the tip of the blade into the top of my arm. Pain shot through my arm and shoulder. Until this point, I was determined not to scream. Screaming means the torturer is winning. I refused to let Lee win, but with the knife digging into my arm, my determination slipped.

I bit my lip trying to hold back the scream on my tongue. Lee slowly pushed the blade down the length of my arm. I could feel my flesh splitting around the blade. He was working his way from the top of my arm to my elbow. When he reached about half way, I could not hold it in anymore. I screamed. I felt the blood pouring from my body, but did not care. I could only think about the piercing pain in my arm. Then, suddenly, Lee stopped cutting.

I heard sounds of feet shuffling around the room. I turned my head and my heart leapt. Finn was fighting Lee. He must have walked into the shed during Lee's carving and pulled him off of me.

Lee still had his knife and was swinging it at Finn's face. Finn jumped back with only inches to spare. Lee was larger than Finn by height and weight, but Finn was faster. Finn picked up the chair Courtney had used and hit Lee in the arm with it. The blow caused Lee to drop his weapon. The fight continued. They were a blur of movements. I did not know if that was because they were moving so quickly, or because of my loss of blood. I think it was the latter.

They were exchanging blow for blow. Finn was doing a good job of avoiding Lee's fist but one connected to his chin. The hit sent Finn to the floor. As Lee ran at him to attack again, Finn reached out and picked up Lee's knife. He spun and raised the blade up and into Lee's neck. The blade went through the front of his neck and came out the back of his head. Lee's body crumpled to the ground.

Chapter 40

FINN SCRAMBLED AWAY from Lee's falling body. I closed my eyes and rested my forehead on the cold, wet cement floor. Finn ran to my side. "Oh, shit!"

I did not know if he was upset at killing Lee or at the sight of my bloody body. He knelt next to me and pulled out his pocket knife. He put the blade between my hands and gave the knife a quick jerk to cut the plastic tie that bound my wrists. The sudden release of tension caused my hands to fall briskly to the floor. Pain shot from my wrists to my shoulders. I had not realized what a strain being tied up has on the shoulders.

Finn pulled my jacket the rest of the way off my arms and dropped it on the floor. He placed a hand on my back. "Blake, can you hear me?"

I moaned a response and placed my hands under me. I tried to push myself up, but pain burned through my left arm. "I've got you," Finn said, as he wrapped his arms around my torso.

He gently lifted me off the floor. A sharp pressure flowed around my left rib cage causing me to suck in air through my teeth. I opened my eyes as my face was lifted from the floor. The cement was covered in blood. Puddles of red liquid were below my face, and I watched blood slowly drip from my cheek to the floor.

"You need to go to the hospital," Finn said.

"No...I'll be fine," I told him. I'd had worse injuries than these. Hospitals were not the best places for injured assassins to go.

"OK." Finn held me upright and slowly led me to the wooden chair I was seated in earlier. He gently sat me down and knelt in front of me. He tilted my face up slightly, so he could look at me. I looked into his eyes, but his were not on mine. He was examining my injuries. "Can you sit here for a second without falling over?"

It was a reasonable question judging by the state I was in, but it hurt my pride a little. *Yes, I got the crap kicked out of me, but I was strong enough to sit in a damn chair.* "Yeah, I'm all right."

Finn nodded and moved away from me. I heard him throwing things around behind me and the sound of a metal cabinet being opened. I did not feel like turning to see what he was doing. I was fairly certain he would not kill me.

He returned a few seconds later with a red duffel bag. He unzipped it and began rummaging through it. "What's that?" I asked.

"It's a first aid bag. Janey made a bunch of these and placed them around the house. About every other room has one," Finn told me, as he pulled out a handful of gauze.

He leaned forward and pressed the gauze against the cut on my right cheek. "Can you hold this? It is bleeding pretty badly," he told me.

I lifted my hand and saw the cuts on my wrist from the plastic tie. The cuts were not deep enough to cause too much bleeding. I hesitated only a second before taking the gauze from him and pressed it against my face. The pressure on the cut hurt, but I held back my complaint.

Finn reached in his bag and pulled out more gauze and a bottle of alcohol. He moved around to my left arm and looked at the cut Lee had given me. "That son of a bitch," Finn mumbled under his breath.

He began to wipe up the blood around my wound. His face was so serious. He was concentrating on what he was doing, but I doubted he was thinking only about fixing me up. He came back here for a reason; he wanted to know something.

"Ask me," I told him. He hesitated cleaning my arm for a split second, then continued.

"Ask you what?" he said.

"What you came here to ask me." Finn stopped and looked at me. For a moment he did not say anything. He just stared at me.

Finally he looked back at my arm. "Is what Courtney said true?"

"I did not kill Janey. Finn, I swear I didn't." Finn nodded his head as a response.

"What about everything else she said? Are you really a..." he did not finish his question.

"Assassin?" I finished it for him. He nodded. I took a deep breath and released it. "Yes, I am."

"This is going to sting a little," Finn said, just before he poured alcohol on the wound.

I clenched my fists and bit my lip to keep from making any sound at the pain. It did hurt, but not bad enough to break me. The sting was only temporary, so it was gone in a matter of seconds. Finn pulled a bottle of something out of the bag and opened it.

"You need stitches, but I don't have a suture kit. This is liquid stitches; it will have to do." He applied the liquid to my arm and placed a few butterfly bandages on the cut to hold the sides together, so the glue would work. "So, are you really here to kill us?"

"That's what I wanted to talk to you about yesterday...or was it the day before." Everything had been happening so quickly I lost track of the days. "I was sent here to kill people but didn't know their names. When I found out it was all of you, I couldn't go through with it," I tried to explain.

Finn moved his attention to my face. He pulled my hand away from my cut. The gauze I had been holding was soaked in blood. Finn grabbed some fresh gauze and wiped away the blood around the wound. "Why would someone want to kill us?"

This was going to be the hard part of the conversation. I did not know if he would believe me over Courtney. I doubted it, but I had to try. "Courtney has not been honest with you," I told him.

He stopped working and looked at me. "What are you talking about?"

"This is going to be hard to believe," I warned. I took a breath before starting again. "Court has been selling illegal weapons to terrorist groups." I said it quickly, just like with a band aid-rip it off quickly.

Finn stared at me for a second. He was trying to read my eyes. I had never been able to lie to him. He always said my eyes gave the lie away. "You are serious?"

I nodded. "I was hired by the NSA. This training thing," I said, waving my good arm around my head before thinking about how painful it would be, "is fake. She is really training men to work for her."

Finn listened to me without interrupting. He applied the liquid stitches to my cheek and more butterfly bandages.

"Also..." I waited until he looked at me. "She killed Janey." Finn's face instantly changed. His eyes were growing angry. "Janey found out about Courtney's arms dealings. They killed her to keep her from telling the rest of you."

Finn was quiet for a second. "I should have known something was wrong. Courtney has been acting differently the past few years. We all have noticed it." He ran his hand across his eyes, he then looked up at me. "God, Blake, I am so sorry."

"For what?" I asked. He hadn't done anything. He wasn't the one who beat the crap out of me. He had saved me. If he had not shown up when he had, Lee would have finished carving my arm. There's no telling what he would have done after that.

"I shouldn't have left. If I didn't, this may not have happened to you," he said.

"No; if I would have told you the truth from the beginning, then we wouldn't be in this situation."

Finn shook his head. "If I-"

"Stop blaming yourself. I'm fine. What he did is not your fault," I told him.

"Don't make excuses for me. I was wrong! Just admit it!" Finn was persistent.

"Fine! What do you want me to say? Yes, it hurt to see you leave like that, to see that look in your eyes, yeah, it hurt."

Finn looked away from me. "I'm sorry."

I reached down and took his hand. "I know. Me too." Finn looked up at me and gave me a small smile.

"Let's get you out of here," he said. Finn stood up and pulled the duffel bag over his shoulder. I stood, and he wrapped an arm around my side to steady me. His hand touched my ribs and I winced. "What's wrong?" he asked.

"Nothing. I probably just have a few bruised ribs," I said. I'd had a broken rib before, and that hurt a lot more than what I was feeling. I don't think Finn believed me. He moved his hand below my elbow and led me to the door.

I stopped before we reached it. "My purse," I told him. Finn turned and saw it lying on the floor beside Lee's body. He stepped over the corpse and retrieved my bag. He handed it to me, and I pulled out my phone. I had four missed calls from Mark and three from Tank. I decided to call Mark back first.

"Where the hell have you been?"

"I had a minor problem," I told him. I heard someone in the background talking to Mark. There was a shuffling as someone took the phone from him.

"Blake, where are you?" *Shit!*

"Tank? What are you doing here?" I turned and walked unsteadily away from Finn.

"Pack Rat told me who the targets were. Why didn't you tell me?"

"It's a long story." I was beginning to get a headache, along with all the other aches I was experiencing. Finn stepped to my side and put a hand under my elbow to steady me. "I will explain everything. I'm going to grab my car and I will be at the hotel in a minute."

"I'm driving you," Finn told me.

"Hold on Tank," I said, as I pushed the phone against my stomach to muffle our voices. "No, I'm fine. I can drive myself."

"Blake, I'm not leaving you again. I won't make that mistake twice."

"This is not about that. Your name is on the kill order. They could kill you if you show up with me." Finn's face did not change.

"I'm not leaving you," he said, as he squeezed my hand. I was not going to win this argument.

I sighed and pulled the phone back to my ear. "Tank?"

"Oh, I'm so sorry. Did I interrupt something more important?" he asked sarcastically.

"I'm leaving now, but I'm not alone. Finn is coming with me." I held my breath.

"Finn, as in Bradley Monroe? The name on the kill order?"

"Yes, but I need you to promise that you will not hurt him," I demanded.

"Blake, his name is on the-"

"I don't care what his name is on, Tank. Promise me he will be safe, or I won't come back, ever," I threatened. I meant the threat. I would not return until I had Tank's word. I refused to hand Finn over to his killers.

"Fine, I will guarantee his safety until we go after Courtney. I can't promise that I won't kill him later. I have a job to do."

That was going to be the best offer I would get from him. I would have to take it. "Thanks, Tank." He hung up the phone without saying good bye. I put mine away and looked at Finn. The stubborn guy was going to get himself killed.

Chapter 41

FINN LED ME to the parking lot. It was just after two o'clock in the morning, so there was no one walking around outside. We walked past my car to Finn's SUV. He opened the passenger door for me and helped me climb in the seat.

I pulled down the visor and opened the vanity mirror. *Wow!* I looked like crap. Blood was matted in my hair. My left eye was slightly bruised. The cut on my right cheek looked worse than it felt, and it felt like hell. There was a small cut at the corner of my mouth that hurt every time I spoke, and blood was dried in patches all over my face.

Finn opened his door and climbed in the driver's seat. He looked at me and gave a small smile. I glanced back at my reflection and closed the visor. I leaned my head back against the seat and closed my eyes as he pulled out of the driveway and through the gate.

"What about Brooke and Jake? We need to let them know about Courtney," Finn said, as we turned on the street.

We could not tell them now. They were both hot-tempered and would confront Courtney. That would probably get them killed. If we did not tell them, they would think Finn betrayed them to help me escape.

"I don't know. Jake was ready to kill me when Court told him I killed Janey. Maybe we should wait to tell them. Courtney will kill them if she found out they knew the truth about her."

Finn ran a hand through his hair. "Let me call Brooke. If you plan on going inside to get Courtney, which I'm sure you are, we need them to be on our side. I don't want to fight them." He looked at me to see what I thought of the idea. "I'll tell her not to say anything to Jake or Courtney until we get there."

"Do you think she will be able to act normal around Courtney?" I asked.

"I don't know."

"Then I don't think we can risk it. I would rather them think I killed Janey than risk their lives."

"There are still a few things I don't understand," Finn said. "What exactly did Courtney say?"

I told him. I told him everything, starting from my arrival in New Orleans to my recent rescue. He nodded at some parts and asked questions at others. By the time we reached the hotel, he understood everything, possibly even better than I did.

Finn parked in his normal spot in front of the hotel. He pulled the red duffle bag off the backseat and ran around the car to meet me as I opened my door. He placed a hand under my elbow and led me to the hotel door. The doorman opened the door and gave me a startled look. My bloody appearance must have shocked the hell out of him.

We ignored the looks I got from the clerks and bartenders and went straight for the elevator. Once we were inside, I turned to Finn. "Are you sure you want to come with me? It's not too late for you to leave."

Finn stepped close to me and wrapped his arms around me. He held me softly against his chest and rubbed my back. "I'm not going anywhere."

The elevator doors opened, and I forced myself to step away from his embrace. I did not want to. I felt safe and comfortable in those arms and wanted to stay there forever, but I had a roomful of assassins to face.

We walked to my room. I did not feel like searching for my key, so we knocked on the door. I heard voices from inside the room and the sound of footsteps approach the door. Nicole opened the door and froze.

"Holy shit! Blake, what happened?" she exclaimed, as she opened the door wider and stepped aside so we could enter the room.

"I'm fine," I said, walking toward the bed. Tank, Mark, and Pack Rat were waiting in the room, and they all stared at me when I entered.

"What the hell happened to you?" Tank asked. He looked angry.

I sat down on my bed. "Just wanted to see what it feels like to be on the other end of a torture session for a change." Tank looked from me to Finn. "Tank, this is Finn. Finn, this is my boss, Tank."

Finn walked over to the bed and extended his hand. Tank looked at it a second before looking at me. I raised my eyebrows at him, which hurt my bruised eye. Tank turned and took Finn's hand.

Tank turned to Mark. "Mark, call the other room and tell Victoria to come here."

"Vicky's here?" I asked. I liked Victoria. She had been a nurse before she became an assassin. I never understood how she went from saving lives to taking them, but she was handy to have around, as we played with dangerous weapons and sometimes ended up injuring ourselves.

I liked her because she was a smartass. I doubted if she had that special filter in your brain that stops you from saying things you shouldn't. She always said the first thing that would pop in her head, and she ended up embarrassing everyone but herself.

"Yeah, for some reason I thought we might need her on this trip. I brought a few others with me." When Tank said a "few others," he meant at least a dozen.

"I'm fine, really. I look a lot worse than I feel," I said. Tank frowned, but didn't insist that Vicky be called in.

"Who did this to you?" Mark asked.

"Lee."

"I'm going to kill him," Mark said.

"Sorry, but you're a little too late," I told Mark.

Finn sat down beside me. I did not tell them who killed Lee. Finn did not like the idea of killing other people, and I doubted he would have wanted me advertising he killed Lee. I didn't think he was ashamed of it, but happy was a different thing.

"Why don't you go take a shower? You will probably feel better after," Finn said to me. A shower sounded amazing.

"Wait, you need to tell me what happened," Tank said.

"I think between everyone in this room, you could piece together what happened," I said.

I had told Finn everything I knew, and besides him, Mark and Nicole knew everything up to Maryland. Tank would be able to figure it out.

I started toward my suitcase, but Nicole stopped me. "Just get in the shower. I will bring you some clothes." I smiled at her and went into the bathroom.

I peeled my clothes off, wincing slightly when I pulled my shirt over my sliced arm, and dropped the bloody clothes on the floor. My shirt was ruined. Even if the blood-stains would wash out, I doubted I would want to wear it again. I removed the necklace Finn had given me and set it on the counter. Blood had gathered between the small stones. I would have to clean it later.

I climbed in the shower and turned the hot water on. I tilted my head to the floor and watched the water turn a rust color as blood was being washed away from my body. The water stung a little when it hit my cuts and scrapes, but the pain faded quickly.

The door opened, and Nicole stepped into the bathroom bringing a gust of cold air with her. "Here are some clean clothes. I'll throw out your old ones."

I pulled my face out from beneath the water long enough to thank her. She left, taking my bloody clothes with her, and I picked up a wash-cloth. I wanted to stay in the shower for hours, but I also did not want to leave Finn with Tank. I trusted Tank's word, and I knew Nicole and Mark would not let anyone hurt Finn but I still was anxious to get back to him. I washed my body, face, and hair before turning off the water and drying off.

The mirror had fogged up from the steam the shower caused. I wiped a hand across the glass so I could see my reflection. My eye was a shade darker, and the cuts on my face were glistening with fresh blood. The hot water had reopened the wounds, but the dried blood was gone from my face and hair. I looked and felt better.

Nicole had brought me my pajama shorts and a tight spaghetti strap t-shirt that I liked to sleep in. I hated when a baggy t-shirt would get wrapped around my body while I slept. I had always preferred sleeping in tight-fitting clothing. I pulled my clothes on and walked out of the bathroom.

Finn and Tank were leaning over the desk, staring at a piece of paper. Mark and Nicole were sitting on the bed, and Pack Rat was standing by himself in the corner of the room. They all looked up at me when I entered. I walked over to the desk to see what they were working on. The paper looked like a map. I examined it closer and recognized parts of it. It was a map of Courtney's house; Finn must have drawn it for Tank.

Finn placed a hand on my back. "Feel better?" I nodded, and he smiled at me, but it quickly faded. He held my arm up. "You're bleeding again."

I looked down at my arm. He was right. The shower had reopened the wound on my arm as well as the cuts on my face. The ones on my face were not bleeding too badly but blood was beginning to push at the walls on my arm wound.

"Call Victoria," Tank told Mark. Before I could protest, Mark had the receiver and was dialing the other room's number. I decided not to argue anymore about my injuries. I would let Vicky tell them I was all right.

I walked to my bed and sat down, leaned my back against the headboard, and closed my eyes. The bed shook as someone sat down next to my legs. A hand touched my knee, and I opened my eyes. Finn was looking at me, his eyebrows crinkled in concern.

"Drink this," he said, as he handed me a cup of coffee. I happily accepted the coffee and took a sip. It was delicious. It was not the best coffee I'd ever had, but it was what I needed at that moment. I looked at Finn, who still looked concerned.

"What?" I asked.

"You look pale." I had lost a lot of blood and gotten the crap kicked out of me, so the paleness made sense.

There was a knock at the door, and Pack Rat hurried to open it. Vicky entered the room. She wore a tight black shirt and dark jeans that looked amazing against her mocha skin tone. Her long dark hair fell in waves around her shoulders. She looked at me and laughed. "Looks like you had a little too much fun. You look like shit," Vicky said, in a slight Southern accent.

"Nice to see you too, Vicky," I replied. She walked to my side of the bed but stopped when her eyes hit Finn.

She raised her eyebrows at him. "And who might you be?"

I rolled my eyes at her. "This is Finn. Finn, meet Victoria. Don't take anything she says seriously." Finn smiled at her, and she gave him her most flirtatious smile.

"Less talking. Blake is hurt," Tank said.

"Good observation, boss," Vicky said, as she sat down on the bed and faced me. Tank swore under his breath, something about smartass women. "Let me take a look at you," Vicky said, tilting my face to the side. She let go of my chin and lifted my arm. "This needs stitches, but I don't have my supplies."

"I have this," Finn said, handing her the red duffle bag.

"My, aren't you helpful," she said, as she took the bag. I watched as her fingers brushed his in the bag exchange. I made a mental note to hit her later.

She opened the bag and removed the supplies she needed, which she used to doctor me up similar to how Finn had. Finally, she put one large bandage on my arm to cover the cut. She did not worry about my face.

"What about this cut?" Finn asked, pointing to the one on my cheek.

She looked closely at it and shrugged. "It's fine. It will heal."

"Will it scar?" I asked.

"I doubt it." Well, that was a relief.

Another knock at the door drew my attention. I did not know who else was coming to the room. Mark answered the door. He only opened it a crack and closed it quickly. He came back with a tray of sandwiches.

"We ordered room service," he explained, as he handed the tray to me. I shook my head and pushed the tray away. I was not in the mood for food. I was tired and sore, not hungry. "You need to eat. When was the last time you ate something?"

I thought about it. The last time I had eaten was when Courtney invited me for dinner. Ever since then, I had been living on coffee. I knew Mark would yell at me for not eating, so I didn't answer his question. Instead, I took a plate with a sandwich on it from the tray. Mark smiled and returned to his seat next to Nicole.

"So, we need a plan to kill Courtney," Tank said.

I looked at Finn to see how he would take the statement. He knew we would be going after her, but I did not know how he would feel about listening to the planning. His face was unreadable, which meant that he was not happy. I reached down and squeezed his hand. He looked back at me and gave me a small smile.

"I have some friends who will be distracting the police while we get in and out. So we just need to figure out how to get inside," Tank went on.

"I can help with that," Finn said.

I pulled on his hand so he would look at me. "What are you doing?" I whispered. I'm not sure why I lowered my voice; everyone in the room was already looking at us.

"I'm going to help. Courtney lied to us, used us, killed Janey, and tried to kill you. I'm not going to sit back and let her get away with that."

"So you are willing to help kill her?" I asked.

Finn's face was deadly serious. "Yes."

"Great, so what's the plan?" Tank asked. Finn looked at me for a second before turning to Tank and explaining what he had in mind. I did not take my eyes off his face. I knew this was hurting him more than he was admitting.

"I don't think we can just walk in. Courtney probably knows you helped me escape, and if she doesn't, she will be suspicious," I said.

"Well, what other options do we have?" Finn asked.

"I may have an idea, but I don't think you are going to like it." I told Finn. He raised his eyebrows at me. I told them what I had in mind.

"I don't think so." "Absolutely not," Finn and Tank said at once.

"What? It will work, I think," I said. I was not sure it would work. It was sort of a Hail Mary pass, but it was all we had.

"No, you are not going. You need rest, and besides you are too close to the target," Tank said.

"Look, Tank, you don't need to worry about me being unable to pull the trigger. I want her dead more than you know. I am not staying, so let's skip the argument and go straight to you giving in. You don't have enough people to leave someone to behind to watch me, and the second you leave, I will follow you." I crossed my arms as I said it. I was not going to falter; I would not be left out of this mission.

"Fine," Tank said. "But hurry up and change clothes. We will be downstairs." Tank turned and again mumbled something under his breath about smartass women.

Everyone walked out the room, leaving Finn and me alone. "I don't want you to do this," Finn said.

"I know, but we don't have a whole hell of a lot of options," I replied.

"We could leave, just you and me. We could forget all about Courtney," he said. He laced his fingers through mine.

"I wish it was that simple," I said, looking at our hands. I marveled at how my hand fit in his perfectly. "Besides, we can't leave Brooke and Jake with her."

"Yeah, you're right."

I looked up at Finn. "Are you sure you can do this?" I asked him.

Finn looked down at his shoes. "I won't leave you again."

"Damn it, Finn, this is not about that. We are going to kill Courtney, do you understand that?"

"Yes, I do. But it still applies. I'm going with you. I will do what I have to in order to make sure you're safe."

He was worried about me, so much so that he was willing to hurt himself in order to help me. I wrapped my arms around his waist. "Finn, I appreciate the concern, but this is what I do. I will be fine," I said.

"I'm still going." Finn leaned down and kissed my forehead. "If you can be stubborn, so can I. Now get dressed."

Finn walked out of the room, and I turned and did as he said. I choose a pair of stretch jeans and a black shirt. I could kill in that.

Chapter 42

FINN DROVE HIS SUV to the house. I was in the passenger seat, and Mark and Nicole were in the backseat. It was deadly quiet; we were all anticipating the future mission. I couldn't stand the silence. Normally, when I had a big mission to go on, I would crank up the music. A little Nirvana and Rage Against the Machine, and I was ready for action. But at that moment, the thought of loud rock music was making my head hurt. But even with the headache, the silence had to stop; so I picked up the phone and called Tank.

"When are these friends of yours going to move?"

"They are going to hit a few liquor stores and maybe a bank or two in about five minutes," he said.

"Who are these people?" I asked.

"Just some gang leaders that owe me a few favors," he explained. The variety of people Tank knew continued to astound me. "We are almost there. You ready?"

"I hope so," I said. My voice was not very convincing.

"Be careful. We got your back."

"Thanks." I hung up the phone.

It was time to get ready. Finn pulled the vehicle off the road and put it in park, then turned to face me. I smiled and held my hands out to him, with my wrists pressed together. He frowned at me but pulled a plastic tie out of his pocket and tied my wrists together. He did not make it too tight, but it was enough to have my stomach in knots. I didn't like the idea of having that thing on my wrists again, but this was my plan, so I couldn't complain.

I looked in the backseat and saw that Mark had tied Nicole's wrists together also. Finn pulled out a razor blade that Tank had given him and carefully cut into the plastic tie. He cut a little more than halfway through the plastic, leaving just enough to hold it together. The idea was to make it appear like I was tied, but if things got out of hand, hopefully I would be able to break through the plastic.

Finn handed the razor to Mark, and he did the same to Nicole's plastic tie. When he was finished, he held his arms out to Finn, who repeated the tying and cutting of the plastic on Mark's wrists. Once we were finished, Finn pulled back onto the road. Mark leaned over and gave Nicole a quick kiss before we pulled up to the gate.

Finn rolled down his window and a guard approached the SUV. I noticed he had an assault rifle strapped to his back. It looked like a M16 semi automatic. It was definitely military issue. I had not seen the guards with heavy-duty weapons yet. That must mean Courtney had everyone on alert. *Fabulous.*

"Sir?" The guard looked nervous.

"Open the gate, Brandt," Finn demanded.

"Um..." the guard shifted his weight from one foot to the other. "Ms. Jacobs asked to be notified if you returned." So Courtney did suspect Finn was with me.

"Well, then notify her," Finn said impatiently.

The guard pulled his two-way radio out of his pocket and pushed the call button. "I am reporting to Ms. Jacobs." There was a short pause.

"Hold," said a deep voice on the other end of the receiver.

After a few moments, Courtney's voice came through the speaker. "Yes?"

"Ms. Jacobs, Mr. Monroe has returned and would-"

"Give me the damn thing!" Finn reached out and grabbed the device. "Court, tell the idiot to open the gate." He released the talk button.

"Finn, where have you been?" Courtney did not sound angry; instead, she sounded very calm. Calm people made me nervous. I would rather fight angry people any day. The more emotional they are, the more mistakes they tend to make.

"Look at the camera screen," he told her.

"OK, what am I supposed to be seeing?" she asked. Finn looked at me before he reached over and grabbed a handful of my hair. He jerked my head toward his window so the security camera would see me. I let out a painful cry at being jerked by the hair. It did hurt, but the cry was more for the benefit of Courtney and the guard. "Interesting. Where did you find her?" she asked.

"I went to talk to her in the shed and found Lee. I know what hotel she was staying at, so I went to get her. I have her friends in the back as well."

There was a pause. Courtney was trying to read Finn. He looked angry which was good. He was angry with Courtney, but he appeared to be mad at me. That would work. "OK, we will meet you outside."

Finn gave the guard back his receiver, and he returned to his watch as we drove through the gates.

I turned around in my seat and saw Pack Rat sneak into the guardhouse. Brandt would be dead in seconds. We pulled into Finn's normal parking spot and he climbed out of the car. *Here we go.*

He opened the back seat and pulled Nicole out of the vehicle by her arm. He led her around the other side and opened the back door. He grabbed the front of Mark's shirt and aggressively pulled him out of the SUV and threw him to the ground. Finn looked like he did not care for Mark. I wondered how much of that was real and how much was an act. Nicole stood at Mark's side as he climbed to his feet.

The front door of the house opened, and several men walked outside, holding M16s. All of the guns were pointed at Mark and Nicole. Finn opened my door next and forcefully hauled me out by my arm. He pulled a 9mm out of his belt and pushed it into my side. I had never liked having a gun pressed into my ribs.

Courtney walked through the front door and stood on the porch. She was partly hidden behind a few recruits. I doubted the assassins who were positioning themselves on the wall would be able to get a good shot. I knew Vicky and David were on the wall. They were two of our best snipers. I might not have liked David, but he was a good shot and Vicky was no slouch.

Finn had two pistols tucked in the back of his jeans-a 45 for Mark and my Llama. Nicole had her knives in their specialty belt that fit inside her jeans. They were small knives, and the belt was so thin, no one would be able to see them if they did not know what to look for.

Courtney stepped to the side of a guard and looked at me. "You killed Lee." I did not respond. I glared at her for a moment before she smiled an evil smile. "Finn, I found this in the shed." She held up his pocket knife. The light from the wall lamp hit the blade, flashing his initials for all to see. He must have forgotten to put it back in his pocket after cutting me free. The recruits suddenly turned their guns on Finn. *Shit.*

This entire plan hinged on the hope that Courtney would think Finn was on her side. *So much for Plan A. Now it was time for Plan B.*

I pulled my wrists apart, and the plastic tie broke. *Woo-hoo!* Mark and Nicole followed suit. I leaned forward and pulled my gun from Finn's back. "Shoot them!" Courtney yelled.

A recruit pointed his gun at me before I could get a firm grip on my gun. Suddenly, the recruit's head jerked back, and blood splattered from his forehead. I glanced behind me and saw Vicky smile. *I'm going to have to remember to thank her.*

I turned my attention back to the recruits in front of me. Mark shot one, and I took out another. Nicole pulled a knife and threw it past my head. It landed in a recruit's cheek. Finn raised his gun and shot an approaching guard.

I was slightly surprised to see him kill the recruit. I didn't know if he would be able to pull the trigger or not. I looked up to search for Courtney, but she was gone. She had escaped inside the house.

"We need to go," Finn yelled. "More will be coming."

Nicole ran to the fallen recruit and retrieved her knife, along with his M16, which she slung over her shoulder. Recruits began pouring out of the front door. Finn shot off a few rounds of his 9mm, grabbed my elbow, and we ran to the side of the building with Mark and Nicole following closely. Assassins ran through the gate and took on the recruits.

We ran to the kitchen entrance that I had used to originally sneak in the house. Finn threw open the door, and we met two recruits. I lifted my gun in my right hand and fired two shots, one for each. They crumbled to the ground before Finn had his gun raised. He turned his head toward me and gave me a startled look. He hadn't realized what I was capable of. I could have explained it all day, but he would never fully realize what I was saying until he saw it for himself. I gave him a small smile. *I hoped I did not scare him too much.*

We ran through the kitchen and into the hall. A recruit stepped out of the guard's office, and Finn shot him before he could raise his weapon. I poked my head inside the office and saw two guards at the security monitors. They were on their walkie-talkies telling recruits where to go. I put a bullet in the backs of their heads. We walked in the room and stood in front of the monitors. *One of them has to show where Courtney is.*

Finn walked past me and opened a metal cabinet. M16s lined the walls. He pulled a rifle off the wall and handed it to me, but I waved it away. "I prefer pistols," I said.

He opened a drawer at the bottom of the cabinet. Several pistols were set in a cloth bottom. He picked up one and loaded a magazine in it. He handed it to me grip first. I took it from him and pulled the slide back. It was loaded and ready. He handed me a few extra clips, which I put in my pocket. Nicole took a pistol and a few clips as well, and Mark and Finn took M16s.

I turned my attention back to the monitors. No Courtney, but I did find Brooke and Jake. They were in the living room, with nearly a dozen recruits stationed around them. All had M16s. They had to come first. Once I knew they were safe, I would go after Courtney.

Chapter 43

I POINTED AT THE monitor showing Brooke and Jake. "Let's go," I told them. Finn nodded and stepped out of the room.

"Follow me," he said. We did. He knew the way around this house; the rest of us did not. I followed closely at his side with Nicole behind me. Mark was at the end of the line to watch our backs.

We walked quickly but quietly down the wall. We reached the end and turned right. Two recruits rounded the corner ahead of us. They saw us and raised their weapons. Finn shot them before they could fire their guns. As we ran past them, Finn stopped and knelt to pick up their rifles. As one of the recruits had fallen on his weapon, Finn was forced to roll him over. He paused as he looked at the recruit's face. His expression dropped.

"Are you OK?" I asked.

"It's Charlie," Finn said, as he stood. "I liked him."

I gave his arm a slight squeeze in sympathy. I knew this would be hard for him. He would know most, if not all, of the people we were fighting.

Finn gave me a reassuring smile and threw Charlie's rifle over his shoulder, He led us to the door marked "Private," and we entered the room. We made our way across the room to the other door, but it opened before we could touch the handle. I raised my gun as Joshua stepped through the doorway. He saw us and held up his hands in surrender. I did not pull the trigger.

"I'm on your side," he said. "Courtney is not letting Brooke leave. I think she is going to hurt her." Finn and I kept our weapons pointed at his chest; we didn't know if we could trust him yet. "Please, we have to help her."

His eyes were filled with concern. During Mardi Gras, I had noticed the way he would look at Brooke. He was in love with her. I saw it in his eyes then, and it was there now. I lowered my gun. Finn looked at me questioningly, and I nodded. He lowered his gun also.

"They are in our living room," Finn told Joshua.

Joshua turned and stepped through the door he had just entered. We followed him. The door led to a hall, where we were forced to turn left or right. We choose left. We had barely taken a step when shots were fired behind us. Recruits had come up the other end of the hall, and Mark had opened fire. Nicole turned also and helped kill the remaining recruits.

We continued down the hall until we were just around the corner from the living room where Brooke and Jake were being held by at least a dozen guards.

Joshua took a deep breath and turned the corner; we followed behind him. Shots were fired from both sides. I grabbed Joshua and Finn's arms and pulled them behind the couch. We huddled behind the sofa, and Nicole hid behind a chair. Mark was still in the hall, firing shots from around the corner.

Joshua jumped up and shot two guards. I poked my head over the couch and shot another. One recruit set his aim on Joshua, but Finn shot him first. On the way down, the recruit pulled the trigger, and the bullet hit Joshua in the chest. He fell to the floor beside me.

I heard Brooke scream. I looked up to see her break free of the grip a recruit had on her arm, and she ran toward Joshua. She was running straight into the line of fire.

I jumped over the couch and collided with her side. We both hit the floor. I landed on my back and pointed my gun at the first recruit I saw. I shot him at the same moment he saw me. Brooke was scrambling toward Joshua, and I stayed close behind her. I was on my back, but I crawled with one arm and fired my pistol with the other.

I was still in the open when my gun clicked-I had run out of bullets. I pulled my spare gun out of my jeans, but a recruit had time to raise his gun at me. Finn shot him before he could shoot me. "Move!" Finn yelled at me.

I turned and ran toward Brooke. I wrapped my arms around her waist and lifted her to her feet. Together we ran toward Joshua. When we reached him, I pushed Brooke behind the couch and grabbed Joshua. He was still breathing, but his breaths were becoming more sporadic and shallow. I helped him move behind the couch. Brooke pulled him into her lap and pressed a hand to his chest over the bullet wound to stop the bleeding.

I turned my attention back to the fight. Jake was trying to wrestle a gun away from a recruit. I raised my gun and sighted the recruit. I would have to be quick; otherwise, I could kill Jake. I pulled my trigger, and the recruit fell. Only one remained, and Nicole took care of that one.

I looked back at Brooke. She was rocking Joshua back and forth. His eyes had glazed over. I did not have to check his pulse; I was very familiar with those eyes. It was the eyes of the dead. I squatted down in front of her. Tears flowed down her cheeks but she made no sound. Brooke was strong. She did not want to openly weep in front of us. She bent down and gave him one last kiss. I felt like I should not be there. This was an emotional moment for her, and I wanted to turn away, but I couldn't.

She looked up at me. "What the hell is going on?"

"Courtney, she is responsible for this," Finn said, looking down at Brooke.

Jake walked up to me. I sucked in a deep breath. I really hoped he didn't try to kill me. If he thought I killed Janey, I had no doubt in my mind that he would try. Finn must have thought the same thing, because he moved to stand by my side.

"Blake didn't kill Janey. Court did," Finn told him.

Jake jerked his head up. "What?"

"She's been lying to you for a long time. Janey found out some information Courtney didn't want her to know," I told him.

"So she killed her?" Jake directed the question to Finn.

"I'm sorry Jake," he said. Finn reached out and grabbed Jake's shoulder. In a man's world, that was considered a hug.

Jake studied Finn before glancing at me and Brooke.

Brooke scooted out from under Joshua's body and took the rifle from his hands. I held out my hand to her, and she took it. Mark and Nicole were pulling weapons off the dead recruits and distributing them among us. I took a few clips and reloaded the weapon I had discarded.

Brooke and Jake exchanged meaningful looks before he turned to me and said, "Let's go find the bitch. She has questions to answer."

Chapter 44

W E LEFT THE living room and Joshua's body behind us. We weren't sure where Courtney was, so we decided to check her office first. The problem was that the office was located at the back of the house. We would have to go through several large rooms to get there.

Again Finn led the way. Mark and Jake stayed at the back of our group to make sure no one would sneak up on us. There was not a lot of activity inside the house, but could hear gunshots and screams coming from outside. It seemed most of the recruits had run outside to fight my coworkers.

We entered the dining room. Several recruits were there, but their attention was on the fight outside. They were shooting through the window at assassins in the yard. Their backs made easy targets. Brooke fired the first shot. That surprised me. I did not think she had it in her to kill, but apparently I was wrong. Her aim was not the best. She hit the recruit in the arm. I raised my gun and finished him before he could turn on Brooke. Once the room was cleared we moved to the next.

A recreational room was at the other end of the hall. A large pool table sat on one side of the room, and a foosball table was in the middle. On the other end was a giant screen television with couches and chairs placed in front of it.

The recruits there must have heard the gun fire from the dining room, because they were ready for us. But we outnumbered them, and half of us were professional killers; they did not stand a chance. Finn and I were the first out the door. I dropped to one knee and aimed. I was able to take out two before they realized I was not standing anymore. Finn finished off the last recruit.

I rose to my feet, and we moved into the next hall. It was a long hall with several doors on either side. "Recruits' rooms," Jake said from behind me. We moved slowly down the hall, listening for any indication that there was someone around other than us. The indication came from behind us. Recruits rounded the corner and saw us. Mark opened fire on them, and they jumped back around the corner.

"Go!" Jake yelled at us. The hall was only wide enough for a couple of people. Mark and Jake would be able to handle the recruits around the corner. The rest of us would only get in the way or be in danger.

Finn led us girls to the next room. I turned to Nicole. "Stay with Brooke in the hall, in case the guys need backup." She nodded. Finn and I entered the library.

The room was not very large. It had a couple desks, and the walls were lined in books, and it did not have any windows. Instead, the wall opposite us had a door in the left corner, and the wall adjacent to us had a door. *What kind of design was this? What room needed three doors?*

I stepped into the room and began to walk toward the door to my right. The door on the left opened, and a recruit walked into the library. He shot first.

I dove to the ground and turned a desk over to shield myself from bullets. I knelt behind it and looked around the side, only to see more recruits shooting at us. I ducked behind the desk in time to hear a bullet hit the thick wooden top. I peeked around and fired at a recruit but missed my target. Finn quickly leaned out of his doorway and shot. He did not miss his man.

I heard a door behind me open, then a gunshot. I felt something slam into my back, and I fell forward. I caught myself with my hands just before my face slammed into the floor. There was so much pressure on my back, it felt like a weight was dropped on me. I turned my head and saw silky auburn hair fall across my face. *Nicole.*

I rolled over and Nicole fell off my back. She was face up on the floor, and her eyes were open. "Nicole?" I shoved an arm under her back to help her up and felt warm liquid on my hand. I pulled my hand away and looked at it. Dark blood covered my palm. I heard a laugh and jerked my head up.

Courtney was standing in the open doorway, holding a pistol. She gave me her evil smile. If Barbie had been an evil bitch, Courtney could have modeled for her. I raised my gun to shoot, but she dashed out the door. I could have followed her, but I would have to leave Nicole. I looked down at her and she looked up at me.

"We're even," she said.

"Finn!" I yelled. I needed help. Finn appeared at my side.

"Shit!" he said.

"Nicole, listen to me. You're going to be fine," I told her. She nodded. Brooke poked her head in the room and looked at us. Her face became serious, and she disappeared into the hall.

Mark and Jake entered the room and ran toward us. Mark ran to our side and dropped to his knees. He took Nicole and ripped open her blouse. There was no blood on the front of her shirt, which meant the bullet was still in her back. "Baby, can you hear me?" he asked her.

"Yeah, I'm right here," she said, with a hint of sarcasm. She turned her head toward me and added, "This hurts like a bitch." I let out a small laugh that ended when she winced from pain. Mark bent down and kissed her.

Brooke ran into the room, holding a red duffle bag. She dropped to the floor, opened it, and pulled out a wad of gauze; Mark lifted Nicole so she could press the gauze to the wound.

Brooke looked at me. "Go. We'll take care of her. Go get Courtney."

I looked at Nicole. "Hold on, OK? You'll be all right." I reached down and squeezed her hand.

I felt tears forming behind my eyes. Nicole had become a good friend. She helped me through this whole situation when the smart thing to do would have been to go to Tank, like Pack Rat did. *She'll be fine. My gunshot wound was much worse.* I had to find Courtney. *The others will take care of her. Mark will make sure she is all right.* He cared about her too much to let her die.

I stood and ran toward the door Courtney had gone through. I did not have to look to know Finn was right behind me. I ran down the hall with my gun raised. *The second I see that bitch, she's dead.*

We approached the end of the hall, where I recognized Courtney's office. I threw open the door and dropped to one knee, breathing heavily from the run. I looked around the room; it was empty.

I rose to my feet and walked into the office. Finn followed behind me. I crossed the room to her enormous desk. Papers were scattered around on top of the surface. I looked up and saw a door on the other side of her desk. I walked around my only obstacle and grasped the doorknob. Courtney had to be on the other side of that door. I took a deep breath and threw open the door.

Courtney's bedroom was huge. A giant sleigh bed made of cherry wood was its centerpiece. A large wooden dresser was on one side of the room, and a vanity mirror was on the other. A large window was next to her dresser. I walked up to the window and found it was opened enough for someone to crawl through. I looked back at Finn. He clenched his teeth together, like he always did when he was angry. I saw the muscles flare along his jaw. We had lost Courtney. She was gone. *Shit!*

Chapter 45

I TURNED AWAY FROM the window and looked at Finn. He stared at me with a look of dissatisfaction on his face. I understood how he felt. I wanted to tear Courtney apart with my bare hands. She had killed Janey and shot Nicole. I leaned my back against the wall and closed my eyes. I saw Courtney's evil smile form out of the darkness in my mind. I growled and slammed my fist against the wall. It hurt, but not enough for me to care.

I opened my eyes and Finn was frowning. I walked past him and entered the office. I wanted to get back to Nicole to see how she was doing. She had jumped in front of a bullet for me. That was crazy. I had done it for her, but that seemed like so long ago.

I had walked out of the office and was walking down the hall when my cell phone rang. I pulled it out of my pocket and looked at the caller ID; it read "Court." I flipped it open but did not say anything. I listened to her breathing.

"How is your friend?" Courtney asked, with humor in her voice.

"You bitch, where the hell are you?"

"The house was getting a little too crowded for me, so I left."

"I am going to find you. There is no place I won't go to see you die. I am going to watch as the last hint of life leaves your eyes."

"Wow, that's a little dark, Blake. Maybe you should see a therapist." She was speaking calmly. I hated that. I wanted her to be as emotionally involved as I was. She sounded like she was reading off a shopping list. "Oh, by the way, I left something for you. A surprise of sorts, although I don't think you are going to like it." The humor was back in her voice.

"What did you do?"

"You will find out soon enough. In about one minute, actually." She let out a wicked laugh.

I didn't bother hanging up the phone; I simply let it fall to the floor. Finn gave me a startled look. I grabbed the front of his shirt before turning to run down the hall. He followed closely behind me.

"Blake, What is it?" he asked.

We entered the library. "Bomb!"

Courtney was going to blow the whole damn place. I looked around the room and saw blood on the floor. Where were the others? I did not have time to ask. We had to get out.

Finn grabbed my wrist and pulled me to the door on our left. We ran down the hall that led to the recruits' rooms. *One minute is too short. We don't have enough time.* We darted into the recreational room. One wall had a large window. That was our way out. I ran toward it, pulling Finn behind me.

In the movies, people jump through closed windows all the time, as if it were no big deal. It hurts like hell. It is basically a wall that, if you don't hit it hard enough, won't break. And if it does break, there is a good chance you will get cut by thousands of tiny pieces of glass. I pulled my gun and shot holes in the glass. The glass did not break, but the bullet holes weakened the resolve of the glass.

We ran at the glass. Just before we hit it, Finn pulled my head into his chest. I closed my eyes and jumped. We hit the glass hard; it shattered beneath the impact, and we fell to the ground with a thud. I felt broken glass dig into my left arm, but I ignored it. Finn pulled me to my knees and dragged me away from the house.

We had moved about a foot when the minute expired. The side of the house we were at exploded. The force of it blew me forward, and I landed on top of Finn. Heat from the bomb rushed along my spine and burned into my face. Finn covered my head with his hands and turned me, so his body was shielding mine. Bits of wood, plaster, and other debris fell on top and all around us.

We did not move. Slowly things stopped falling on us, and Finn leaned off of me. He pushed a large piece of wood off his shoulder and placed his hand on the side of my face. "Are you all right?" he asked.

I was breathing heavily, my left arm was numb where I had hit the glass and landed on it, and there was an obnoxious ringing in my ears, but I was alive. "Yeah, you?"

He smiled and put his forehead on my shoulder. I took that as a yes. He leaned to the side so I could sit up. I looked at the destroyed house. The bomb had taken out the entire west wing.

I heard my name being screamed across the yard. I looked in the direction of the scream and saw Brooke and Jake running toward us. *Thank God.* They had made it out of the house before the explosion.

I crawled to my feet before they reached us and looked down at Finn. He was staring at the house. It had been his home for the past five years. "Finn." I smiled at him and held out a hand. He returned the smile and placed his hand in mine. I pulled him to his feet.

He took a step and stumbled. He let out a small moan of pain and I grabbed him around the waist to hold him up. His eyes were closed tightly, and his hand went to his leg. My eyes followed his movements and saw the problem. A large shard of glass the size of a butcher's knife was sticking out of Finn's right thigh.

"Shit," I said, holding him up. Brooke and Jake reached us and saw Finn's leg. "Come hold him up," I told Jake.

He took my place below Finn's left shoulder and helped hold him. I moved to the other side and knelt on the ground. I needed to pull the glass out. It would cause him to bleed, but he would not be able to walk with it sticking out of his leg. I could grab the glass, but it would probably cut into my hand.

My shirt was already torn from recent activities, so I grabbed the bottom of it and ripped a strip off. I wrapped the fabric around the glass and gripped the end like a handle, then looked up at Finn, who took a deep breath and held it. *Just like a band aid.*

I quickly jerked the glass out of his leg. About four inches of glass came out, covered in blood. Finn made a small noise but otherwise held it together.

I stood and placed myself under Finn's right arm. He put some of his weight on my shoulder, and I helped him walk. I turned to Brooke. "Where's Nicole?"

"Over there with some woman," Brooke said, and pointed to the parking lot. I saw Vicky loading Nicole into the cargo hold of Finn's SUV. *Good Vicky has her, everything will be fine.*

I looked around the yard and saw several bodies. Recruits' corpses were scattered all over the ground. We would need to get out of there. I didn't know how long Tank's gangster friends would be able to hold off the police, but I was sure the heavy gunfire had gotten some attention. If that hadn't done it, I knew the explosion did. We made our way toward the vehicles.

I sucked in a deep breath when I saw Tank walking toward us. David was on one side, and Pack Rat was on the other. Tank was holding a pistol. *This is not good.* Tank would put his gun away if he did not need it. I tensed, and Brooke saw it.

"Do we need to be worried?" Brooke whispered, as she looked at the approaching men. I did not respond, which was in itself the answer. I saw her reach for the gun at her waist. I quickly grabbed her hand to keep her from grabbing the gun. That would be a fatal mistake. I looked at her and shook my head.

"Where is the Mother?" Tank asked.

"She got away," I told him.

"What?" Tank, Jake, and Brooke said almost simultaneously.

"I tried." That was all I could say. I had no explanation of why she got away. She just did.

"Who are they?" Tank asked, looking at Brooke and Jake.

"It doesn't matter," I said firmly.

Tank rubbed a hand across his eyes. "Blake, the kill order..."

"I don't care about the damn kill order!" Tank looked at me. I would not let him kill these people.

"Fine, I don't know their names. There are several dead here who I could say was them. But Finn," he didn't finish the sentence. He knew I understood what he was saying.

"No."

"I'm sorry Blake, I am, but his name is on the kill order." Tank raised his gun and pointed it at Finn's chest.

I stepped in front of Finn. If Tank wanted to shoot Finn, he would have to go through me. Finn placed his hands on my shoulders and tried to push me out of the way, but I held my ground. "Tank, just let him go. He'll leave, and you won't see him again, please."

"I'm not leaving," Finn said.

I rounded on him. "Yes, you are. He will kill you, do you understand that?"

"I love you." He looked me in the eye. I knew he felt that way, but hearing him say it was different. My butterflies flared to life. I had to calm them down. This was not the time for them to play. "I won't leave you again."

"Finn," I place my hands on his chest and looked at my fingers. I had to tell him I did not love him. I had to make him leave. It would hurt me to lie, but it would kill me to watch him die. If lying and hurting him would keep him safe, then I would hurt him. "I don't-"

Finn did not let me finish. He took my face in his hands and pressed his lips against mine. He held me against his mouth and I melted into him. I tried to keep myself from kissing him back but couldn't. I kissed him like it would be the last time I ever got the chance, because it very well could be.

He pulled away from me but brushed his lips across mine. "As long as you kiss me like that, I'm not going anywhere," he whispered. I felt his warm breath against my lips and was unable to speak.

"He means that much to you?" Tank asked me. The fact that I had forgotten all about him showed just how great of a kiss it was. I turned and nodded. Tank smiled at me and sighed. "Fine, he can come with us. But you have to talk to the boss and convince him to let Finn live."

I smiled. "Thanks, Tank." I turned back to Finn who was giving me that wicked smile I loved so much. I leaned forward and kissed him again.

"We better get going," Tank called back to us. I heard sirens in the distance and agreed.

"We're coming, too," Brooke said, as she and Jake followed him.

Tank mumbled under his breath but did not say anything. He turned to David. "Take Blake's car and go to the hotel. Get all their things, clean both rooms, and the car, then catch a flight home." David nodded and ran toward my rented Acura.

I placed myself under Finn's arm and helped him over to the SUV. He was walking fine by himself. I was there just in case he needed support-and because I liked having my arm wrapped around his waist.

I opened the back door to Finn's SUV, and he climbed into the backseat. Tank took the front passenger seat, and Pack Rat climbed in the driver's seat. I climbed in after Finn, and Brooke and Jake followed. The backseat was not meant for four people, so I sat partially on Finn's lap and partially on Jake's. I turned to face the cargo hold of the SUV.

Mark had Nicole in his lap. She was positioned on her side and Vicky was behind her. Vicky had the red duffle bag out and was applying pressure to the wound on her back. I looked at Nicole. She was pale but otherwise did not look too bad. Mark looked worse.

"How are you doing?" I asked her.

She smiled at me. "I'm fine. I get to have this man wrapped around me," she said, patting Mark's arm. He bent down and kissed her forehead. "How did you ever let him go?" she asked me.

I smiled back at her. "He was never mine. I was just holding him for you." It was a little cheesy, but I knew Nicole liked all that romantic stuff. I was willing to suck it up for her sake.

I turned back around in my seat and leaned against Finn. His leg was bleeding pretty badly. I looked up to tell him so, but he was looking at my arm and frowning. I followed his gaze and saw that my arm was bleeding again. The knife wound had reopened, and there were tiny cuts up and down the rest of my arm. *I hate jumping through windows.*

I heard Tank telling Pack Rat to head for the airport. Our jet was there waiting for us. *Thank God.*

Chapter 46

WE PULLED THROUGH the private airport gates. Three other vehicles full of assassins followed our SUV toward the company jet. We climbed out of the SUV, and I ran around the back to open the door for Nicole. Vicky climbed out first, followed by Mark, carrying Nicole, and we headed for the jet. We quickly climbed the stairs and entered the cab of the plane.

The cab had one long couch on one side, with several rows of seats on the other. Each row had three seats facing another three seats. Mark sat on the couch and laid Nicole in his lap. Vicky sat next to her and resumed applying pressure to the wound. Finn, Brooke, and Jake chose a row at the back of the plane. I began to follow them, but Tank called me. He was heading toward the front row, and I followed. He was on the phone with someone.

"We need a cleanup at the Mother's address," Tank told the man on the phone. After a short pause, he continued. "I will let the person assigned to her case explain the results." Tank handed the phone to me. He mouthed the words "Agent Powell."

I took the phone from him. "Hello," I said.

"Am I speaking with Ms. Raven?" Agent Powell asked.

"Yes, but my name is Blake Morgan." There was no need for secrecy now.

"Of course, Ms. Morgan. So tell me, is the job completed?"

"Not exactly," I said.

"Explain," he demanded, sounding angry.

"The target got away," I told him.

"All of them?"

I paused for a moment. I could tell him that Lee and Janey were dead. They were on the list as well as the others. That might help my plea, but I doubted it. He wanted Courtney dead. *Join the club.* "I need a favor," I told him.

"Really? What favor would that be?"

"I want everyone but The Mother's name off the Kill Order. They had no knowledge of her activities and are completely innocent. In fact, they want her dead more than you do."

"Is that so?" I don't think he believed me.

"If you do this for me, I will tell you everything I know about the target."

"I seem to recall you promising me information before and not delivering."

"Yeah, I'm sorry about that. I freaked out when you told me about the reasons for her death sentence."

"You know her don't you?"

"Better than anyone else on the planet, with the exception of three people you want me to kill-the same three people who helped us try to kill her tonight. If you grant me this favor, I will kill her for free." I would do that anyway for Janey, but he did not need to know that.

Silence filled the phone while he thought about my offer. "Fine, we have a deal. Now, tell me what you know."

"You will take the names off the kill order, you can leave Lee Chauvin's name on it, because he is already dead."

"Yes, consider it done. What do you know?" he asked me again.

"Telling you about her could last all day. I will write up a full biography on her and e-mail it to you. But if you want some information now, search the name Courtney Marilyn Jacobs."

"That's her name?"

"Yeah, she is in the system. Her father killed her mother when she was five. Custody went to the state. Her file should be with Child Services in Michigan."

"How do you know her?"

"We grew up in the same orphanage," I told him.

"Great. I will be waiting for your report." He hung up the phone, and I handed the cell phone back to Tank.

I closed my eyes and smiled in relief. Finn, Brooke, and Jake were safe. I let out a deep breath, and it felt like a weight was lifted off my shoulders. Tank patted me on the leg, and I looked up at him. He smiled at me and left his seat to enter the cockpit.

I left my seat and walked over to where Nicole was lying. I knelt in front of her. Mark was stroking her hair and whispering assurances in her ear. She looked horrible. All color had drained from her face, and her eyes were slowly closing. She jerked them open and looked at me. She was trying to fight sleep; that was good. She gave me a weak smile.

"How are you feeling?" I asked her.

"Great, I think we should go bowling when we get back," she replied. I had said something similar to her when I was shot. I smiled at her.

"That's a good idea," I told her. I looked up at Vicky. She gave me a serious look. Vicky is never serious. The look on her face made me more nervous than the look on Nicole's.

Vicky handed me some gauze, alcohol, and bandages. "Your boy is bleeding. Go fix him up," she told me. I rubbed Nicole's arm, then accepted the medical supplies from Vicky.

I stood and walked to the back of the plane where my people were located. I passed several assassins in their seats. Pack Rat looked up at me and gave me a sad smile. He was worried about Nicole too.

Brooke and Jake were seated next to each other, with Finn seated across from them. I knelt at Finn's side and leaned back on my heels.

"What are you doing?" he asked me.

I reached up and grabbed the place where the glass had pierced his leg. I slipped my fingers through the hole in his jeans and ripped the fabric until the wound on his thigh was fully exposed.

"You are bleeding. I'm helping," I said, as I pressed gauze against the wound. I poured some alcohol on a piece of gauze and cleaned the wound.

His leg tensed a little, but he didn't make a sound. I finished by covering the cut with the bandage. I patted his knee and climbed into the seat next to him.

"How's Nicole?" Brooke asked. I looked back at Nicole. She looked so frail.

"I don't know," I said softly. "We just have to get her back. The doctors we have can fix anything." We just had to get her there. Finn wrapped his arm around my shoulders and pulled me to him. I leaned my head on his shoulder.

"I really don't understand what's going on," Jake told me. "Why are these people looking for Courtney?"

I had forgotten they did not know the truth about her. I hadn't had time to tell them, but that could be fixed. I told them everything. They took the news rather well.

"That bitch!" Brooke yelled. Several people in the plane turned to look at us. OK, she did not take the news that well. "She was using us?"

I nodded. Jake remained quiet the entire time I spoke. He was a man of few words, when he was not arguing with Brooke.

"So you really are an assassin?" Brooke asked and I nodded. "That explains a lot. How many people have you killed?"

I looked at my hands. Of course, Brooke would think my job was interesting. "A few," I said.

Truthfully, I had no idea how many people I'd killed. I could probably figure out how many hits I had been on, but kills are different. Tonight, for example, I had one target but killed who-knows-how-many recruits. Many jobs were like that. I had to go through a few people to get to the target.

Brooke laughed at my answer, but Finn did not look so happy. I knew he did not approve of killing, but he had done it tonight, too. The rest of the plane ride, I was forced to answer questions about my career. I did not mind so much. There were certain things I kept to myself, such as names of past kills and other assassins. I also did not answer the question about my first kill. That was something I did not like to talk about. It was one of the hardest things I had ever done, and the pain of that hit was still in the back of my mind. I learned to separate emotions because of that hit. Talking about it would make the emotions come back. I avoided that at all cost..

Chapter 47

I CHECKED MY WATCH as the plane began to make its descent. It was just after nine in the morning; I had not slept in over forty-eight hours. The plane landed in our private air field. When we exited the plane, we were met by the cold Chicago winter air. In New Orleans a person could get by without a jacket in February, but it was insane to try it in Chicago-and we were in short-sleeved t-shirts.

Four large white vans were waiting for us as we climbed down the stairs. The nearest van opened and a doctor stepped out. He met Mark and helped him place Nicole in the back. Vicky was right behind him, telling him about her loss of blood and pulse rate. I wanted to get in the van with them, but they closed the door and drove off before I could reach the vehicle.

I stood in the parking lot and watched them drive through the gates. I guess it was good they did not wait for me. They needed to get Nicole back as soon as possible.

The driver of the next van stepped out. She was short, with blond hair that framed her round face. Tank made his way toward her and she climbed back into the driver's seat. We followed Tank and claimed the back seat.

"We need to get back ASAP, Sarah," Tank told his assistant.

"Yes, sir," she said, as she handed him a few papers. He was shuffling through the papers and did not pay any attention to us. Sarah acted as if we were not in the vehicle. She had always been too professional for small talk.

I did not feel like talking anyway. Nicole had me worried sick. She looked awful.

The twenty-minute drive seemed to take hours. We pulled directly up to the front door of our building. The doctor would have gone around back for secrecy, but we did not care if we were seen. We were illegally parked, but I doubted Tank worried about a few parking tickets. He opened his door while the van was still moving and stepped onto the curb. I followed closely behind him along with the others. We looked like baby ducks following our mother.

Tank threw open the doors and walked straight to the side door. "Open the door," he told the security guards, before he reached it. Both guards did something behind their desks and the door unlocked. I always thought you had to have a palm print to get in, but apparently that did not apply to Tank.

We all entered through the door and walked down the hall past the elevator, and straight through to the medical wing. The door opened in time for us to see the doctor wheel Nicole into surgery on a stretcher. Mark followed her until the surgery room doors closed in his face.

I walked up to his side and touched his arm. He looked down at me. Pain swarmed his eyes. "She is going to be fine. She's strong," I told him. He nodded and turned to take a seat in the waiting area. Vicky was standing in the corner. I walked up to her.

"Is she going to be OK?" I asked.

"I don't know," Vicky said, as she wiped her hands across her eyes. "She lost a lot of blood."

Vicky led me to a chair and sat down beside me. Finn took a seat on the other side. He reached down and wrapped his fingers around mine. It was what I needed at that moment. Tank walked up and stood in front of me.

"Go have your arm looked at, and take him too. His leg is bleeding," he told me.

"I want to wait for Nicole," I said, shaking my head.

"It could be a while. Just do what I say for once," he said. I sighed but agreed.

I stood up with Finn and walked down the hall. A nurse I recognized from when I was shot, was standing at a counter, doing paperwork.

"Hey, Jessica," I said to her.

She turned, and her eyes widened when she saw me. "Blake, what happened?"

"The usual stuff," I said. "Do you have time for a quick fix-up?"

"Yeah, come on."

Finn and I followed Jessica to an empty room. It was a typical hospital room with one bed, a chair, and a window. I sat down on the bed, and Finn sat beside me. I introduced them to each other. Jessica gave him a smile that was not just polite but slightly flirtatious. I did not mind too much. He was mine, and he was as loyal as they come.

"Finn has a bad cut on his leg," I said to Jessica.

"Blake first," he told her. Jessica came to my side and looked at my arm. "Vicky and I used liquid stitches on the cut, but it opened again," he said, as she looked at my knife wound.

"Yeah this needs stitches." *Great, everyone loves stitches.*

She pulled out a syringe and gave me the shot to deaden the nerves in my arm, so the stitching would not be so bad. The shot was bad enough. I hated needles. She cleaned the wound and stitched up my arm quickly; then it was Finn's turn. She removed the bandage I applied and looked at the cut.

"A piece of glass did it," I said, trying to be helpful.

"How did you clean it?" she asked.

"Alcohol," I answered.

"I better do it again. I need to make sure there are no glass fibers still in the cut before I stitch him up."

I looked at my watch again; it was a nine-forty-five in the morning. Finn saw me check the time. "Why don't you go wait with Mark? This won't take long."

"OK," I said, as I got up off the bed. I knew that all I could offer Mark was, at most, a hand to hold, but I thought he needed the support more than Finn did.

I returned to the waiting room. The room was filled with people waiting to hear that Nicole would be all right. I took the empty seat next to Mark, and we waited in silence. It was so quiet, I could hear the second hand ticking on my watch. Mark's leg was twitching, and his eyes were focused on nothing. I could have waved my hand in front of his face, and he would not have noticed.

Finn walked into the room and took a seat next to Brooke. Pack Rat walked up to us, carrying cups of coffee. I took one gratefully and sipped it slowly. It felt like we waited for hours before the surgery rooms doors opened and the doctor walked out.

Mark stood quickly, and Tank and I stood beside him. I reached down and took Mark's hand. He squeezed mine in return. The doctor approached us.

"I'm sorry. We did everything we could." My heart dropped. Mark dropped my hand and walked to the wall and leaned against it with his head lowered. I couldn't move. "The bullet caused too much damage, and she lost too much blood. I'm sorry."

Nicole was dead. She died saving me. This was wrong, just wrong. I shook my head back and forth, as if I could change it. It did not make sense. I had survived a gunshot; she should have been able to also.

I looked up at Mark. I heard him yell something before he punched the wall hard. Tank made a move toward him and I grabbed his arm. Mark picked up a chair and threw it at the wall. I stepped forward and reached out to him. "Mark."

He turned and looked at me. Pain and grief filled his eyes. I took another step and placed my hand on his arm. He did not move. I went to hug him, and he pulled away from me. He walked straight for the back door, and I did not stop him. Everyone deals with grief differently, and Mark needed to be alone.

Finn walked up behind me and placed his hand on my shoulder. I did not need to turn to know it was him. I reached up and covered his hand with mine. I would not cry; Nicole did not need my tears. She was dead. I would cry when Nicole had justice. I would cry for her and for Janey when I killed Courtney.

"Go home. Get some rest," Tank told me. He suddenly sounded very tired. "I had Sarah go to the store for shirts and pants for the guys. She is going to pick up something for you to eat as well." He handed me the keys to the van. I took them and walked out the way we came.

Finn, Brooke, and Jake were silent behind me. I was thankful for that; I did not want to talk. I wanted to crawl into bed and not think about anything for a long time. I wasn't sad. I should have been, but I wasn't. I felt numb. I assumed it was from sleep deprivation and lack of food.

We walked down the hall and ran into a pack of girls headed for the elevator. The one leading the others was thin, with long blond hair, and walked with an attitude. I didn't feel like dealing with Tabitha right then, but she saw me before I could turn around. Her two clones behind her turned to look at me as well.

Tabitha laughed when she saw me. "My, my, my, you look like someone beat the hell out of you. Sorry I missed that."

I did look like crap. My left arm was covered in tiny cuts, with one large cut taking up the upper half of my arm. My lip was busted, my eye was no doubt black by now, and I had a gash on my cheek. Not to mention my shirt was torn to shreds.

Brooke made an aggressive step to my side. I guess she did not feel like putting up with crap from Tabitha, either. She didn't even know Tabitha but could sense she was a bitch. "Get out of my way, Tabitha," I said.

Tabitha saw Brooke's movement and smiled. "Well, it looks like you're not only stealing people's boyfriends but drawing in girls, too." She scanned Brooke's body. "But frankly, I think she could do better." Her clones laughed behind her.

I'd had enough and stepped forward. "I did not steal Mark from you. He ran away as fast as he could, because you are an evil bitch. You care about nothing but yourself and enjoy making others as miserable as you are. Now, yesterday was probably the worst day I have ever had, followed by an even worse night and I am not in the mood to put up with your shit. All I want is to sleep for two days, but if you make me, I will take a few minutes and beat the ever-living shit out of you. So I will tell you one more time. Get. The. Fuck. Out. Of. My. Way."

Tabitha's jaw dropped, and eyes widened. I heard her swallow, and she slowly stepped to the side. I did not look at her as I passed. The others followed behind me as we walked through the door and through the lobby.

"So that was Mark's ex?" Finn asked. I nodded. "You were right. She's not very nice." That was the understatement of the year, but I did not tell him so.

We approached the van and Finn grabbed my wrist.

"Maybe I should drive. You're upset," he said.

"I'm fine. Besides, you don't know where to go," I told him, and climbed into the driver's seat. I fastened my seat belt and waited for the others to get into the vehicle before I pulled away from the curb.

Chapter 48

I<small>T DIDN'T TAKE</small> very long to get to my condo, although it seemed like it took forever. I parked the van in front of my garage. One of the reasons I loved my condo so much was because it had its own two-car garage. I climbed the stairs to my front door before I remembered I did not have my keys. I had left them in my purse at the hotel in New Orleans. I backtracked to the last stair and reached underneath it; I had a spare key taped to the bottom of the stair. I removed the key and opened my door. I walked in and dropped the key on the counter.

The smell of pizza hit me as soon as I walked through the door. Two large pizza boxes were on the counter next to a couple of grocery bags. Tank must have given Sarah the extra key I had made for him. I walked past the kitchen and into the living room, where I fell down on the couch. The others remained in my kitchen.

Jake opened the first box and took a slice of pepperoni pizza. "There should be Cokes in the fridge," I told them. Finn walked over and sat next to me. Jake took a seat at the bar in my kitchen, and Brooke joined us in the living room. She chose the recliner.

I pointed to the room across the kitchen. "That's one spare room, and that," I pointed to the door across from me, "is the other. You will have to share the bathroom." My room was the one behind the couch, and I had my own bathroom.

"I'm going to take a shower. Brooke, do you want some clothes to sleep in?" I stood up and walked toward my room. She nodded and followed me to my bedroom.

I opened the door and turned on my light. I had a normal bedroom. A king-sized bed took up most of the center of my room, with nightstands on either side. A wooden chest, in which I stored my weapons, sat at the foot of my bed. I always had a gun in the top drawer of my right nightstand-I always slept on the right side of the bed. My closet was at the far end of my room.

I opened the door and entered the closet. That was the other reason I loved my condo so much-my walk-in closet was enormous. Brooke let out a gasp when she saw it. The closet was large enough to be considered another room. I walked to my dresser and pulled out the top drawer, pulled out some clean underwear, then opened another drawer and retrieved my boxer shorts and one of the night shirts I liked to sleep in.

"What do you want to sleep in?" I asked Brooke. She was still staring, opened-mouthed at my closet.

"This is amazing," she said, stepping inside the closet. I don't think she heard me.

"Take whatever you want. I'm hopping in the shower," I said, leaving her to a slice of her own paradise. Too bad she did not approve of the attire I filled the closet with.

I stepped in the bathroom and turned on the shower. I saw steam rising from the top and decided it was hot enough. I stripped out of my clothes and threw them in the trash. They were ruined.

I climbed in the shower and let the hot water beat on my face. It felt amazing, but I was too tired to stay in there for long, so I washed and stepped out and dried off and got dressed. I ran the towel through my hair to get rid of the excess water. I would let it dry on its own. With my face as beat up as it was, I did not care what my hair looked like. I pulled my thick, warm, cotton crimson robe off the hook on the back of my bathroom door and put it on. I felt a hundred times better, now that I was clean and warm.

I went back into the living room to join the others. The smell of pizza made my stomach growl, so I went to the kitchen and took a slice. I'm sure it was delicious but I was too tired to enjoy it. I pulled a Coke out of my fridge and sat at the bar. As I ate, I looked through the shopping bags Sarah had left us. They contained toothbrushes, a few pairs of boxer shorts and plain white t-shirts for the guys, underwear for Brooke, and a couple of sweat-pants and sweat-shirts that had "Chicago Cubs" written on them. Sarah assumed I would let Brooke borrow clothes, but the guys needed something to wear. I was glad she had picked Cubs sweats.

Finn walked up to me and looked through the bags. "You can take a shower if you want," I said. He pulled out a pair of boxer shorts and a t-shirt.

"Thanks," he said. He took the things to the bathroom and I heard him start the shower and Brooke went in the guest bathroom to shower as well.

I joined Jake in the living room. He was watching cartoons and still eating pizza. I swear, he could eat his weight in food. He did not talk to me as we sat there, and I was grateful. I didn't feel like chit-chat at the moment.

Finn walked back into the room, wearing the new clothes, with his hair was wet. I saw the stitches in his leg. Even with the ugly stitches, he still looked good. I wanted to cuddle against his chest and fall asleep. I was too tired for anything else.

"I think I'm going to bed," I said to everyone in the room. I heard the water stop running. Brooke was finished with her shower.

"Me too, as soon as I take a shower," Jake said, as he grabbed some things out of the shopping bags and went into a guest room.

Finn stretched out on the couch and adjusted the pillow under his head, then picked up the remote and turned off the television. He crossed his feet and pulled the small blanket off the back of the sofa and covered himself. He was planning on sleeping on the couch.

"You don't have to sleep in here," I told him.

"You sure?" he asked. "I thought you might want to be alone."

I walked into my room and held the door open. I nodded for him to join me. He rose from the couch in one smooth motion and walked into my room. I closed the door and turned off the lights.

It was almost noon. Light seeped in through the curtains allowing me to still see with the lights off. I removed my robe and hung it back on the bathroom door, walked around the bed, and climbed under the covers.

Finn was still standing by my door. I leaned over and pulled the blanket out for him. I patted the mattress, and he smiled. He was so cute.

He climbed into the bed and moved until our bodies were pressed together. He leaned over me and pressed his lips to mine, and I reached out and brushed my fingertips down his cheek. He pulled away and laid his head down beside mine.

I rolled over and rested my cheek on his chest. I wrapped my arms around him, and he did the same to me, holding me close enough that I could hear his heartbeat. I closed my eyes and images of Nicole flashed in my head. The images soon turned to Courtney's evil smile. I opened my eyes to get rid of the picture.

"Are you all right?" he asked me. He must have felt my body tense.

"Yeah. What about you?" I asked. He turned his head to the side, and I looked up at him.

"What do you mean?" he asked.

"You've been really quiet since we left New Orleans."

"I've just been trying to wrap my head around everything that happened," he said, as he rubbed my back.

"OK." I closed my eyes. His warmth surrounded me, making me feel safe. I felt that as long as I was in his arms, nothing bad could happen to me.

"Can I ask a question?"

"Of course," I answered.

He hesitated. "Do you feel anything? When you...when you complete a job, do you feel bad or anything?"

I thought about it. Did I feel anything when I killed someone? I knew the answer that would make him feel better, but I didn't want to lie to him. I wanted to be honest with him.

"No," I answered.

"No, you don't feel bad? Or no, you don't feel anything?"

"No, I don't feel anything. Not since my first assignment," I told him truthfully.

"It must have been bad."

"Yeah," was all I said.

I closed my eyes again, and Finn held me tighter. He did not respond to my answer. Instead, he trailed his fingers up and down my arm. That movement calmed me more than anything else. The simple strokes of his fingertips were soothing. I was drifting asleep.

"Finn?"

"Yeah?"

"I love you." The butterflies were acting up again, but I was too sleepy to care. I loved Finn. I wanted him to know that before I fell asleep. I wanted him in my life; I needed him in my life.

Finn leaned down and kissed the top of my head. "I love you, too."

I smiled and listened to the beat of his heart. I was worried about closing my eyes again, not wanting to see Courtney's face. I closed my eyes anyway and thought about Finn. He loved me, and I loved him. I would worry about Courtney tomorrow. Today, the only thing I wanted to think about was Finn's smile. I held onto that image, and soon all others faded away. The soft, rhythmic drumming of Finn's heart combined with the safety of his arms caused me to slowly drift to sleep.

If you enjoyed the DEADLY CONSCIENCE, don't miss ...

DEADLY JUSTICE

WWW.AMYLANEWILLIAMS.COM